I dedicate this book to
Peter and Mary Worrall, my parents,
who have made me what I am.

Acknowledgements

Grateful thanks to the following kind people
who have helped me along the way;
My family, David, Charlie, Suze, Lewis, Rumer and Indi
who have supplied ideas and constant support.
My mother Mary Worrall and sister Pamela Palmer
who have been my biggest fans.
Richard and Gilly Webb who got me started;
Val Wills and Alan Stewart, the patient cover designers;
Sarah Smith proofreader extraordinaire and the quiet voice of reason;
Elisabeth Hütterman and Jesus Peréz for their enthusiasm, fantastic vision
and beautiful illustrations;
Mark at Short Run Press for his measured advice and assistance.
There are others who have helped me over the years and
to all of them I say thank you. I finally got there.

Catherine Bond

Moonmirror

PART ONE

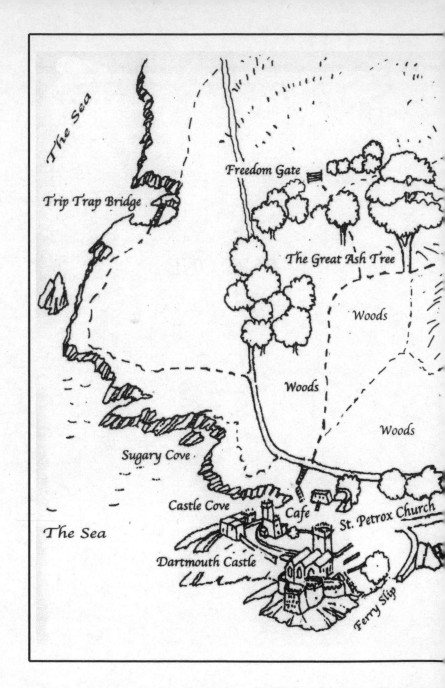

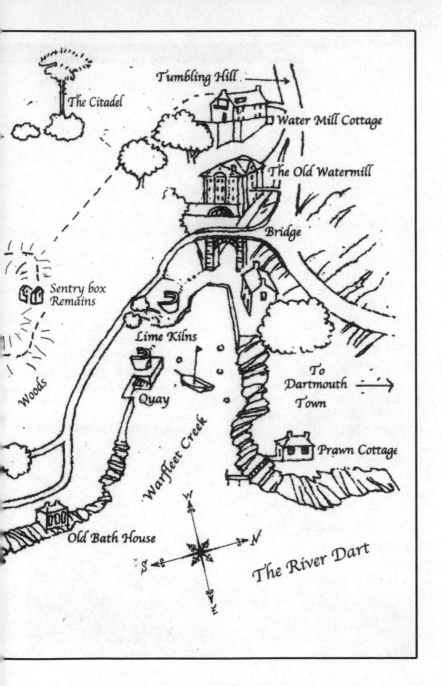

Chapter One
An introduction to Warfleet

Watermill Cottage was an ordinary sort of house when you first looked at it, situated just off the main road leading out of Dartmouth. It overlooked the old watermill, a large stone-built building with an iron bridge across to its entrance. A small stream which had fed the mill ran down the hill, and just before the cottage, it disappeared into a culvert and gushed out again at Warfleet Creek. Quite ordinary you might think, but you would be wrong.

Nothing was known of the two kingdoms that the stream divided – the ancient dynasties of the Woodlanders and the Seafarers, existing hidden away from human eyes. The Woodlanders' territory began behind the cottage, rising steeply into dense woods, eventually leading to a group of old pine trees known as the Citadel. A pair of magnificent buzzards lived here who were the sole rulers of the whole woodland, fiercely territorial and not interested in humans at all. That is, until the children arrived.

When the family moved into Watermill Cottage in 1978 they had no idea of the animal worlds surrounding them. No one could have imagined the old kingdoms which stretched far back into ancient times. Every so often in history, things occur which alter events and link the past and the present. The arrival of the children at Watermill Cottage was such an event. It changed everything.

Outside the cottage, a narrow lane led to the sheltered inlet of Warfleet Creek where the rushing waters of the stream emerged from beneath the road and spread out flowing gently towards the sea. The world of the Seafarers began at this beach, the oldest kingdom of all ruled over by the mighty Spirit of the Sea.

There were many sea birds wading in the muddy oozes of low tide and a pair of swans often visited. It was said that they were linked by an invisible thread, endlessly long and immensely strong, which tied them together for life.

News soon reached the Citadel that two small children had taken up residence in the empty and neglected cottage by the stream. The buzzards were naturally curious and sent a robin down to investigate. He flew to the cottage, landed on the window sill and peeped in, listening and watching for a while, gathering his information. Then he flew back to the great pine trees to give his report.

"My Lord there are two adults and two children, a boy called Edmund and a girl called Eleanor, but they are too small to pose any threat."

"Very good, but I am going to appoint you as their guardian so watch them well and update me regularly."

"Yes my Lord." The robin felt very important and chose a sheltered spot on the garden wall where he sat often looking into the kitchen window. He saw Edmond and Eleanor's first day at school and shared the excitement. Not long afterwards their names were altered to Eddie and Ellie by their school friends. Nothing unusual happened and the robin reported boring annual

8

observations to the Buzzard. Little disturbed the rhythm of the Woodland; not yet.

Their father, Peter, built them a tree house in the corner of the garden and the children discovered the National Trust footpath behind the cottage where they made a tree swing from an old rope. Their shrieks could be heard far and wide as they took turns swaying out over the steep hillside.

One afternoon after Easter, when their father was home on leave from the Navy, the family were having a cup of tea and some cake in the garden. The robin watched them from the branch of an apple tree and before he could help himself, he swooped down, snatched up some crumbs and flew off. He was soon back, this time he perched cheekily on Peter's foot. Everyone was very surprised and held their breath as the bird looked at them all in turn with his beady black eyes.

"We'd like to be friends." whispered Ellie. From that moment the robin was no longer afraid of the children. He appeared everywhere, following them and watching them.

"Let's call him Faithful Freddie," said Eddie one day. "Dad's got a compass on his ship called that which is always reliable. No matter what we do that robin seems to be there, it's really weird."

Ellie agreed and later the robin landed by the front door, hopping up and down and cheeping in an agitated way; blinking his shiny black eyes he stared at them intently, head on one side. He kept doing it.

"You know," said Ellie, "I think he's trying to tell us something."

"You're right. Let's follow him."

The bird led them all the way down to the creek, to the slippery wet rocks at the foot of the old quay, where, under the mooring ropes, they could see a seagull. The robin perched on a branch and waited.

The seagull lay very still, his grey feathers moving up and down. Eddie inched nearer, bending down, talking gently to him, trying to soothe him. He saw at once what the matter was.

"He's got a fishing hook stuck in his leg, all tangled up with fishing lines. It's a terrible mess – not one of mine I hope," said Eddie suddenly feeling guilty. "Shall we take him home and see if we can untangle the lines?"

Ellie thought carefully.

"I suppose we'd better. The tide might come in and wash him away."

Eddie agreed and raced home for a cardboard box and then back down the creek, clambering over the rocks. Above their heads some gulls were circling, calling out in their loud voices.

"They've seen him," said Ellie. "I hope they don't dive bomb us."

Gently and carefully they lifted the gull into a nest of crumpled newspaper and carried him back up to the cottage. He wouldn't keep still enough for Eddie to try and untangle the fishing line or the sharp hook from his leg. The gull squawked loudly as he tried to get out of the box. Both children were rather scared of the seagull who snapped his beak.

"What's all this?" said Mary, their Mother, who appeared in the kitchen from upstairs.

"Oh Mum, we found him down at the creek. He's hurt his leg and we'd like to help him. But it's so difficult, he won't keep still and we want to untangle the line. What shall we do?" Without hesitation Mother decided. "Into the car you two," she said. "Bring the box we'll have to take him to the Slapton Ley Field Centre. I'm sure they will know what to do. Let's go straight away."

Reluctantly Eddie and Ellie carried the bird into the boot of the car and off they went. At the field centre a very nice man in a white coat took the box from them.

"My goodness, you've got yourself in a bit of a pickle. Steady old fellow," said the man. "Jean," he called into the next room, "I'm going to need some help in here."

He looked over his big glasses at the children.

"This is very kind of you," he said. "He is very lucky you found him. We might have to do a little surgery on his leg, but leave him with us and we'll see what we can do." He smiled at them.

"Can we come back for him later on?" asked Eddie insistently.

"Why don't you ring up and see how he's doing? We'll soon sort him out, don't worry."

"That's a good idea." said Mother, relieved. "Thank you very much indeed." And she exchanged phone numbers with the vet. "Goodbye."

They looked back for the last time at the forlorn seagull and walked slowly to the car. Mother drove home.

"It wasn't really us, Ellie, who saved him you know," said Eddie looking out of the window at the grey sea passing by. "It was Freddie."

"Yes," said Ellie rather gloomily. "He must have known we would try and help him."

They were rather sad and felt they had failed. When they got home, there on the windowsill looking in, was Freddie. He tapped on the window pane with his beak.

"Hello Freddie," said Eddie, who found himself talking to the robin quite naturally. "Your friend has gone to the bird sanctuary, he's not here anymore."

The robin flew off and news soon spread to all the Seafarers that Eddie and Ellie had rescued him. Through Eddie's persistent nagging mother phoned the Slapton Ley Centre the next day.

"Well," said the vet, whose name was Mr Jameson, "It's a very strange thing. Firstly we had to amputate the injured leg – it was a great shame but we just couldn't save it. Secondly, when the gull woke up from the anaesthetic, we took him outside to a special recovery pen and before we could close it up, he gave a flap, took off and just flew away. It's never happened before and I am very sorry. Naturally I'm worried how he will manage with one leg. Probably he'll be alright, birds do adjust. I'm really sorry."

"Oh, what a shame," said Mother, giving a quick look at Eddie as she spoke. "Thank you anyway for what you've done. Ring me at once if he turns up. Good bye."

She put the phone down gently. She sat down to break the news to the waiting children. They were not pleased. In fact they were very cross indeed – especially Eddie.

"How could he lose him?" he shouted. "How stupid. What a stupid, stupid man! He will probably die now and it's all our fault. We should never have taken him to that stupid place. Ellie and I would have taken better care of him than that."

Eddie flounced out of the house almost in tears, feeling frustrated and helpless. Ellie watched him go. She knew better than to pester Eddie when he was angry. He climbed up into the tree house and sat miserably, his hands around his face and his elbows on his knees. Freddie flew down and landed where Eddie could see him.

"Hello Freddie," said Eddie gloomily. "Bad new I'm afraid. He's disappeared from the bird sanctuary, and worse than that he's only got one leg now. Sorry, we didn't help much."

The robin put his head to one side and looked at the sad little boy who cared so much for the seagull he had lost. He stayed for a minute or two and then flew away, leaving Eddie alone and fed up. Eventually the boy curled up in the tree house with the old cushions and blankets and closed his eyes.

The robin flew high up into the woodland and winged his way to the Citadel where the buzzards were waiting for him. They already knew of the seagull's escape. They had sat in the dusk watching, as over the headland flew the grey gull returning to his home at the creek. They gave this news to the robin. "Couldn't I be allowed to tell the boy?" he pleaded. "Let me tell him that the seagull is safe. Please master." he beseeched.

The buzzards entered into a great and lengthy discussion.

"There are great dangers and risks in revealing to the humans that we can speak their language," said the male buzzard. "He will tell his sister and she in turn will tell other people. Our deepest secret will be revealed. Lead him to the seagull, show him he is alive and well and end his misery. Go now and arrange it as we have decided. You have done well." He nodded in an approving and benevolent way

"As you say, Master. Wisdom is yours," bowed the robin and flew back to the creek. He found that the Seafarers had already guided the seagull into the shelter of the old lime kiln where he was warm and comfortable in dried leaves and moss. The robin flew back to the cottage to find Eddie but didn't see him; where was he?

The Citadel

Chapter Two
Two important discoveries

Eddie woke up very early, feeling rather unhappy. He got up and crept outside, drawn to the beach, his favourite place. Freddie hopped down from the wall and flew in front of the boy immediately, hoping he would follow him. When he reached the furthest kiln by the old steps, the first thing Eddie saw was the sleeping gull nestled in a pile of dried leaves. He was so excited he could hardly breathe and as Eddie approached, the gull woke up, flapped its wings and hopped up onto its one leg. Eddie put his hand down unafraid and gently stroked the gull's smooth head. The gull sat quietly letting him.

"It's you," whispered Eddie, "it's really you. You've come back home. How did you find your way? It's miles. You are like those eels that come home from the other side of the world, from the Sargasso Sea. I am going to call you Sargasso from now on." He tickled the bird's feathers. "Go back to sleep now and I'll come and see you later."

The gull obediently hopped back into his cosy bed of leaves and lay down.

"Goodbye Sargasso," whispered Eddie, "Goodbye. Come on Freddie, lets tell Ellie."

Eddie was so delighted, he ran back home and rushed into the kitchen where his mother and Ellie were making a cup of tea.

"He's found his way back," he beamed at them both with a face full of joy. "He's back in the creek and he's OK."

"Do you mean the gull, Eddie?" said his mother, "Can it really have come back by itself?"

"Yes!" shouted Eddie, "Isn't it great? He's alive after all."

The robin took up his perch again by the wall and was very satisfied with the outcome. He flew off at once to the Citadel. The buzzards, who of course knew everything, remained calm.

"All is as it should be," said the buzzard wisely. "Leave it well alone now."

That is how Eddie made his bond of friendship with Sargasso; a strong and unbreakable flow of feelings ran between them, a rare link that would never be broken. Eddie and Ellie were now held in very high esteem by the Seafarers of the creek.

***

As Eddie's passion for all things connected with the sea grew, Ellie developed her own interests. She particularly liked visiting the old church at the castle. The beautiful stained-glass windows told stories of tragedies and glories, and grateful memorials thanked brave soldiers from the town. She wondered many things as she looked around. How did they dress, where did they sit each week in the pews, why did one of the gravestones have a skull and crossbones on it?

One spring Saturday morning Ellie picked some primroses from the garden and feeling bored, she thought up a romantic

16

reason to visit the church. She liked an excuse to go out by herself.

"I think I'm going out to put these flowers on somebody's grave."

"Well, I've got to finish my French homework. And then I want to catch some prawns when the tide is out later on. Do you mind, Ellie, if I don't come with you? I've got a new net and I am dying to try it out."

"OK, tell Mother where I've gone. I'll be back in an hour. Bye." And off she went.

Ellie set off on the familiar route along the narrow shady lane which led to St. Petrox. She searched among the old headstones until she found one she liked. It was a man who had drowned at Dartmouth. The date was 1788 – yes, he would do. She wanted a little bowl to put them in and went inside the church to get one.

Ellie knew exactly where the key to the flower arranging cupboard was kept. The church was dark and gloomy inside compared to the bright sunshine she had just left. She took the key from its hiding place and pulled the heavy gold curtain aside which screened off the choir vestry. It was very quiet and there were no visitors about. Ellie put the little key in the padlock and opened the wooden door of the big dark flower arranging cupboard to look for a bowl.

Two eyes stared back at her. On the middle shelf was a tiny mouse sitting bolt upright nibbling something held in its dainty paws. They were both extremely startled to see each other and neither could move for a few seconds. The mouse stopped nibbling. Ellie stood still. The mouse stared back at her unafraid. How was she to get her bowl? She finally closed the door gently and sat down on the long bench in the dark choir vestry to think.

What's it doing there? she thought. *I had better have another look.*

Very carefully she took the door edge between her fingers and opened it just a couple of inches. It was still there. She opened the door just a little bit wider and peeped around the edge again. Goodness, there were two of them now, staring at Ellie. One was wearing a green and gold brocade waistcoat which had been made from an old collection bag that was passed around the church for the congregation to put their offerings in.

"Well don't just stand there," snapped the larger mouse. "We are in the most frightful draft. Hurry up and get whatever it is you want." He waved his tiny pink claws at her impatiently.

Ellie put her hand inside the cupboard and picked up the nearest bowl, slammed the door and ran outside the church. She sat down on the grassy bank next to the water tap.

That mouse actually spoke to me and he was so rude. It's our cupboard. What are they doing in there?

She put some water in the bowl and carried it round to the grave she had chosen and spread out the dainty primroses beside the old worn headstone. Ellie decided to leave the mice and go home. She didn't like being told off. She wandered up the path from the church to the café at the castle. When she got there, one man was painting the walls and another was painting the seats outside. A man with white hair and a moustache seemed to be in charge – he was waving his arms about and talking loudly. He was not happy.

"I've been in business for thirty years," he shouted. "I want to get this place open this year, not next year. Do you hear me?"

He seemed very angry. In her anxiety to get away she tripped over a scaffolding bar which was lying in the road. It made a loud clanging noise as it rolled over. Poor Ellie cried out in pain as she fell on the path, grazing her knee and hurting her hands.

"What's going on now, for heavens' sake?" called out the man as he stomped out of the shop to investigate the noise. He caught sight of Ellie nursing her poor gritty hands.

"What are you doing here?"

"Nothing," she answered, trying not to cry, "I was only walking by and I tripped over this pole and now I've hurt myself." She cradled her dirty hands together, which were bleeding a little, and sniffed miserably.

The man suddenly became much nicer. "I'm sorry you tripped over the pole. Brian!" he called, "Move these scaffolding poles will you. Somebody else will fall over and sue me for damages."

He brought Ellie gently with him into the café and down into the little dark kitchen. He sat her down and ran some warm water into the sink. "Put your hands in there," he said, "and we'll wash them."

Soon she was tidied up and George, who had introduced himself, presented her with a plate of strawberries he fetched out of the huge fridge. "Cream and sugar, madam?" he asked, bowing to her in an exaggerated gesture of politeness.

"Yes please," sniffed Ellie.

George went back outside to see what the workmen were doing. When he came back, Ellie had finished the strawberries and was scraping the bowl.

"Mmm, that was lovely," she said. "Thank you. Strawberries are my absolute favourite."

"My wife loved them too," he said wistfully. "She's dead now I'm afraid, but she was a nurse. Very fussy she was about everything."

He paused for a minute, looking sad, Ellie noticed.

"I had better go home now I think." She was a little embarrassed.

"Well Ellie," said George, smiling at her, "I'm going to be here all summer. Come and see me again won't you? I might need some help here in the kitchen – you never know. Now off you go."

19

"Goodbye George," said Ellie, getting up from the table, "and thank you."

Ellie had forgotten all about the mice in the flower arranging cupboard; she had met George and made a new friend, and hurrying back home she went down by the creek dying to tell Eddie all about it. He was in the water with his new prawn net and had a bucket with masses of prawns in it.

"Hi Ellie," he called up from the rocks as soon as he saw her, "I've done really well. Come and look." Eddie was excited and pleased, standing up to his waist in water with his new prawn net made from an old net curtain. Standing on a black rock quite near to Eddie, she noticed the seagull. She sat down to rest on the old manhole cover they always sat on. She watched the seagull, and he watched her.

"I am so glad we saved him," and she felt pleased. She watched Eddie working his way around the rocks with the seagull hopping along by his side. She closed her eyes and rested back against the wall feeling the warm sunshine suddenly making her drowsy.

She remembered the mice. She sat bolt upright. Could it have been real? She knew she had nodded off in the sun. May be it was a dream, she didn't know anymore. Eddie came back carrying his heavy bucket.

"Is that our seagull?"

"Yes it is," said Eddie, "He's the only one with one leg. But he seems to manage. He likes my prawns!" He threw one, dripping from the bucket, towards the gull who caught it in mid-air and swallowed it down in one gulp. Eddie and Ellie both laughed.

"See," said Eddie, "nothing wrong with him." The seagull cocked his head and looked inquiringly at him. "I've given him a name. I've decided to call him Sargasso because of his long journey home. I think he likes it, it's hard to tell." He laughed again.

He threw the gull another prawn. "Good catch isn't he?" Eddie said to Ellie, admiring his accuracy.

All the seashore inhabitants of the creek had heard of the seagull with one leg. He had become quite a celebrity in his world and had made friends with some humans.

"We are going to have a great summer Eddie," said Ellie. "There's new man at the café and he is opening soon. They are painting everything and have a new sign and... they are going to sell ice creams again."

"What's he like?" asked Eddie, packing up his things and peering into the bottom of his plastic bucket with great satisfaction.

"Oh, he is quite old with white hair and a moustache," said Ellie. "I fell over and hurt myself but he was very kind to me and I had some strawberries in the kitchen." she added triumphantly.

"Oh did you, you lucky thing." said Eddie. "Help me carry some of this stuff back will you? It's heavy now I've got so many prawns in it."

So together they carried the bucket and the net and the canvas bag all the way up the lane, slopping water out, the bucket swinging to and fro. Eddie was soaking wet. When they finally made it to the back door he took off all his wet things and ran shivering upstairs. Their mother came into the kitchen and rolled her eyes.

"Where's Eddie? No, don't tell me, I can see by the clothes on the back doorstep. Now listen, I want both of you to help me for a while."

"What do you want us to do?" asked Ellie reluctantly.

"I want to dig over the vegetable patch and make a little wall around it to keep the edges tidy. It's a nice afternoon and we'll soon get it done if there's three of us. I'll cook the prawns first and then we can get started."

When Eddie came downstairs he admired the prawns which

were sitting on a plate cooling. Then Ellie told him about their afternoon digging duties and he knew there was no escape. They climbed up the brick steps to the top garden which overlooked the old watermill. From there, Eddie could just see the water at the creek and he longed to be back there. He sighed.

"Come on Eddie." Ellie pushed him in annoyance. "We've got to help Mum today."

"Oh alright," he grumbled, "I'm going to. What have we got to do?"

Mother and Ellie marked out the boundaries with string and some sticks where they wanted to dig. Eddie's heart sank. *We will never do all that,* he thought miserably. It was slow work and they became hot and thirsty. Freddie turned up of course, to eat all the grubs and beetles.

"It's coming on very nicely," said Mother. She smiled at them both encouragingly. "It's really looking good. Could you find me just a few more big stones Eddie, for the wall?"

"Alright," sighed Eddie and wandered off deep into the undergrowth where mossy stones had fallen down. He pulled out the edges of several stones and a lot of soil tumbled down after them. Something caught his eye – white and long. It was dirty and muddy.

It's some sort of bone, he thought. He rubbed the mud off it but it wasn't a bone, it was a piece of chalky china broken at one end with a hole in it. *I know what it is, it's an old pipe. I wonder if there are any more?*

He put his hands back into the space and scooped out handfuls of dry crumbly soil. Out fell something fat and round and very muddy – the other half of the pipe. As Eddie rubbed it clean he could see it was a carved face of a man with a beard.

"This is lovely," he said out loud. "Look what I've found!"

He ran back to show them the broken pieces of pipe. "Isn't it beautiful?"

They both agreed that it was.

"Where did you find it?" asked Ellie, very excited. Are there anymore? Let's go and look." She and Eddie ran back to the hole under the tree roots and began digging and pulling out the earth. They found nothing.

"Do bring those stones over," called Mother, "Come on you two – half an hour and you can go and do what you like."

Eddie and Ellie reluctantly came back to the vegetable patch. Soon the stones were neatly arranged around the whole area, which was tidy and smooth, with rake marks running up and down it like the top of a shepherd's pie. Mother was very pleased.

"Well, I didn't think we would do all that today. Well done. Off you go now. Don't be late for tea and put the tools away for me in the shed." she added cheekily.

The two children hurried off and took a small trowel and fork out of the garden shed. They were very excited as they scrambled back up the bank to the old stone wall which was almost hidden by branches, brambles and moss. They pulled handfuls of inter-woven ivy trails off the floor to try to find a place to dig and they started jabbing with the trowel and fork. Several metallic sounds resounded from their frantic digging.

"There something here!" shouted Ellie ecstatically, "Can you hear that metal noise?" She was very excited. Dirt flew every-where.

Eddie tried to restrain her. "Be careful, we don't want to da-mage anything."

A black metal object came into view, long and rounded. As they unearthed it in great excitement, Eddie said, "I know what this is. It's part of an old pistol. Look, can you see the barrel? Oh

I hope it's all there, wouldn't it be fantastic?"

They worked hard together, scraping and digging carefully. Finally they exposed the whole thing. Part of the wooden handle had been eaten away and was full of mud. The trigger, barrel and hammer all seemed to be there. Eddie carefully lifted it out of its ancient hideaway and placed it gently on some dry twigs.

"Wow," he said, "it's really, really old, but considering that it's been buried it's not in bad condition. Let's dig some more Ellie."

They carried on, Eddie hit something hard again. The next things that revealed themselves were hard long objects. Eddie rubbed them on his tee shirt.

"These are bones," he said. "I thought they were more pipes but I don't think so. Have a look here."

"Ugh!" Ellie made a face. "Do you think they're real?"

"Of course they're real. "What you mean is, are they human? Well I don't know. It could be somebody's dog."

"Don't be silly," said Ellie, "whoever heard of a dog that smoked a pipe and had a gun?"

"Shut up!" said Eddie, "Make yourself useful and do some more digging."

"Dig yourself!" she answered him, giving him a push. They stopped arguing and got back to work and as they made a deeper hole a round white patch appeared. They looked at each other and stopped immediately.

"You don't think… It couldn't be…"

They carefully edged around the protruding creamy-coloured thing, with their fingers this time, and eventually there it was – a skull. It looked horrible; holes where eyes had been, a hole where a nose had been and teeth still good, closed together in a ghastly smile. Zigzag lines crossed the top and it was pierced with little holes.

"I don't like it. What shall we do now?" whispered Eddie, as he clutched Ellie's arm.

"I don't know," whispered Ellie back, "I don't like it either, but it's dead and it can't hurt us now. We had better not tell Mother, she will want to get the police and the History Society and the vicar and heaven knows who else. Do you think we should put it back and leave it?"

"No, let's just keep it a secret for now," said Eddie. "I'll get something to put it in," and made a step towards the garden shed.

"Don't leave me!" cried Ellie and grabbed his arm and they went together to the shed. An old sack, which had held daffodil bulbs, seemed to be the kindest thing.

"I don't know that a sack is quite the right place for someone's skull," giggled Ellie.

Eddie, being the braver, dislodged the bony skull from the earth and put it into the sack. Underneath it were more bones and also a chain.

"Look, there's a necklace. Get it out Ellie." She tugged it out of the earth. It was a long chain with a medallion on it.

Eddie, curious, gently took it from her and put it in his pocket. "I'll check on this later."

He knew his father had a lot of history books and he was determined to piece together this mystery.

"What shall we do now?" asked Ellie, who was by now tired, dirty, and fed up with the whole thing.

"We'll fill in the hole and then hide everything in the shed behind the lawnmower and nobody will find it."

Eddie soon hid every sign of their discovery. They went inside, and washed and tidied themselves for supper, both sitting down exhausted.

25

"What a busy day!" said Mother, smiling at them as she produced the prawns with bread and butter, and banana custard to follow.

"Did you find anything else interesting?"

"No actually we didn't," said Eddie, not daring to look at Ellie. "Are you pleased with your vegetable patch?" he asked, changing the subject.

"Oh yes, it's just how I wanted it, thank you. You both look very tired. Better have a hot bath." she advised kindly, grateful for their help. Ellie quickly lost interest in their discoveries and went to watch television, but Eddie couldn't wait to have another look at the medallion. Where had it come from? Who had it belonged to?

Chapter Three
An unexpected night-time visitor

After supper was over and they had cleared up the dishes, Eddie took himself off to his bedroom. Mother put the pipe on the dresser in the kitchen. Upstairs, Eddie examined the medal and chain that he had put in his pocket but it was too dirty to see much so he went into the bathroom and washed it gently with some soap. Back in his room he got a magnifying glass out of his drawer. It looked like gold. It was round and heavy and very beautiful. One side was written in very old English and the other side was in a foreign language.

"I think it might be Spanish," he murmured. He turned it over and tried hard to read the English letters: *'To Captain John Avery. In gratitude for your devotion to duty. Governor of Jamaica. Port Royal. 1630.'*

Eddie suddenly looked up and was drawn to stare out of the window. It was getting dark and the trees were spiky and black against the sky. He felt a funny feeling coming over him. Maybe hundreds of years ago this man might have lived somewhere near this house? He could have sailed here from Jamaica, all that way across the Atlantic and died here in this place.

He held the medallion tightly in his hand and covered it with his fingers. It was cold but as Eddie squeezed harder it became warm and then it got hot, very hot. Eddie felt it burning his hand. "Ouch! How weird." He dropped the medallion and it rolled into the bottom of his wardrobe. He didn't bother to pick it up. By now Ellie had had her bath and was in bed reading. Eddie knew better than to disturb her.

"Night Ellie," he called.

"Night, night Ed," she called back. "See you in the morning."

He had his bath, called goodnight to his mother and climbed into bed. He left a tiny gap in the curtains. His bed faced the window and looked out over the garden, the wall to the woods and the hill beyond. He thought he could hear a dog barking in the distance. He snuggled down underneath his duvet and got nice and warm and lay for long time thinking about the chance discoveries they had made that day. How long had the person's bones been buried there? Who had put him there? Why did they bury the pipe and pistol and medallion with him? As Eddie thought about everything and it all swirled round in his head he fell into a deep sleep. His mother peeped in but he was far too sleepy to even reply as she said "Goodnight" again. She visited Ellie who was also dead to the world. She went downstairs again to watch television and do a little needlework; a dog barked again in the distance and then everything fell quiet.

Eddie awoke in the middle of the night. He lay still, his heart beating loudly. He could hear the noise in his ears of his heart pounding. What was it? What had woken him? It was still dark and he sat up in bed. He could smell a very strange smell and hear a long steady squeaking noise, and then it stopped; and it came again. Eddie reached his arm out and turned his bedside light on.

"What the devil's that?" said a voice, and Eddie saw in the corner of his room a strange man sitting in the green rocking chair. The chair had come from Grandma's home and had a squeaky rocker. Eddie was not frightened, merely curious, as the man was smoking a pipe – a clay pipe with a carved face on it.

It's the one I dug up yesterday, thought Eddie. *He is wearing some very strange clothes,* was his next thought. Starting at the feet, he wore black shoes with square silver buckles, white stockings and knee-length baggy brown suede trousers, a white shirt with a brown leather belt, into which were tucked two pistols and a powder horn. Eddie eyed the pistols suspiciously. On top of the shirt he wore a black velvet coat with silver buttons and a blue sash and a black tricorn hat with a white ostrich feather in it. Clouds of dreadful smoke were coming out of the pipe and made them both cough. The man had a trimmed beard and long black hair tied behind his head. He jumped to his feet.

"Well sir, explain yourself!"

He seemed to be talking to Eddie who remained icily calm. It was possible that he was still dreaming, but on the other hand he felt very awake.

He must be a ghost, thought Eddie. *It's the only explanation.*

He took a deep breath and began, "My name is Edmund. I live here, this is my bedroom and you are sitting in my chair. Your smoke is very annoying and I would be grateful if you would kindly put out that pipe." He spoke firmly and clearly. "If you don't mind," he added for politeness, trying to remember his manners.

"Yes, yes, young man or Edmund, you are right and my most humble apologies. Captain John Avery, sir."

The man made a sweeping bow with his hat which he had snatched off his head. He began at once to tamp down the pipe.

"I shall sit; my pipe and I are old friends sir, and it is many a year since I have had a good smoke." He chuckled, thinking this a great joke. He rocked back and forth in the chair, which began squeaking again.

"There are many mysteries here I do not understand," he said. "What is this strange candle that has no flame?" pointing to Eddie's bedside light.

"This room, this house," he made a sweep with his arm. "I did not leave this place like this." He shook his head and slumped back in the chair. "It is a veritable mystery."

Eddie showed him how the light switched on and off. Captain Avery sat stunned. "Amazing!" he kept saying, "Amazing!"

"Are those your own pistols?" asked Eddie, pointing to his belt.

"These, oh yes indeed, young sir." He patted them both. "Wheel lock repeating pistols. Uses ball and wad and black powder, saved my life in Jamaica sir and been my best friends since." He stroked the walnut stocks. "Finest pistols money can buy."

He pulled one out and held it out to Eddie. It was exactly like the one Eddie had dug up yesterday only clean and well-oiled. Eddie was suddenly confused and shook his head.

"Where did you come from, sir?" he asked, feeling a little shaken. "Are you the bones I found yesterday? I found that pipe but it was broken and that pistol and it was no good. They were all buried in the garden. Are they the same ones?"

"I know not." answered the man, shaking his head sadly. He gripped the arms of the chair and sat up straight.

"I tell you sir, I awoke at the foot of that cupboard, fully clothed, my pipe and pistols lying beside me. You must have brought me hither. But I lived here with Bartholomew, my servant and my dog. My dog, my dog," he was getting upset now, "Where is my dog? Syracuse." he called, looking wildly around him.

"Shush," said Eddie sternly, "You'll wake everybody up."

It must have been the medallion, thought Eddie. *It got so hot. It must have brought him back from the dead. I wonder if there is anything left in the sack in the shed? I must find out.* The man had sunk back into the chair, looking tired. Eddie hopped out of bed and opened the wardrobe door wide. The medallion was lying on the floor. He picked it up and put it in his hand again.

"Is this yours, Captain, sir?" he asked. He opened his fingers and showed it to him. The man sighed, looking at the medallion.

"Indeed it is," he answered. "All I had left of the treasures I once owned." He shook his head sadly, "Lost forever now. All lost."

Eddie closed his fingers around the medallion. It became warm and then hot and before he could warn him, in a quick flash, the chair was empty. The man was gone, completely vanished – all except the faint smoky smell from the clay pipe that still hung around in the bedroom.

What had happened? Eddie could not quite understand. It had to be the gold medallion. When he squeezed it, it got hotter and hotter and strange things began. He took a pencil and notebook out of the desk drawer and carefully copied the writings and engravings on the medal. He also wrote down the name Captain John Avery again. He didn't risk rubbing it; he didn't quite feel up to another meeting with the strange gentleman. His task completed, he put everything away and lay down again in the dark. The bed was cold now and Eddie shivered. He looked at the time, it was 3.35 a.m. He closed his eyes tightly and tried to go back to sleep. An owl hooted in the woods behind the curtains. The dog barked again. In his mind he tried to recall everything that had happened. He pictured the clothes the captain had been wearing. He tried so hard that he eventually fell asleep, rather restless and confused.

Eddie and Ellie's discovery that afternoon in the garden was not the secret they thought it to be. At that very moment in the dark and windy heights of the pine trees it was being discussed at great length. Faithful Freddie had of course been perched in the branches above their heads, as the children dug and discovered more and more. The robin was duty bound to report the news of the uncovering of the bones to the Citadel. He wasn't looking forward to it.

He bravely flew to the top of the hill as it was getting dark, to disclose the news. The buzzard opened his huge majestic wings, flapped them a few times to stretch them and then settled down to give audience to the robin. The tiny bird was rather overawed and nervous. He knew it would stir up trouble the minute the children had made their discovery and had started disturbing and exploring the old woodland. He tried to explain that they had been gardening and had broken into the old grave by accident. Eddie's curiosity had led them to investigate further and the consequence of unearthing the bones had not been foreseen. He had no idea how Eddie had recalled the spirit of the old sea captain or how he had sent him away again. It was all a mystery – wasn't it? The robin cowered low, waiting.

The buzzard was displeased. He said nothing at all. His partner, the female buzzard sat nervously beside him, blinking her eyes and shaking her head from side to side. Eventually he spoke:

"I have nurtured this dread in my heart. For years, ever since those human children arrived, I have known this day would come. Now there will be disruption; disturbance of ancient angers, which had been laid to rest long, long ago and forgotten. Those children are innocent of the power they may unwittingly release. I can foresee great troubles ahead. I must think precisely and carefully on this matter and on our future. Go now Robin and be vigilant, take up your position, post the blue tits on duty as well and miss nothing. Too much is at stake."

He dismissed the robin, who bowed and said,

"Yes Master, it will be done." and flew away, grateful to have escaped. He flew down to the wall by the kitchen and tucked himself up under a leafy shrub.

They were all asleep now, each with their own secrets – Ellie and her meeting with the two white mice and Eddie dreaming of the strange sea captain who had entered his life.

***

The next day Eddie woke up tired and grumpy. Gradually the memories of the previous night flooded back to him and he jumped out of bed and pulled back the curtains.

I must go out to the shed at once and look.

He hurried downstairs into the kitchen. The pipe had gone! He unlocked the back door, ran up the steps and opened the shed door. He pulled aside the lawnmower and found the sack. It was quite empty!

What shall I tell Ellie? She will wonder where it's all gone.

He was keen to go to the library and find out all he could about Captain Avery and events in Jamaica around the time dated on the medallion. He didn't like keeping secrets from Ellie but she might be frightened. He went back down the steps and into the kitchen for breakfast.

He put the kettle on and filled up the toaster. He heard Ellie and his mother upstairs. They soon smelt the toast.

"Thank you Eddie," said his mother as she came into the kitchen. "What are you doing today?"

"I'm going down to the library," said Eddie, "Coming Ellie? I've got some research to do for a project at school."

"All right," said Ellie, "I'll help you."

As soon as they were ready, they set off for the library. The library lady found the big reference books they wanted. They carried the books to the desk and Eddie turned the dusty pages over. The first book had nothing at all so they started leafing through the second book which had black and white pen engravings in it.

"What exactly are we looking for?" asked Ellie.

"I want to find out if any famous sailors or pirates lived here in Dartmouth."

He returned to the book. "It says here that fleets of boats set sail to Newfoundland and came back after long voyages loaded with valuable cargoes of tobacco. That was in the 17th century. Look up the section on pirates, Ellie." They turned the big pages and found a picture of a pirate called Long Ben Avery. Eddie nearly jumped off the chair.

The picture showed a pirate standing in front of a man-of-war with three masts, sails rigged and flags flying. He was wearing a black tricorn hat and a buttoned coat. A belt was fastened round his waist with two pistols tucked into it, a powder bag and cutlass in his hand.

"Read what it says. Ellie." he said excitedly.

Ellie began, "At the end of the 17th century 'Long Ben Avery', an Englishmen called John Avery but nicknamed Long Ben, was the most famous pirate of them all. He operated his piracy on the Isle Ste Marie halfway down the coast of Madagascar. He captured a ship called Gunsway which belonged to an Indian Prince, full of gold, silver and diamonds. Avery swindled his partners out of their share and set off on a voyage which led him to the Bahamas, Boston and eventually Ireland and England. It is rumoured that Avery himself was cheated by the merchants he entrusted to sell the treasure. He died a pauper in his native Devon. Oh isn't that sad Eddie?"

Eddie sat back in the chair. So he was a pirate after all but he had lost everything. That was what Captain Avery had told him. "Is there anything about Jamaica?"

She flipped back to the index at the back "G, H, I, J... Yes, here we are, Jamaica. 'In the early 1600s Henry Morgan, a famous pirate, was part of an English force that took Jamaica from the Spanish. He later became Lieutenant-Governor of Jamaica. He was a popular figure in England and received a knighthood from King Charles II. He amassed huge wealth and estates and lead many daring raids on Panama City'. Is that what you want Eddie?"

"Yes that's great." he replied.

So the medal was given to Captain Avery by Henry Morgan, presumably for his help in capturing Jamaica from the Spanish. No wonder he kept it, thought Eddie. He wrote all that down too.

"I think that's enough for now Ellie, let's pack it up and go down to the Sea Shanty for some chips. Got any money?"

Off they went to the chip shop. Such a wonderful smell came out of the door luring them in. They searched around in their pockets and found two pounds in coins.

"Salt and vinegar?" asked the young girl.

"Oh yes please. Lots," said Ellie, "thanks." And off they went.

Eddie picked a seat right at the end of the river front by the big bronze cannon where they both sat down and dived into the chips.

"Mmm." They both agreed there is nothing as good as chips when you are starving.

Sitting together in silence, Eddie mulled over what he had learnt in the library.

"Eddie, do you believe that animals can talk?" Ellie asked him suddenly. "Do you think it's possible?" She looked at him closely.

"Well I'm sure it's possible, I don't know, I haven't heard any animals talking. Why?"

Ellie started to explain her visit to the church, the cupboard and the two mice. She said she thought it was real but she wasn't sure. "I need to go again to make sure."

"Well let's do it then," said Eddie. I'll come with you and then if I hear them too we'll know that it's true. Do you want to?"

"I think so," said Ellie rather seriously. "I want them to be there, I want to believe that it's true." She looked at Eddie to see what he thought.

Eddie saw her earnest face wanting him to agree with her. He knew she believed she had seen the mice. He felt guilty for keeping his own secret from her and as she stood up ready to go he caught her arm and restrained her, sitting her down again on the wooden seat.

"Just a minute, I want to tell you something but you mustn't tell a single soul Ellie, I mean it. Do you promise?"

"Yes," said Ellie wide eyed. "Of course. What is it?"

Eddie began, "Well you know the bones and things we dug up the other day and we hid them in the shed?"

"Yes," said Ellie, nodding.

"They're not there anymore. They've gone."

"What do you mean, they've gone?"

"They have turned into the spirit of the person they used to be."

"What, resurrected you mean?"

"Well… sort of. They've turned into a real man. He came to visit me in the night. He is from a different time, ages ago. He dresses in funny clothes and speaks in an old fashioned way. I think it's the medallion we found that brings him back. It's all a bit strange. I can't quite believe it. Is it possible Ellie?" It was his turn to look into his sister's face for the answer he wanted.

"But it must be," she replied, holding his arm, "Just like my mice in the flower arranging cupboard. We must believe it's true. You come and see my mice and I'll come and see your man."

She laughed. Eddie felt better, now he had told his secret. Ellie wasn't like other girls; she seemed to understand what he felt. He was very proud of her.

"Come on, let's go." They both jumped up from the seat, putting their chip wrappings into the bin. Eddie patted the bronze cannon as he passed.

***

Back at Watermill Cottage the robin was worried. He had been summoned back for another meeting at the Citadel. The buzzard was adamant – no more digging around in the woodland by the children. One more happening, one more spiritual reincarnation, and he would have to take steps. He didn't want to, but he alone knew that unearthings could lead to terrible things. There were many bones buried in the woods, young and old, good and evil and many spirits that could easily appear. The buzzard, as ruler of the kingdom, however, could unleash an immense power of his own; every bird and animal would do his bidding without question. They had their own way of dealing with unwanted spirits.

He had no power below the shoreline, however. All the sea creatures answered to a different master – the mighty Spirit of the Sea. The two kingdoms would have to work together if they were to defeat the spirits from the Other World should they be released. Sargasso was the one to mediate, he had no doubt; a bird like himself but a Seafarer, he linked the sea, the sky and the land and most important of all, he understood humans.

Freddie was sent down to find Sargasso and arranged for him to go to Sugary Cove at an appointed time. The buzzard would fly down the valley and meet the seagull perched on the wooden railings where the rocky coast met the sea. The time was set as the last rays of light faded in the west, at the time which is neither day nor night, but in-between. Sargasso was to fly over the waves, search out the voice of the sea and bring back his findings. It was to be a momentous occasion. Would the Spirit of the Sea agree to help him?

Chapter Four
First visit to the Tea Shop

The two youngsters made their way over the bridge and along the road, hair flying and coats undone, and eventually stopped breathless and panting at the wall by the church. They opened the big door and went down the steps, entering the shadowy stillness of the old building, smelling the musty air which today was heavily laden with the fragrance of white lilies from the altar.

Ellie got the keys from their safe hiding place, pulled aside the heavy gold curtains, and found the padlock key from the large bunch. Eddie stood beside her, looking over her shoulder. She opened the door.

"Can you see anything?" whispered Eddie loudly.

"Shhhh," Ellie hissed at him angrily. "Shut up for a minute and stop pushing me!"

They both stood in silence. A very small sneeze echoed around the cupboard. "Atisshooo!" Then another and another. "Atisshooo, atisshooo!"

Eddie and Ellie looked at each other, mouths dropping open.

"Oh dear, those wretched lilies do make me sneeze so," said a small voice, sniffing. "People are so inconsiderate of those of us who suffer with hay fever. It really is too bad," she complained.

A little figure hurried along the shelf and looked out at the two stunned faces. She screamed a small high pitched scream and rushed back into the darkest recesses of the cupboard.

"Ferdinand, Ferdinand, they are back again!" she screamed.

A voice was heard sighing. "Oh Isabella, what is it now? You make such a drama, dear, of everything. What can be the matter now?" replied the long suffering voice.

"I'm not making it up, they're outside again – you told me they had gone."

As the fascinated children watched, two figures ran along the shelf together holding hands. The lady mouse was dressed in an embroidered gown and hat that Ellie had only seen in history books. The gentleman mouse was wearing an embroidered waistcoat of green and gold threads and tiny leather breeches of pale cream. In his hand he held a small walking stick.

The gentleman mouse was brave. He had spoken to Ellie before and stood quite fearlessly in front of them, shouting angrily.

"You have frightened my wife Isabella." He shook his little stick at them. "I will not have it. Do you hear me? She suffers with her nerves and is not to get excited. Now go away and leave us alone!"

He hopped in rage. The pretty little white mouse in the beautiful dress sneezed again and again. Eddie and Ellie looked at each other, nodded and closed the door. They tiptoed out of the church into the bright fresh air and laughed and laughed. Eddie gasped and wiped his eyes. He hadn't laughed so much for a long time.

"Oh dear," he said to Ellie, "It's too much really." He started to laugh again just at the thought of it. "Well I can't argue with you now Ellie, they are definitely there and they can most definitely talk."

They walked up the narrow path past the gravestones round the wall which overlooked the castle and climbed up the steps to the tea shop. There was a man up a ladder fastening some new gold letters onto the front: THE CASTLE TEA SHOP. It all looked very impressive.

"Hello George," called Ellie, recognising the man up the ladder, who turned around.

"Hello again Ellie," he replied smiling. "Feeling better?"

"Oh yes thank you," she said. "This is my brother Eddie – we were just passing."

"Well well, how about an ice cream, you two? Come on, what flavour would you like?" He led them into the café. It looked so clean and new, everything ready for the first customers.

"When are you opening the café?" asked Eddie, "It's looking great in here."

"Soon as my sister Bridget gets here. We've rented the old bathhouse just along the road. Now there's vanilla, toffee, strawberry, and chocolate chip, bubblegum, thunder and lightning – they are the new ones to try." George added very pleased with himself. "What would you like?"

"Oh, let me see, thunder and lightning please," said Ellie. "It's so hard to choose."

"Bubblegum for me," said Eddie.

"Right," said George, and he loaded two crispy cones with the fragrant dollops. They took them from him, thanked him and sat down to lick the wonderful concoctions.

"Mmm," said Ellie, "this is really good."

"So is mine," said Eddie, licking round and round the cone. "It's amazing."

George watched them closely.

"I am pleased you like them. Well, tell your friends we're open now for ice cream."

Eddie liked George.

"If you ever need help washing-up, if you get too busy, I'll always help out," Eddie offered.

"That is a very kind thought Eddie," said George, rather touched. "I'll write the phone number down for you." and he got up, found a pad and pen and scribbled the number for him.

"Me too," said Ellie, kicking Eddie under the table furiously. "I offered first." She made a face at him.

"Well now, I've got two extra staff for emergencies, fancy that. Good, good. Bridget will be glad because she's worried about how we'll manage in a rush at holiday times." George beamed at them both with his big cheery face.

"I am glad I have met you two," he said, "I think we are going to get along, don't you?"

The youngsters got up from the table and saying their good-byes they left the café, promising to come back to meet Bridget in a few days time.

"He's nice," said Eddie, as they hurried back home.

Ellie said very little, until they walked down the gravel path by the creek, when she turned to Eddie and said, "I was going to help him, you know. I asked first," and she seemed to be rather upset.

"Well I didn't know, did I? I don't care anyway. You can do the washing-up all summer if you want to. I want to be outside sailing and fishing." They walked up the path to the cottage and went inside.

"Where have you been?" said Mother quite crossly. "You're late for lunch and your father is on the way home."

Ellie was still a bit sulky and Eddie tried hard to bring her out of her moodiness.

"Come on Ellie, let's look at the notebook with the notes from the library."

A car pulled into the driveway and the engine cut out.

"Dad's home!" They both scrambled down from the chairs and rushed to the door. In a few moments their father appeared laden down with briefcase, jacket, bunch of flowers and two carrier bags. He came up the steps into the hallway.

"Hi, you two terrors," he said laughing, and putting his luggage down he kissed Ellie and ruffled Eddie's hair.

"Where's Mum?" he asked.

Eddie and Ellie explored the interesting carrier bags they had each been given. Inside them were two Balinese kites made out of silk and wood, with dragon's faces and sharp teeth; one was blue and one was orange. Down at the bottom of the bags were two boxes of chocolate sea shells.

"Thanks Dad." They both hugged him.

"That's alright, it's very hard to know what you want now you are both getting so grown up," he replied.

Later as he sat with their mother, Mary, drinking tea and eating cake, he sighed.

"Just one more cup and we'll go and give those kites a try – yes?"

It couldn't have been a better afternoon. Breezy and bright, the sun filtered through every branch and lit up the mossy hiding places in between. The family started the effortful climb up the hill behind the cottage, followed now by the robin and blue tits hopping along behind them. By the time they reached the top everyone was out of breath, panting and very grateful to stop.

"This is what I've been waiting for," said Father, "this view of the river, looking out to sea, the cliffs, and the woods – it's all in

43

my mind when I'm away." He sat down on the grass and held his face up to the sun. "This is just heaven. I've really missed this."

They sat down in silence enjoying the fresh air and sunshine after the strenuous walk. Gulls called and swooped over the river mouth and tiny boats chugged out to sea. At the top of Gallants Bower, sitting on the old earthworks, the view was magnificent.

"Right, what about those kites?" asked Father, springing to his feet. "Let's have a bit of action."

For the next hour they tussled with strings, handles, tangles, terrified seagulls, collisions and eventual success. The kites flew wonderfully. The wings of the dragons were hand painted and made a spectacular splash of colour in the sky. It was a great afternoon and eventually Mother set off down the hill with Eddie and Ellie, leaving her husband to enjoy a few minutes of quiet contemplation and relaxation alone in the spot he loved.

He was thinking about Eddie's birthday and that now was the time to give in to his constant begging for a boat; just a small one, the right size for the running mooring in the creek. Both children could swim now and in minutes his decision was made. He got up and walked down the hill towards the castle just as large black clouds seemed to be gathering on the horizon and a chilly breeze sprang up and whipped around him.

Better get home quickly, it's going to rain. I wonder what's for supper?

The sea was churning up and a storm was definitely brewing. He marched steadily on towards home where a lovely smell welcomed him as he opened the back door. It was warm and cosy inside and he felt very glad to be back with his family and to forget about rules, regulations, paperwork and planning, ships and the sea.

As they sat in the kitchen around the table Freddie peeped into the window. In the distance the robin heard a dog barking. He had heard it before. It became louder and more insistent.

Eddie looked up from his delicious fish pie. He stopped eating.

"I've heard that dog before. Can you hear it? I wonder whose it is?"

The barking stopped. They resumed their supper and the usual chit chat carried on.

"It seems to have stopped now," remarked Eddie. "He shouldn't be out in the dark on his own anyway. I wonder where his owner is? Maybe he's lost."

Quite suddenly he had rather a scary thought. It couldn't be the dog Captain Avery was looking for, could it?

Chapter Five
Unrest in the woodland, and a newcomer

Down at Sugary Cove, exciting things were happening. At in-between, the set time, the buzzard flew down through the trees, circling the small sheltered bay a few times to establish a good vantage point. He settled himself on the sturdy wooden railings above the cove, from where he had a good view of the beach and out to sea. Wooded and rocky outcrops edged the small bay and on the farthest tip the buzzard spied Sargasso sitting on a rock. The seagull waited and the buzzard nodded to him. At once the gull took off, and skimming over the darkening water, flew straight out to sea becoming smaller and smaller until he was out of sight.

Black clouds rolled in from the horizon; the wind whipped up and sent skittering wavelets zigzagging over the surface of the sea. The sky grew darker and darker. Nothing happened. The buzzard was nervous; his feathers were ruffling in the strengthening wind. He didn't like the sea. As the tide came in nearer and nearer, waves bounced off the rocks and sent white spray upwards. Noticing a twisted tree overhanging the cliff the large bird flew down to perch in its branches for a better look; he was

Sugary Cove

now as close to the sea as he had ever been.

Meanwhile Sargasso flew on and on, further and further away from land. The sea was rough out here with a big swell and high winds and he was buffeted by its strength, making it more difficult to fly. He saw a shoal of glinting fish below him, a sparkling silver and black moving pattern. They patrolled the seas looking and searching for strangers. Immediately the fish started to leap out of the water and in tiny tinkling voices called,

"Who are you? Whom do you seek?"

The seagull told them his name and asked to speak to the Spirit of the Sea. The tiny fish called his name. "Sargasso! Sargasso! Sargasso! Come with us, with us, with us, follow us, us, us, us."

Grateful for a sign of what he had to do, he hovered just above them as they turned round and headed back towards the shore. What a dance they led him! They dived and raced and leapt and swerved, twisting and turning. Sargasso followed, enjoying the chase as they entered the quiet waters of the cove, leaping higher and higher.

The buzzard saw his return and felt relieved. Sargasso rested on a rock opposite him waiting for the next sign; he didn't know what to do. Suddenly there was a clap of thunder and a flash of lightning and the cove waters were lit up. Out of the water, by the edge of the high tide, two whales reared up, their heads bursting through the water, terrifying the buzzard who tried not to fly away with fright. A flock of black-backed gulls screamed in overhead, dark against the sky and flew round and round in the air, circling the whales.

"We have received a signal from the Silver Tinkling Shoals," thundered the voices of the whales exactly together. "What do you want from the Seafarers?"

The buzzard opened his beak, and gathering his courage, he

spoke.

"I seek your assistance in the event of any disturbances or conflict that might befall us in the future – I have no control over the sea creatures, and we live in such close kingdoms that we may need each other should disaster befall us."

"It is granted," boomed the voices of the whales in unison. "The Great Spirit has sent us. We speak for him. We will turn to stone here on the shores of this cove, watching and waiting, until you need us."

"My kingdom is grateful for your sacrifice," replied the buzzard graciously. "You have given up your freedom for us."

"We have long lives yet, Bird King, and much to do."

As their tails disappeared beneath the waves, white hard icy stones hammered down from the sky and their voices became fainter as they sank into the water. Soon only their two heads were visible; they had turned into black rocks and moved no more.

The sky flashed and thunder roared as the huge shoal of fish leapt and sparkled and darted beneath the wild seas, disappearing into the darkness. The screaming flock of gulls became silent and flew far out towards the horizon leaving the buzzard staring at the two black rocks lying on the shore, being pounded by the waves of the high tide. Sargasso came to join him and they flew together up, up, up into the woodland and came to rest in the tall pine trees. Their ordeal had wearied them.

"Something strange is coming. It will not be long. I feel it," said the buzzard, shaking his head. "Thank you Sargasso. At least we have a great ally now to help us."

Sargasso left the buzzard and was flying down the hillside through the trees towards the sea when he saw a black dog. The wind came through the tree branches and they swayed together as the strong forces of the wind rumbled like the sound of a

49

far-off train. The black dog was searching and sniffing, looking for his master. He looked up at the seagull. The gull screamed out loud, for the dog had red eyes and they shone up through the twisting boughs. It barked at the bird, baring its teeth. Sargasso turned sharply and headed back towards the creek finding shelter in the lime kiln. He was utterly exhausted and fell into a deep but troubled sleep.

***

The next day at breakfast Father made his announcement:

"I think, Eddie, that it's time we bought a boat. How about we start looking today in time for your birthday? Eddie can you hear me?" Eddie was speechless. He went bright red with sheer delight.

"Do you mean it, Dad?" he asked cautiously, not daring to believe it.

"Of course I do – you've been on and on about a boat since you were six years old. I think it's a good idea. We'll have great fun learning to sail it – Ellie can come too. Lots of girls sail now, some are nearly as good as us."

"Dad!" Ellie punched his arm.

"I'll make a few phone calls in a minute," said Father confidently. "Leave me to get on with it. I'll let you know. Hop it!"

Eddie and Ellie both went upstairs.

Peter went to the red telephone hanging on the wall beside the back door and dialled a number, leaning against the warm stove as he waited.

"Hi Alan, ringing about the boat, I'd love to have a look at it. OK, about four-thirty, when you've finished. I'll be there. Thanks very much. Bye."

"That's good," he said, "Just the price to settle if the boat's in good nick. She's called Skylark. Just the right size for the kids.

What do you think, Mary?" He sat down and waited.

"Well... if it's what you want and you think that Eddie can manage it."

"Don't worry, they'll be fine," reassured her husband. "They won't go anywhere until I'm absolutely sure they are competent." He drank his tea and patted her hand.

"They are growing up and have got to have some freedom. It'll be great for them you'll see, don't worry about them so much."

He looked very pleased and went off upstairs to tell Eddie. Mary sat still at the table, worried and upset.

This is stupid, she thought, jumping up and pushing her brown hair back from her face. *They are not young children any more. Peter's quite right.*

She opened the back door and went outside to look around the garden. Eddie and Ellie came dashing out to find her.

"Mum, isn't it brilliant, Dad's going to look at Alan's boat this afternoon! You know the one, he's been doing it up down at the creek. It's even got a launching-trolley with it. I've looked at it a hundred times."

"Well there's nothing definite yet so why don't you go round to the tea shop and see if you can make yourselves useful? It will pass the time for you until this afternoon?" suggested Mary.

Ellie agreed nodding excitedly, and Eddie, who would much rather have looked at the boat again, reluctantly followed her to the tea shop. George and Bridget fetched Coca-Colas and ham and cheese toasted sandwiches from the white kitchen and then George came over to their table and whispered in her ear.

"We could do with ten minutes washing-up Ellie, if you want to."

Ellie, filled with pride, followed George into the kitchen, her face pink and blushing. What fun – a real job! Bridget welcomed her into the warm privacy of the kitchen and made her wash her hands and put on a large white apron.

"There now, you're ready to start. Here's some nice hot soapy water and a cloth. Clean drying clothes in the drawer here." She pointed to the correct drawer.

"We've been too busy to do much washing-up. Quite a rush we've had."

Eddie ate his sandwich and called goodbye. He left at once feeling cross and in the way as Ellie started very carefully handling the pretty crockery and glasses and soon had a great pile of steaming clean dishes. She gazed out of the kitchen window. *What a fantastic place to work,* she thought. It took about half an hour to dry and put everything away exactly where Bridget had told her and then there was a lull in the trade.

"Well dear, that was well done, here's a little something for your trouble," and she pressed some pound coins into Ellie's hand. "I think we're going to get along just fine, don't you?" and she smiled at the young girl. Her first wages! Ellie was thrilled. She stayed and chatted for a while and Bridget asked her all about her family.

"It's Eddie's birthday soon," she told Bridget and George. "Mum and Dad are getting him a boat. He's very excited."

"Well I'm all for sailing and the sea, used to sail myself up at Robin Hood Bay." George smiled at her. "Good for him."

She skipped home to tell her mother what had happened but everybody seemed to be somewhere else. Ellie went up into the woods and found the tree swing in the cool shadows. She climbed onto the smooth wooden bar and swung gently backwards and forwards under the trees, hypnotically enjoying the rhythm of the movement. She drifted backwards and forwards, backwards and forwards. She closed her eyes. It was so peaceful. The trees rustled and there was a soft breeze.

She opened her eyes, jolting awake and on the path just in sight and slightly further up the hill she saw a dog – a black dog, standing quite still, with his nose in the air and his ears alert. He stood there and turned his head to look at her. He stared unmoving and even from that distance Ellie could see his eyes. There was something strange about the eyes. Were they red? The dog turned away and disappeared behind a tree. He was gone.

Ellie sat still, waiting to hear movements in the undergrowth or for its owner to appear, striding down the hill. Nothing happened. She heard no one. She waited.

That's very funny, she thought. *It's gone – vanished.*

Her quiet dreamy swing now over, Ellie felt nervous and alone. It was too quiet, too still. Nothing was moving anywhere. She didn't like it. She felt frightened. With her heart beating faster and faster she jumped off the swing and ran home feeling as if something was watching her.

Chapter Six
Eddie has an unwelcome visitor

Eddie was sitting in the kitchen watching football on television as Ellie came running inside and slammed the door. She was so relieved to be safe at home.

"Have you seen a black dog in the woods?"

"No I haven't but I've heard one barking, don't you remember?"

"Yes, I do now. Maybe it's the same one."

Trying to take his mind off the boat, Eddie remained fixed on the television, not really listening.

Peter walked down to the creek at four-thirty where Alan was waiting by the boat. He had untied the tarpaulin and pulled it back. He stepped forward and shook hands with Eddie's father.

"I've just been giving her a tidy-up," he explained. "The paint is all dry now and the varnish is set hard. Looks good doesn't she?"

"Are all the sails there?" asked Peter, "In good nick are they?"

"I think so, haven't used them this year, but they were new so they should be alright." He unrolled the creamy canvas and Peter examined them carefully.

"Yes, they look fine."

The boat was a 12ft Bermuda rigged clinker sailing dingy, with one mainsail and one foresail. The top edge was varnished, the outside painted green and the inside cream. Some ropes were knotted neatly together, a pair of oars inside, a wooden rudder and a tiller bar to steer with. Peter checked it all over in silence, taking his time to look at everything.

Eddie and Ellie crept out of the house and down the lane, hiding round the wall at the bottom. They watched and waited. Eddie's heart lifted when he saw the two men shake hands.

"Great!" he yelled and they both rushed over to the boat. Ellie, Eddie and Peter covered her up again to prevent rainwater and seagulls from spoiling it and when all was secure they walked up the short hill back home. Both of them were so excited they fell into the kitchen laughing and fighting to be the first one to tell Mother. She appeared on the landing and said,

"I can guess, I think. You are boat owners now. Sailing lessons for you two then, starting tomorrow I hope."

Father appeared, grinning.

"Well I've done it. It's ours now, just a few things to sort out. Hopefully we will get her afloat before I leave tomorrow evening. Got a tide table Eddie anywhere? Make a list Ellie," and she ran to get her famous note book and wrote down the list that her father dictated. "Petrol can and leads, small anchor, spanner, pliers, spark plugs, marlin spike, and stern rope, bow rope, a box of distress flares (in date), knife, life jackets, baler and spare oars. That will do to start with."

"Golly," said Ellie, "There won't be any room for us."

"We will have to buy the lifejackets and flares in town tomorrow," Peter told them firmly.

"Can't we go out without them, just once?" asked Ellie.

"Certainly not. You must get into the habit of always wearing them."

"But we're good swimmers," argued Eddie, "I'd just swim to the shore and wouldn't panic."

"Well you think that now Eddie, but I can assure you, better sailors than you'll ever be have drowned. You get tired and cold and just slip under the water. Gone. The orange life jacket is bright and keeps you afloat when you're tired or unconscious. That is what they are for."

On that gloomy note, Peter announced that he was starving and wanted to go down to Dartmouth for fish and chips.

"What a good idea," said Mary, "no cooking tonight!"

"I don't want to go," said Eddie. "I'm going to fly my kite for a bit."

"Alright Eddie, we'll see you back here."

He went upstairs and picked up the blue-painted kite. He was feeling very happy indeed. Some days were good days, days to remember all your life. This was one of them. He felt very satisfied.

He looked out of the window of his bedroom which overlooked the garden and the woods and saw Sargasso on the garden seat. Something was wrong. He never sat there. He raced downstairs and up into the garden and sat down beside the seagull.

"Is everything alright?" asked Eddie, looking anxiously at him. The seagull lifted his head and made quiet croaking noises.

"Come with me Sargasso, come up into the woods with me to fly my kite," he pleaded.

The seagull shook his head. He wasn't brave enough to enter the Woodlanders' territory again – not after meeting the dog from the spirit world. Eddie picked up his kite, and the seagull flapped its wings and flew away. Eddie was unable to make any sense of Sargasso's strange behaviour.

Eddie entered the woods at the foot of Gallants Bower and felt a quiet breeze rustling the trees. As he reached the first bend there was a loud smacking noise and two pigeons flew out from the branches, their wings clapping together, making him jump. He plodded on, up and up, reaching the rooted steps leading from the bluebell woods to the grassy heathland. Two black rooks flying low passed him, cawing much louder than usual. He looked back suddenly, and saw behind him a black dog in the shadows of the woods. It was standing quite still, nose up in the air and his tail up too. It was quite alone.

There's a dog. Is it him? Could his bones have been disturbed too?

From where he was he could see the sun setting over the valley below him; the sky was rose tinted, golden and bright. As he continued on along the path and round the corner, the huge ash tree at the very top of the earthworks was illuminated eerily in a strange pink light. Then the wind began to blow noisily along the ridge, louder and stronger, coming up through the trees. Eddie felt slightly panicky and a little unsure.

All of a sudden the dog appeared from nowhere and threw himself at Eddie, knocking him to the ground. At the same moment, a seagull dived down, screaming and screeching and went for the dog's eyes. Sargasso pecked and bit the dog and it growled and retreated to the woods again as fast as it had come. Eddie lay on the ground winded, unable to move, not quite knowing what had happened to him. He sat up eventually and saw Sargasso circling round in the sky, calling to him. He watched the seagull for a few moments and then it dived towards the sea and out of sight. The dog had vanished.

57

This was Syracuse. He roamed the woods constantly searching for his master during the darkening evening light and on into the night. Some of his bones had been released from the grave, where he had been buried beside his beloved master Captain Avery. The dog had spent many years voyaging with his master until they had reached their final resting place in the thatched cottage at the top of the creek. He was restless and out of his time, uneasy and alone. He persisted in his search, unable to make contact with the sea captain, who unknowingly had left the dog behind.

Eddie, shaken and scared, could only remember the dog's eyes: they were red, the eyes of the spirit world. He got to his feet and hurried back into the woodland and the path which led home. The path and the undulating terrain all seemed to melt into one in the pink dimming light. He stumbled over roots and rocks which he couldn't seem to see. He could hear his breathing, noisy and panic-laden. He looked around nervously and thought he saw giant tree snakes looking at him in the half light, their branches hideous stick insects and their trunks full of knobbly faces with great yawning mouths waiting to pounce on him. The woods, dead and silent, gloomy and lifeless, seemed to be waiting. Time was suspended. He walked faster and faster, wheezing as the air went in and out of his body. Shadows fell across his path. Large black beetles crawled along the pathway in front of him. Eddie hardly knew what he was doing, he was so frightened.

Then, two blue tits appeared, trailing a piece of bryony in their mouths, each berry lit up, like a string of bright Christmas tree lights, red and green. The birds flew in front of the terrified Eddie, holding their necklace of brilliance up before him and guiding him gently down the twisting path through the woods. At the foot of Gallants Bower they flew away as the day's last light came into view. He was nearly home.

Eddie walked rather unsteadily towards the cottage, opened the door and stumbled upstairs and into his bedroom.

His parents and Ellie were not back yet. He sat down onto the bed sighing with relief. He was still clutching his kite as he closed his eyes, hardly able to believe what had happened to him. His whole body ached and he was drenched in the sweat of extreme fear; but whatever it was or had been, it was over.

Freddie, who had sent the blue tits in his anxiety for Eddie's well-being, peered in at the window. There he was, safely back in bed. The birds twittered to each other, proud of their success, and returned to their evening resting places, very satisfied with themselves.

Not long afterwards Eddie was woken up by his sister calling to him,

"Eddie, Eddie are you there?"

He heard her coming up the stairs. He groaned and tried to wake himself up as she knocked on his door.

"Eddie?"

He called back to her, "Yes I'm here," scrambling off the bed and tidying his rumpled hair.

She burst in, "We've got the fish and chips, they look scrummy, come on we're ready for supper now". She looked at him.

"Are you alright, you look…well, you don't look well, what's the matter?"

"I'm just tired, that's all. I laid down on the bed and fell asleep. I'll just wash my face and I'll be down." He guided her out of the room. "You go on, I'm coming," and he went into the bathroom, splashed water on his face to liven himself up and joined his parents in the kitchen. The smell was wonderful.

"Here's yours, Eddie," said his mother. "Did you have a good expedition with your kite? I'm sure you're getting the hang of it now." She passed a large plateful of golden battered fish and crisp fat chips towards him.

"No it wasn't that good actually," he replied quietly.

They sat around the table and dived into the chips and golden fish, all that is except Eddie. He had very little appetite and picked at his supper, eventually pushing it away.

"Whatever's the matter with you?" asked his father.

"Don't know really," said Eddie. "I'm not hungry, that's all. I think I'll go and watch telly. Is that OK Mum?" And he looked at his mother with big blue eyes and a sad face.

"Of course."

Eddie left the room.

"What's the matter with him?" asked Ellie with her mouth full.

"Well, no point in wasting it," said Peter and tipped some of Eddie's supper onto his own plate. "Anyone else want any?"

After supper was over the evening passed away and soon it was bed time. Eddie was asleep long before everyone else and soon the house was covered in darkness with the owls hooting across the valley at each other. Just the faint barking of a dog broke the silence from time to time as they all slept soundly. Syracuse tried desperately to find a way back to his beloved master. Why had he abandoned him?

Chapter Seven
The boat launch and sailing lessons

In the morning they gathered in the kitchen, yawning and getting in each others' way. Finally, after a trip to the ships' chandlers in town, they had most of the things they wanted. Ellie had bought a little flag as a secret present for Eddie's birthday. It was a dark blue triangle and she had planned to stitch a fabric seagull onto it.

Somehow everything got transported by wheelbarrow down to the slipway. Several people passed by with their dogs and chatted to Peter about the Navy and life at sea in general. It seemed that Dartmouth attracted all types of seafarers like some sort of magnet; there was a kind of refreshing community spirit, born of the river and the sea.

"Can we have a proper launching ceremony, Dad?" asked Eddie, as they transferred their equipment from the wheelbarrow.

"Oh yes, I'll get some lemonade," said Ellie. She was delighted.

Down at the creek, neighbours and friends stood around laughing and joking. It was a wonderful moment when Dad gave the signal and the boat was pushed by many willing hands into the water. The string on the bottle was swung, and with a clonk the lemonade frothed over the boat.

"I name this ship *Sargasso* and may God bless all who sail in her," said Eddie proudly in a loud voice. Everyone clapped and the children were thrilled. They spent a couple of delightful hours just rowing around in the river. Peter taught them the tricky manoeuvre of getting out of the boat and then putting the rope on and pulling her out into the middle of the creek again on the running mooring.

"My arms ache," announced Eddie, rubbing them and groaning.

"So do mine," agreed Ellie.

"I'll make sailors of you yet!" said their father. At last everything was put away and they trooped into the kitchen for hot sausages, jacket potatoes and onion gravy.

"You had better read this book while I'm away, everything you need to know is in here, it's the Royal Yachting Association Day Skipper Manual," Peter insisted. He was absolutely determined that his youngsters would not put themselves in any danger, or anyone else for that matter.

Ellie sneaked upstairs after tea with a bird book and paper and traced out the profile of a seagull. She pinned it onto an old white pillow case, cut the bird out and stitched it onto the flag. After all this she was very tired, and yawning continuously she gave up, had a bath and tumbled into bed. The fresh air and excitement had been exhausting.

Eddie meanwhile was lying on the sofa, reading the yachting manual from cover to cover. Making a decision, he went upstairs to find his father, who was packing his bag.

"Dad, I want to go out in the boat by myself." Seeing his father's face he hurriedly continued, "Only in the creek, I promise. I know I can do it, but I must practise. I really want to do this, Dad, so I want you to tell Mum. She won't like it."

Peter could see the determination on his son's face. After a lengthy discussion Peter decided that Eddie could mess about around the creek and, yes Ellie could go too.

At last he could go out in his very own boat. Eddie ran downstairs to his mother.

"Dad says it's OK. He really did, Mum." He looked to see her reaction.

"Then that's alright," she said calmly, trying not to mind. Eddie went upstairs and got ready for bed. His father came in to say goodbye as he would be leaving at six o'clock in the morning. He ruffled Eddie's hair again, gave him a ten pound note and told him to be good and to look after the girls. Eddie was very sad indeed and as his father closed the door he buried his face in the pillow and held back the tears. He could hear him talking to Ellie now.

Why did his father always have to go away just when everything was getting so exciting? He'd be gone for ages. It just wasn't fair. He found it very boring sometimes with just his mother and Ellie. Well, he would have to teach himself. He'd got the manual and the boat now. It wasn't that difficult, how could it be, with so many sailors filling up the river and the estuary? He'd just have to try.

Chapter Eight
Several birthday surprises

His mother made his birthday cake and booked a table at the Scallop Shell Inn for Eddie's favourite meal, and the surprise was set. Ellie had wrapped up the precious flag in some pink tissue paper and hidden it away, very pleased with her efforts.

A few days later Eddie's birthday dawned. He crept downstairs, opened the window and broke some crumbs onto the window sill. A few minutes later Faithful Freddie landed on the edge, gobbled up the crumbs and whistled a lovely song.

"Morning Freddie," Eddie greeted him. "I'm thirteen today."

Ellie and Mother came to see him with cards and parcels.

"Happy birthday," they hugged him.

"Thanks," said Eddie, "what's in here then?" as he tore at the wrappings.

Ellie sat on the bed, excited, hoping he would like her flag.

"How clever of you to make this!" He kept turning it over and over in his hands. "It's really beautiful Ellie. Thank you very much."

"Our present is sitting in the water, dear!" said his mother smiling. The phone rang and the call was for Eddie.

"Hi Dad, yes, thank you, lovely. I've got a smashing flag from

64

Ellie. What? You'll be here tonight for supper? That's great. Yes, I'll see you later. Bye."

He was so thrilled and excited that his dad was going to be here after all. He was driving a long way from Portsmouth – the best birthday present.

Eddie fried the bacon, keeping the rinds for Sargasso, and decided he must see him and look at the boat.

"Morning Sargasso," he greeted the bird as he paddled out in his bare feet to the boat.

"Did you know it is my birthday today? No I don't expect you did, well here's a treat for you."

He dangled the crispy pieces in front of him. The bird gently took them from Eddie's fingers and swallowed them whole. Delicious!

"I'm going to change the name on the boat now it's really mine." He carefully sandpapered over the name *Skylark* and opened the small tin of white paint, dipped the brush in and painted *Sargasso* with his best lettering. He stood back to admire it. It was a good name.

He took Ellie's flag out of his pocket, put the rope through the narrow tape strip and pulled it back up to the top of the varnished mast. It fluttered gently in the breeze, the seagull quite perfect.

"There," said Eddie satisfied, "that looks great." Ellie appeared from the lane onto the slipway.

"Oh, I like that, it looks really good." She admired the flag, feeling very pleased with herself.

"What shall we do now? Shall we go and see George?" Ellie thought Eddie might like that.

"OK, we might as well do something before lunch."

So they went to the tea shop which was full of visitors, drinking coffee and enjoying Bridget's lovely cakes. It was very busy. George wished Eddie a Happy Birthday and handed him a large, heavy box and Bridget gave him a great big kiss.

"Thank you George. How did you know it was my birthday? You are kind."

There was no time for more chatting, it was much too busy, but Ellie spied a boy in the back kitchen washing-up.

Hmm, who's he? she wondered, a little put out. *He's taken my job!*

He vanished from view and she turned to Eddie,

"They've got a boy in there doing the washing-up. I don't know who he is I've never seen him before. What a cheek!"

Eddie made a face at her. "Maybe you were rubbish at washing-up!"

"No I wasn't!" She went to hit him and he ran off. Ellie chased him furiously all the way home.

When they reached the top of the creek they could see the roof of Dad's car in the driveway.

"Oh good, Dad's here." said Eddie.

The children found their parents on two deckchairs in the garden with a tray of tea.

"Hi you two," greeted their father.

Mother put the candles on the cake and Eddie admired the marzipan boat.

"We've got one surprise left," she said.

Eddie perked up.

"Supper at the Scallop Shell Inn," interrupted Ellie, bursting with excitement. "We're going at seven-thirty."

"Right, before that, we're going for a sail," announced Peter.

Waving to their mother, they marched off down to the creek where Peter put them through the rigours of seamanship. It took the whole afternoon, but eventually he was satisfied. Eddie jumped out, grabbed the mooring line and soon they were dragging the engine back to the store at lime kiln.

"Well done both of you," praised Peter.

"Not bad," was Eddie's reply.

When they were ready later on, the family got into the car and drove off to the village inn which was famous for its superb fish and chip suppers. It was always busy and tonight was no exception, and after an impatient wait they enjoyed huge platefuls of haddock and chips, with sticky toffee pudding and cream to follow. Leaving the pub, they walked along the walled sea-front and Father told them that he was joining a NATO squadron and would only be home a few times until Christmas. Ellie held Peter's hand as they walked along, and Eddie threw stones in the water.

Nobody said much as they drove home in the dark. Eddie and Ellie were sad – they would miss their father being around.

"You'll be a first-class yachtsman by the time I come back Eddie," joked Peter and ruffled his hair.

"I'm really pleased with the boat, Dad," said Eddie. "Thanks very much."

They said their goodbyes as Peter had to leave very early the following morning. Ellie was upset and said it wasn't fair. He kissed her and said she wasn't to turn into a tomboy while he was away. They both went upstairs to bed, resigned to his departure. They could hear their parents talking downstairs. Eddie's birthday had been a success, despite the news that their father was going away for a long time.

Chapter Nine
Meeting Patrick, and bad news for Freddie

Eddie didn't sleep properly, and heard his father leave at five-thirty in the morning, quietly shutting the front door. He got up grumpily and went down to the creek where he sat on the quayside and unwrapped his present from George. Inside was a small ships' light for his boat, but it was not an ordinary light, it seemed to be wired up to a little glass plate. Eddie wasn't sure how it worked. He would have to ask George when he next saw him, and shrugging his shoulders he hurried home for breakfast.

"Do you know what this is, Mother?"

Mary peered into the box that Eddie offered to her.

"Umm, looks like a ships' light of some sort. I think it has a little solar panel on it. What a good idea."

"That's what it is!" said Eddie exasperated, "I've been racking my brains."

Ellie appeared and they sat down to scrambled eggs with lots of crispy bacon.

"This light is really brilliant, it's solar powered, and I've never seen one like it before. Look." He showed her the box. She admired it and returned to her breakfast not terribly interested.

As their return to school was imminent, Mother and Ellie went off to buy some new school shoes.

I really ought to do some practice for cross country next term. Eddie thought.

So dressing in shorts and a vest he set off for the castle. He ran along the road puffing a bit by the time he passed the café. George was just putting out the green tables and chairs.

"Morning, my lad," he greeted him, "Getting in shape I see!"

"Trying to," grinned Eddie, "We've got cross country this term."

"Fancy a cuppa?" asked George.

"Why not?" replied Eddie, forgetting his fitness at once, and in no time at all he was sitting at a table with George, mug of tea in his hand, looking out to sea.

"Thank you for the light, I really love it, but can you tell me how it works?" asked Eddie, sipping the hot tea.

"I'm afraid it's one of my inventions. I thought you might like it. It's actually quite simple."

"It's solar powered, isn't it?" inquired Eddie.

"Yes. It stores the energy in these special-type batteries. They will charge in ultra violet light, it doesn't have to be brilliant sunshine." George seemed very convinced that it would work

"Do you think you could use other sources of energy – say other sources of light to charge things?" asked Eddie earnestly, really trying to get his thoughts together. "If you can use the sun, I don't see why you can't. What about moonlight for instance?"

"In theory, yes, I suppose there isn't any reason why not," replied George slowly, tapping his fingers and thinking, as he looked skyward.

69

"Of course it would be a more difficult light to harness, much weaker. It might be possible to magnify it."

"Or reflect it?" added Eddie hesitantly.

"Yes, that's possible too. Maybe both would work – reflect the light onto a magnifier to intensify it and then store it somehow."

They sat and chatted, mulling over many ideas, some ridiculous, some seemingly impossible. It was a very enjoyable half hour.

"Look out, Bridget's coming," whispered Eddie, and looking up saw a flowery dress advancing, with a blond-haired boy at her side.

"Ah Patrick," said George. Standing up and gathering up the mugs, he patted Patrick on the back. "Meet Eddie, our young friend from Watermill Cottage, down by the creek."

The two boys grinned at each other easily, liking each other instantly.

"Patrick is my godson from Scotland. He's agreed to help us out this week. I can't leave it all to Ellie. He's staying with us until Sunday," Bridget told him.

"Come and sail with me if you like one day. I'm just learning." Eddie invited Patrick. Then saying goodbye he continued his run around the woods, finally reaching home out of breath and puffing. He sat down on the small seat next to the pond, watching the goldfish glide below the water, their silvery scales reflecting the light like tiny mirrors.

Mirrors? thought Eddie. *Hasn't Dad got a light just like that?* He jumped up and went inside the garage, hunting around the shelves, finally spotting the chrome light he wanted. It was a big round searchlight designed to be mounted on a ship's bridge. The small light bulb had a piece of mirror in front of it which reflected the light onto the large concave shiny surface, covering the back of the light. It shone when lit, a large pool of intense light.

Why, it's exactly the same idea that George and I had today. Eddie was disappointed that somebody else had thought up the same idea. *But has it ever been used to reflect the light of the moon?*

Consumed with the idea, he went inside, his mind working constantly. His room faced south and gathered a lot of sunshine so it was a good place to set up George's light. He fastened the light to the drainpipe outside with some garden wire and black masking tape, knowing he would have to wait a while for it to charge up. He was satisfied he had done everything to get the light working.

***

As the afternoon turned into early evening and the sun's rays turned to golden and rosy hues, the buzzards called a meeting high up in the pine trees at the Citadel. Everyone's attendance was requested and Faithful Freddie and the blue tits speculated on the reasons. No one knew what the meeting was for. Had something happened they didn't know about? Had they been careless in their duties? They didn't seem to be able to come up with an answer. At the appointed time of in-between, which is neither night nor day, they all assembled around the foot of the trees. The black rooks, who were the guardians of the Citadel, checked the Woodlanders in. At last the buzzard arrived and began the meeting.

"I have called you here today because we have chosen one of our members for retirement after long and dutiful service to the Woodlander Kingdom. It is time that he is relieved of his appointment, and promoted to join us on the council."

A ripple of intense excitement passed from face to face, and then a look of panic, as each one questioned himself as to who it was going to be. The buzzard continued:

"The children of Watermill Cottage are of an age now when

they no longer need a guardian, so I suggest that the robin is awarded a Retirement Branch on the lower pine tree. This is his for the remainder of his life and the title of Exalted Woodlander is to be added to his name in the Royal Register!"

Appreciative clapping echoed around the meeting, and murmurs of "well done" and "he deserves it" were heard from various parts of the crowd. However the robin was stunned. He was paralysed with shock. Relieved of his duties? Retired from his post? But it wasn't possible. He didn't want to go. He loved his work, and he loved Eddie and Ellie, and the cottage and everything that went on there. He couldn't say a word. The blue tits nudged him.

"Say something."

The robin fluttered his wings and tried to open his beak, but he just couldn't do it.

The buzzard realised the bird was in shock.

"Come on old fellow," he said kindly to him. "You've been on duty a long time you know, many years of devoted service, time for a rest now, take your place in the pine tree and help us with the decision-making. You'll be good at it; all your experience, it won't be wasted. Now, accept your award and join us, we'd love to have you with us, what do you say?"

He tapped him gently and the robin gulped back his tears, and accepted his new position in a quavering voice, thanking the buzzard for the honour.

Everyone clapped and cheered, the buzzard ordered dewdrop wine and squashed flies and they all celebrated long into the night; everyone that is except the robin, who wanted to curl up and sob his heart out. What was he to do? The very thought of leaving the cottage was unbearable. Could he refuse to go?

Chapter Ten
Danger for the mice and an evening of inventions

The next day Ellie decided to go and see how the mice were. As she walked along the driveway Freddie swooped down and landed on her shoulder. He pecked her gently, then flew away into the distance and was gone.

That's very odd. She looked for him to come back, but he didn't appear. She continued on her way, along the dark and shady lane to the church.

Oh!

She stopped, surprised to find a car parked outside. She went through the large studded door and found the new vicar and his wife standing talking in the aisle.

They had not been in the parish very long. He was bright, quick-witted and kind and was keen to wake up his parishioners from their apparent Christian slumber. Attendances had fallen away in recent years. The cold and the damp in the heart of winter took its toll, and there was no heating or lighting. As the new vicar got into his stride, he decided that St Petrox was somewhere very worthwhile to maintain as everyone enjoyed the summer evening services by the sea. He had come out with his wife that morning to have a good look round and hopefully in the calm surroundings, a little divine inspiration would be sent to him as to how to progress.

What they had found was not encouraging. They discovered that dust, cobwebs, rubbish, and discarded books, old garments, old carpets and old curtains were all getting in the way in the vestry and lots of this clutter had been collecting in corners of the other small choir vestry. Stepladders, buckets and brooms, Bibles and boxes were scattered and closeted in each and every cupboard. The vicar and his wife decided that it was just too much of a muddle, and they should undertake to organise a huge clean-up! It would be an example of teamwork, leadership and community spirit. They were just becoming inspired with enthusiasm when Ellie walked in.

"Hello," she greeted them brightly, "You're the new vicar, aren't you?"

"Yes, though it's nearly a year, you know. This is my wife, Prue. Have you met?"

Ellie and Prue smiled at each other.

Yes, I know your mother, Mary isn't it?" said Prue. "Actually I shall be coming back this afternoon to arrange some wedding flowers. We were just saying, weren't we Andrew, that this church needs a bit of a sort out – it will make such a difference, don't you think?" She searched Ellie's face anxiously, looking for any objections or resentment in her reply.

Terror had struck at Ellie's heart – the two mice! What would become of them? They would surely chase them out as vermin and destroy their simple home.

"Don't you think it's time we moved St Petrox forward a little, Ellie?" asked the vicar gently, sensing her hesitation. He and his

St Petrox

wife exchanged glances at Ellie's silence.

"No I don't!" she suddenly burst out, "We like it as it is." And she turned and ran out of the church and along to the ferry slip, where she sat on the top step and cried bitterly, tears running through her fingers and down onto her jacket.

Back in the church there was some consternation.

"What did we say?" said the vicar.

"I have no idea," replied Prue, and she added waspishly, "It's got to be done Andrew, it's such a mess."

"Oh I do agree my dear," placated the vicar, "and we shall do it, we certainly shall. I shall ask the church council to decide on a strategy, and we'll begin as soon as possible," decided Andrew firmly. "Ready dear?"

They both left the church and got into their eco-friendly green runabout car, hurtling off to Dartmouth at once.

In a short while Ellie gathered herself together, and drying her eyes and blowing her nose with a large tissue, she sat to have a good think.

He didn't mention the flower arranging cupboard; maybe if I get Mum to do it, we can save Ferdinand and Isabella. She cheered herself up, feeling a little more hopeful.

As she made her way to the tea shop, great drops of rain started to make round black spots on the path in front of her. George let her in, frowning at the spattered windows and emptying car park. A chilly wind had struck up, and he sighed,

"That's it for today, rain is very bad for business and we're in for a wet afternoon."

"Never mind," replied Bridget briskly, "Patrick can have the rest of the day off. Ellie, this is Patrick our godson from Edinburgh."

Patrick came up the steps from the kitchen into the tea shop.

76

"Just saying, lad, that you can have the rest of the afternoon off."

"Well, if you're sure, that would be fine with me, just fine," nodded Patrick. "I'll get my coat," and he leapt down the step into the kitchen and was ready in a trice.

"Are you walking my way, Ellie?" he asked her.

"Yes, if you're going back to Bridget's," she said, and they both shouted goodbye from the doorway and hurried off, hoods and collars up against the rain, which was still falling relentlessly.

"That was a lucky escape," laughed Ellie.

"Indeed it was," replied Patrick.

"What are you going to do now?" she asked him.

"What, with my afternoon of freedom?" laughed Patrick," I don't really know, I feel I can't waste this opportunity. Maybe I'll visit the museum; at least it will be dry. I think I met your brother this morning." He smiled at her.

She told him where she lived and all about her family as they walked along.

"Call in and see us if you want to on your way back," she told him. Parting company below the bridge, Ellie walked to her house, and Patrick went to visit the museum. Ellie rather admired his determination on this horrible afternoon.

When she got home Eddie was upstairs with his solar light on his desk, unwrapping the masking tape and wires from it.

"Does it work?" she asked him.

"It does, it really does," beamed Eddie. "Look," and he switched the black switch and the bulb glowed brightly.

"I've just met Patrick, that boy who was in the café the other day. He's their godson, and he's staying for a while. He's the one who pinched my job," she laughed.

Eddie had gathered together a mirror, an old magnifying glass, and a funny crystal hedgehog that somebody had brought him back from the seaside once. Among the other odds and ends were a torch and a round wooden cheese box, and a small cardboard box with a lid. To complete the strange assortment were a pair of scissors, a piece of tin foil, and the end of a roll of cling film.

"What are you doing?" asked Ellie with interest.

"I don't quite know," pondered Eddie. "I'm trying to invent something else to do with light. Just messing around. George has given me some ideas. Have you got a diary with the date of the next full moon in it?"

"I think so."

She disappeared for a minute and came back with the calendar off her bedroom wall.

"Four days from now," she counted, "that's not long."

"Good," said Eddie, "I might have worked something out by then."

Ellie went off downstairs and put the kettle on, found an extra jumper, and when she had made some tea, she snuggled up on the sofa with her library book as the rain and dark clouds brought the day to an early end.

Eddie stayed in his bedroom arranging and rearranging his experiment. He cut a hole in the side of the small cardboard box and sellotaped the magnifying glass to the inside to cover it. He then stuck the mirror in the same way opposite the magnifier, and lined the round lid with tin foil, squeezing it to make it concave. This was the reflector. As he was thinking about light and reflection, he heard a tapping at the window and looking up he saw Freddie, beak against the pane. He opened the window and the little bird flew in and sat on the window ledge, blinking his round black eyes and staring intently at Eddie.

"What is it? What's the matter?"

Freddie hopped onto Eddie's hand and pecked him several times. How could he tell them he had to go?

"You're such a lovely little thing," and very carefully Eddie stroked his tiny head.

Just then the front door opened and his mother's voice called up from the hallway.

"I'm home. Anybody in? I've found a stray," and voices were heard downstairs. Freddie hid himself behind the large-checked curtains. Ellie appeared from the sitting room, book in hand.

"Look who I found coming into the driveway. I couldn't let him drown so I brought him in out of the rain," Mary laughed.

"Oh, I'd have been alright," growled Patrick in his deep Scottish accent.

"Well, come in now and get dry. This is George and Bridget's godson, but you've met I hear. Take off those wet things," persuaded Mary. He didn't need much persuasion, the warm kitchen and pot of tea looked too inviting.

Eddie came downstairs and made some toast.

"Was the museum interesting, Patrick?" asked Ellie.

He thought for a moment and then replied, "Well, I had no idea that Dartmouth was so full of history. The Mayflower, trade with Portugal, Newfoundland, fish and tobacco, but I liked the boat models the best." He seemed very interested in it all.

"I'd better phone Bridget and tell her you're here, Patrick, in case she worries and... would you like to stay to supper?" Mary asked.

Patrick looked up at her shyly. "I'd like that very much."

Eddie and Ellie looked pleased.

Mary went to telephone and Patrick sat back relaxing.

"How is your physics?" asked Eddie, leaning across the table on his elbows.

"Are you serious?" replied Patrick with a surprised look.

"'Course I am, I've got a project on," began Eddie. "I need a bit more brain power to solve it. Want to see?" He got up from the chair and beckoned him towards the door. "Come on, have a look."

Patrick shrugged his shoulders and followed Eddie upstairs. As they entered the bedroom Freddie peeped out from behind the curtain and chirped a few times.

"Hey, what's he doing in here?" Patrick pointed at the window ledge.

"Oh that's Freddie our pet robin – follows us everywhere."

"Come on!" said Patrick. "It's not real."

Eddie kept quite a serious expression on his face. "I suppose it is a bit strange. You live in a big city, so maybe you don't understand about animals and birds and things."

Freddie, hearing his words, really thought his heart would break. He didn't want to leave their lives, despite what the buzzard had decreed. Patrick put out his hand rather cautiously. Freddie hopped onto his outstretched palm and stayed there looking at him with bold blinking black eyes, his heart beating madly in his little fluffy chest.

"Wow!" said Patrick, utterly captivated by the feel of the tiny feet on his hand. "Isn't he cute?" Patrick very gently ran his finger over the bird's head, and Freddie sang a little song for him, showing off a bit.

Then the robin took off back to the windowsill and pecked on the glass, and Eddie opened the window and let him go.

"Well?" he looked at Patrick. "Satisfied?"

"I quite believe you now," he said. "Anyway, about your project now, what's it all about?" Patrick changed the subject, hoping he had not offended Eddie. So Eddie explained about the solar-powered light and how he was hoping to make another sort of light using the light of the moon.

Patrick was silent. He rubbed his chin and thought for a while.

"Aye, it sounds a bit far-fetched, but in a way I see what you are getting at maybe; shall we have a go?"

"Okay, so we know some things for sure – the sun's rays are converted into energy in the form of electricity with a solar battery and then used to power a light. Light can be reflected or refracted." Eddie reeled this all off.

"But the moon only shines on certain nights and it has no heat, its light is reflected from the sun…, so we've really only got the light to consider. We could try to catch the light and reflect it, and maybe magnify it, or try to store the energy in a battery or something. Was that what you had in mind?" queried Patrick gently.

"Sort of," agreed Eddie.

"When is the moon full next?"

"Four days' time. Ellie checked on her calendar."

"Perhaps we could go up onto the turret at the tea shop if it's a clear night, that would be a good place."

"Yes, that's a great idea."

"We could make a sort of reflective dish with this round lid and cover it with tin foil and bend it a bit. What do you think?"

They talked, practised with the torch, with the crystal hedgehog, and water in a cut glass, making patterns and lights on the wall. They shone lights through holes onto mirrors and magnifying glasses and got totally carried away, enjoying themselves enormously. Suddenly Ellie walked in and announced,

"Supper's ready, you two. What on earth are you doing?" She stopped in her tracks.

"Inventing things!" grinned Patrick.

81

"Come on, Mum's waiting," and she shooed them downstairs. In the kitchen they sat down to sausages, chips and mushy peas, with ice cream and melted Mars bars for pudding. Mary enjoyed the company of the young people.

Afterwards they sat and played cards. Newmarket was Ellie's favourite game, which she usually won. At about ten o'clock the doorbell rang and it was George, who had come to collect Patrick.

"I came out to get some petrol so thought you might like a lift home." All too soon they both piled into the car and waved goodbye.

"That was a good idea Mum, thanks."

Yawning, Eddie and Ellie decided it was time for bed, and soon the lights went out. Watermill Cottage stood in darkness once more; just the owl hooting in the huge fir tree across the road. After that evening, Patrick became part of the household.

Chapter Eleven
A frightening evening on the river

When Ellie came downstairs the next day, her mother was on the phone.

"Yes I could…Well I suppose I could fit it in next week… Goodbye, Andrew."

"Was it the vicar?" asked Ellie nervously.

"Yes, it seems he and Prue think that St Petrox needs a bit of a tidy-up in certain places, so we've organised a cleaning-up party next Monday."

"I suppose you're in charge of the flower arranging cupboard, are you?"

"Well I assume so."

"Where's Eddie?"

"He's getting the sailing stuff ready for this evening. He has invited Patrick to go sailing at tea time."

"Can I go with them?" She crossed her fingers in her pocket.

"If you really want to, just don't go too far out to sea."

"Can we take a picnic?"

"If you get it all ready yourself, yes you can."

So Ellie got the breadboard out, made some sandwiches and began assembling her picnic. Mary found some chocolate Swiss rolls and three packets of crisps.

"Have you got everything? A warm jumper, woolly hat, waterproofs?"

"Yes I'm ready, really I am," she insisted, hurrying off to find Eddie quickly; she knew what a worrier her Mum could be. He had gathered up the equipment and was loading carefully from the slippery edge, down by the rocks.

"Hi," he called, "Are you coming too? What's in the bag?"

"Supper," answered Ellie, laughing. "We're having a picnic."

"Good, that means we can stay out longer," grinned Eddie. Ellie scrambled down onto the treacherous, slippery rocks, glad of her rubber-soled shoes.

"I've got to talk to you Eddie," she said, carefully climbing into the boat, "about Ferdinand and Isabella."

"Whatever's happened now?"

"The new vicar and his wife want to have a tidy-up and cleaning session at St Petrox."

"Well, it is a bit of a mess in places, you have to admit."

"Yes I know, but if they find their mouse holes and block them up, everything will be ruined. I'm getting very worried about it."

Eddie could see that she was. "We can warn them to go and hide in the bell tower that day, can't we?"

Patrick came down the path at that moment calling to them, a yellow plastic bag slung over his shoulder.

"Are we ready?" he asked, "Can I do anything? Are we taking the engine?"

"No, there's plenty of wind tonight, I think we'll be alright."

"OK then," agreed Patrick, and he carefully negotiated the rocky edge and eased himself into the boat.

They released the rope and pushed themselves off from the side with an oar, and with the sails up and flag aloft, the little green boat slipped through the shiny waters dodging the other mooring ropes. As they rowed to the centre of the river the wind picked them up and started to fill the sails, and away they went.

It was such a good feeling being propelled along, the wind blowing in their hair and faces, watching the banks of the river rush by and the water gurgling behind in the wake. Patrick took the tiller and Eddie manned the ropes and the boom and shouted "Duck!" if he needed to change course. They were at the castle in no time. The sea was calm and the breeze good, so there seemed no reason not to carry on a little bit farther. They turned the corner towards Castle Cove and Sugary Cove.

"Shall we have our picnic here?" asked Ellie.

"Yes, get the anchor out Patrick." Eddie was ready for his supper.

They laid out their feast and rested back in the boat, munching away, enjoying the freedom of the sea. It was a beautiful evening. Boats chugged by, their wakes rocking them from side to side, and making them all laugh.

"That was fantastic," sighed Patrick, completely full up.

"It was," agreed Eddie, screwing up the paper wrappings and tidying them away in the bags.

"Shall we go on a bit more?" suggested Eddie.

"Oh I'm not sure, you know what Mum said," Ellie replied anxiously.

"Oh come on Ellie, let's go on, just another half hour, yes?"

As Eddie pulled up the sails again and Patrick sprang into action, Ellie just rolled her eyes and bit her lip nervously.

"I'm going to switch my light on," announced Eddie proudly and as he pressed the switch a lovely white beam appeared. Very gradually the wind seemed to disappear and the sails flapped as if they lacked energy.

"I think the wind has dropped a wee touch, don't you?" Patrick questioned, as they drifted along rather slowly.

"A bit," replied Eddie, trying not to appear worried.

The wind had deserted them. Eddie looked despondently at Patrick, who shrugged his shoulders, and they both looked at Ellie.

"What's the matter?" she asked, suddenly frightened by their silence.

"The wind's dropped but we can row back, can't we?" asked Patrick, directing his question at Eddie.

"We can try," was his reply, but in his heart Eddie knew that by now the tide would be turning and flooding out of the river for a couple of hours. It was virtually impossible to row against the tide. "We can take it in turns."

Ellie, determined to be brave and sensible as her father had taught her, hunted in the bottom of the boat for the oars. Nobody mentioned the little Seagull Century engine, nicely tucked up in the lime kiln.

Eddie looked at his watch. It was eight o'clock. Mother would be expecting them at nine. After lowering the sails, they fastened the rowlocks into the holes and set up the oars. The two boys took first places, gritting their teeth and trying to keep together. They were making very little headway, and after ten minutes they needed a rest, arms aching.

"No, you can't stop! We'll just drift out to sea again! Keep going!" Ellie urged them. "Come on!" and so they set off with a will.

Back at the creek, Sargasso had flown in for the night and noticed the boat was missing. He flew out to the castle and perched on top of the tower, scanning the sea with his brilliant eyes. Then Sargasso caught sight of the boat, the flag hanging limply from the mast. He flew towards them and screeched to a halt, landing on the front of the boat.

"Sargasso!" Eddie and Ellie cried out together.

But Sargasso was powerless on his own. There was little he could do, but he knew where to ask for help from his friends. He took off again and flew along the coastline and disappeared into a dark craggy outcrop.

"What are we going to do?" asked Ellie, looking upset.

"Don't worry, we'll get back – Sargasso might help us." Eddie patted her arm.

Patrick looked sceptical.

"Not another of your friends is it?"

He smiled at Ellie and picked up the oars again. She ignored him coolly.

"Shall I have another bash at it? Move over, Eddie." And he positioned himself to row. He pulled the oars through the water, making a real effort. Again and again he reached forwards and backwards.

"We're moving!" shouted Eddie. "Well done!"

"We're going quite fast now," screamed Ellie laughing, "What's happened?"

Sargasso flew over them, circling gently, wings outspread. As Eddie looked behind them he saw two black heads in the water and felt a dull thudding noise on the wood of the boat.

"Look!" he called, "there are two seals here. They're pushing the boat along. I can't believe it!"

Ellie moved to the back of the boat and peered into the water.

"You're right! How wonderful, just when we needed them!"

The seals looked beautiful with their whiskers and big brown eyes. Eddie took an oar at once and he and Patrick continued to row. They rounded the castle entrance and entered the river.

The two seals who had come to the rescue, Solomon and Bathsheba, often swam into the deep gully underneath the Trip Trap bridge. Sargasso had gone to look for them hoping they might be there. He was in luck. He told them of the children's plight, and they agreed to push the boat back to Warfleet.

The very strange group eventually reached the mouth of the creek where the seals barked twice and flipped their tails upside down. They then swam around the boat, to the delight of the children, and disappeared. Sargasso flew back with them, happy that his beloved children were safe.

Quickly and in great panic the boys pulled the boat back onto the mooring, sending Ellie up home first to prevent Mother phoning the coastguards.

Patrick skipped off home as fast as he could. It was nine-fifteen, would Ellie be in time? She ran up along the creek with her heart beating fast and as she reached the pathway to the house she saw her mother standing by the window. Mother flung it open.

"Where have you been? I've been so worried about you, it's getting dark now and... Well come inside Ellie, and where's Eddie? Oh, and Patrick? Good heavens, he'll get into trouble with George."

Mary went on and on and Ellie was just trying to explain when Eddie came puffing up the hill. He didn't want to be grounded by his father for not taking enough care. He kissed his mother and apologised. He was very contrite, but thankfully she had not called the coastguards.

Mother bundled them off to bed. Ellie lay awake, thinking about the seals. They had been wonderful, pushing and nosing them home through the green dark water, and with the beautiful sky deepening in colour it had been a magical experience. She drew her knees up tightly, and finding a soft deep hollow in her pillow, she sighed and went to sleep, comfortable and warm. How lucky she was.

Eddie too lay awake. He had not realised how big and wide and frightening the sea was. They had been near to the land and yet it had proved so difficult to get home. The tide could have swept them all out to sea; it didn't bear thinking about. How could he have been so stupid? And what if Sargasso hadn't found them? Eddie turned over and closed his eyes, thanking Sargasso for everything, and went to sleep.

Mary also tossed and turned when she went to bed; she had been so anxious about the children. If only Peter were here it would be so much easier.

***

The first thing everybody heard in the morning was the door knocker banging. Eddie raced downstairs in his tee shirt and boxer shorts to find Patrick on the doorstep.

"I'd forgotten. I'm going back to Edinburgh today. George is driving me to the station at Totnes, so here I am to say cheerio to you both and your mother."

"Come in," invited Eddie, running his fingers through his tousled hair.

"Mum, Ellie," he called upstairs, "Patrick's here to say goodbye."

Patrick promised to come back again for a holiday as soon as possible. George called round ten minutes later to collect Patrick. He thanked the two youngsters for giving his godson such a great time and after making faithful promises to write and phone the three youngsters waved goodbye as the car pulled away.

"When will he be here again, do you think?" asked Ellie quietly.

"Summer holidays maybe."

Eddie gazed out of the window eating his toast.

Mary looked up, smiled at them both and said nothing.

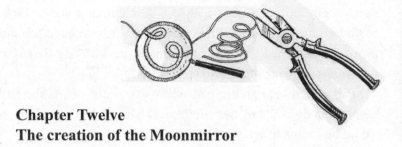

Chapter Twelve
The creation of the Moonmirror

"Why don't you come with me to tell Ferdinand and Isabella about the big clean-up?" Ellie cajoled her brother. "Come on, I'll race you there, see how fit you are," she laughed.

They chased each other, pushing and shoving, until they reached the church doorway panting and gasping for breath. Inside, the windows were all decorated with white flowers and the pillars were garlanded with ivy. They quietly called out the names of the mice. Peeping around the foot of the gold curtain, two noses and whiskers appeared.

"We've come to warn you," said Ellie very gravely. "Do not come out on Monday morning under any circumstances – it's the clean-up day. My mother is coming to do this cupboard, but she doesn't know about you, so please take care."

"We will, we will," said Isabella, dancing round. Ferdinand took a more serious approach.

"Which day did you say, Eddie? I will be sure to take her away."

"It's only for the morning," said Eddie, "Monday. Just don't forget."

"We won't," squeaked Isabella again. Eddie rolled his eyes and Ellie took his arm.

"Thank you Eddie," she said, as they left the church and walked him home.

"Pity Patrick had to go so soon, we were going to try the experiments."

He stopped dead in his tracks. "Ellie, when did you say it was the full moon?"

"I think it was four days from when I looked at the calendar, so … it must be…"

"Today!" finished Eddie excitedly. "Come on, I've got to make a phone call!"

**

The buzzard called an Extraordinary Council Meeting and was checking the attendance list with the black rooks. Most of the members had arrived; even the little robin was perched on his lower branch, rather out ranked by his superior and longer serving colleagues. The buzzard began in his deep voice:

"Welcome to this short meeting. This is to inform you all that the black dog, who had been roaming the woodland in search of his master, has returned to the spirit world, through a crack in one of the gravestones in St Petrox churchyard. Hopefully they have been reunited and the dog's ghost is at peace again."

Everyone applauded. The red-eyed dog had been generally much feared and many Woodlanders had ceased going out after dark, dreading they could be forced to return to the spirit world with him, ensnared forever.

"If any crisis arises, I shall call you with the woodland alarm signal and your immediate attendance will be expected. That is all. All dismissed – everyone except the robin. Squashed flies and dewdrop wine are under the tree, help yourselves." And with that the meeting closed.

The robin stayed nervously behind. The buzzard was kind to him; he realised how the little bird had suffered and he also knew that he continued to live at the cottage, unable to break the habit of watching over the children. He was prepared to let it go. In time he would forget.

"We have some new members in our midst, robin, an expectant bat family who wish to live in the bell tower at the ancient church. It will be your first duty to perform their Welcome Visitation and to appoint a Kinship Cousin to help them settle in. You will go tomorrow at twilight with your chosen one. The bat's name is Belvedere. Is all this clear to you?"

He smiled and nodded approvingly and meaningfully at the little bird.

"Yes my lord," bowed the robin and he flew to the foot of the tree. He snacked on a little of the prized food and wine and the buzz went around about the robin's new assignment. He stayed and answered questions and chatted until he felt exhausted and finally took his leave as soon as he could.

He flew rather unsteadily down the hill, correcting his course for his favourite perch on the wall by the kitchen window. He determined not to even think about the evenings' events and he tucked his head under his wing, and ruffling out his feathers, fell fast asleep.

**

Eddie, back at the cottage, was on the move. He had phoned George, who agreed to meet him at the café. He gathered up his unlikely equipment into a backpack and got his clothes and jacket out. He asked his mother's permission if he could go and see George, glancing at the big clock in the kitchen and noticing that it was nearly seven o'clock.

"I'm off now Mum." He kissed her cheek. "Don't worry about me, George will walk me home."

"OK dear."

Eddie had arranged to meet George outside the café at seven o'clock. He was hopeful that the weather forecast was favourable.

Sure enough George was sitting on the green bench outside the café. He stood up as soon as he saw Eddie and said,

"Hello young man, what's in the bag?"

"Just a few bits and pieces I thought might be useful George – you know, part of an inventor's kit!"

George laughed and they stepped inside. They went into the back part of the kitchen, where a tiny door led to the turret. Bending low, they carefully trod on the old stone steps which curved around and upwards, opening out onto a sort of balcony.

"Wow! What a fabulous view!"

Eddie leaned onto the parapet walls and drank it all in. Sea and sky as far as the eye could see.

"What have you in mind, young Eddie?" questioned George, breaking the spell of the perfect evening.

"Well, I don't exactly know."

He looked at George for inspiration and the old man said kindly,

"Unpack the bag and let's have a look."

Together they knelt down on the roof and fished out the magnifying glass, the tinfoil, the crystal glass and the crystal hedgehog, bulbs, batteries, wire and pliers. Eddie talked as he unpacked, and soon George began to piece together the ideas that had jumbled themselves up in the boy's head.

"Patrick gave me a few ideas too," he added.

"So – we're waiting for the moon before we can try any of this out, yes? We've got time then to set several trials up alongside,

Castle Tea Shop

haven't we? The first thing I think we need is a table."

Eddie was sure that the light of the moon could be harnessed in some way. How, was the question.

"Here we are," beamed George, returning with a small table. "We'll face the table and chairs to where the moon will be at ten o'clock."

George had brought some cookies and two bottles of lemonade.

"Could you reflect the light of the moon with a mirror through a magnifying glass to make it stronger?" began Eddie very seriously, drinking the lemonade.

"Not sure."

"But in theory it's possible" pressed Eddie.

"In theory, yes."

"Well that's my idea. You see, Dad's got a light at home in the garage for signalling at sea, and it's got a curved mirror back for reflecting the light, and that set me thinking. Could you use the moonlight to make a signaller?"

"Yes, if you could store the power somehow."

"You mean like solar power?"

"Exactly. We might be on the brink of discovering something new."

George was smiling. Eddie didn't know if he was joking or not.

Very gradually the sky darkened, and the light faded over the horizon; twilight surrounded them. George and Eddie were busy. They put a mirror inside the battered light, and made a box up with a mirror, a magnifier and the crystal hedgehog. Eddie filled the precious cut glass with water and set it to one side, ready to use it later. Then they both sat down and waited. They watched the sky turn to midnight blue, tiny stars becoming brighter and the pale white circle of the moon growing in intensity, until the water was lit up with a silver streak across its ripples.

"Now?" asked Eddie nervously.

"Of course, let's start experimenting."

George rubbed his hands together in glee. They caught the moon's light on a small piece of mirror and reflected it onto various experiments set up on the table, connected to batteries and a small light bulb. The light was much weaker than the sun, being only reflected light. At the end of an hour they had invented a Moonmirror light, working on the principle of magnification and reflection. The light was to be stored and the power held in the batteries, charged with the light of the moon. They had also invented a battery-powered intensely bright light, which flashed all the colours of the rainbow. It was incredible, what they had achieved with a few basic ideas and the makeshift experiments from household equipment. They shook each other by the hand, and Eddie punched the air with glee.

"Yes! We've done it!"

"Aye lad, we have."

George sat down exhausted, and finished the chocolate biscuits off.

"Well what do you think of that, George?"

"I think it's the best evening I've spent for a long time," and he added, zipping up his jacket, "however, your mother will have the police out, it's eleven-fifteen."

"Never!" gasped Eddie, "Oh no, she'll go mad. Come on, I've got to get home."

They were suddenly aware of something brushing past them in the air. Eddie waved his hand just above his head as he felt a wind rush by. They looked up and two bats, swift and black against the night sky, just missed them.

"Our lights must have disturbed them. I've never seen bats out here before. Strange."

The man and the boy, who had crossed the boundaries of science that night and didn't know it, packed up their kit hastily, and George insisted Eddie came back with him to stay the night. Bridget would phone his mother. They had to make notes on all their findings. Eddie was too tired to argue. They walked back to the Old Bath House and were greeted by Bridget, who telephoned his mother at once and pacified her very convincingly. The findings were all charted and each step recorded on a large sheet of paper with expanded diagrams by Eddie. Unable to stop yawning, Eddie was bundled by Bridget into the spare room.

"Bed for you young man," and she hugged him and kissed him resoundingly on his cheeks. Eddie didn't argue; he got into bed and lay down, but he couldn't sleep, not yet. He thought about the exciting night he had had, and how wonderful it had been to find out that at least two of their ideas had worked. He wanted to tell Patrick about it so badly and resolved to ring him up as soon as possible. He was overjoyed with himself, and stretched his toes out far into the bed and smiled. They had named their inventions – a Moonmirror and a crystal signaller. Not a bad night's work! His eyes closed, and sleep overtook him at last. The seagull on the rooftop tucked its head under its wing as it stood on its one leg.

Chapter Thirteen
Bats in the belfry

High in the darkness in the stone tower of the church, with the dull drone of the sea colliding with the rocky foundations, the two bats secured a hanging space. During the hours of blackest night the female strained and gave birth silently to two tiny babies whose high pitched infant cries were audible only to her and her mate. She suckled them cosily as they unfurled and became accustomed to their new life.

Belvedere looked on proudly. Boadicea would be a good mother, he was sure. She had approved of their move from Tintern Abbey and they felt very lucky to have found a vacancy. Earlier that same evening they had seen the humans on the top of the tower next to theirs making such pretty lights and colours in the sky; it had been rather exciting. The female bat had persuaded her mate to go outside and watch.

"We could do with an evening off," agreed Boadicea, "let's look at the lovely sky for a while."

They were the only witnesses to Eddie and George's remarkable discoveries.

Dwelling as they had for such a long time in an old country

ruin, they were looking forward to joining the woodland network available in every location. Eventually they settled down after an eventful night, snuggling up together, now a furry family.

***

Ellie woke up the next day to find that Eddie had stayed the night with George and Bridget. She was rather envious.

"Can I go round there?" she asked her mother after breakfast.

"No dear, I don't think so. He'll be back soon."

Ellie was quite annoyed. She sulked off to her bedroom and slammed the door.

Eddie always has all the fun, she thought angrily.

However Eddie felt desperate to get home and speak to Patrick about his exciting evening. There were so many new things crowding into his life at the moment. What a shame Patrick wasn't here to share them! Roger, his school friend, lived too far away and George was locked into the endless hours of the tea shop. Even his own father was never home to share things with him.

"Hi Mum," he called as he entered the house.

She came to find him immediately. "Ellie's a bit upset. She's got a face like thunder. She's not happy you stayed at George and Bridget's. Better go and see her."

He sighed.

"But I must ring Patrick and talk to him. George and I have made several brilliant prototype lights up. Honestly Mum, it was such an exciting night."

He continued to tell her all about it. She realised he was completely enthralled with his experiments and focused only on his inventions. Ellie would have to put up with it. Their lives seemed to be taking different directions for the first time. It was all part of growing up.

Chapter Fourteen
Eddie attempts to re-call the Sea Captain

Eddie found Patrick's number and dialled it quickly. He smiled as he heard the strong Scottish-burred voice slowly say the number.

"Hi it's me, Eddie."

"Hello there!" was the delighted reply.

"Patrick you'll never guess, but George and I made the light work. We've called it the Moonmirror. Honestly, I can't believe it and we made a sort of crystal signaller too. It was so exciting! Most of the theories seemed to work."

"Really?"

"Yes, I just wish you had been here, you helped me, some of the ideas were yours."

"Well, I don't know about that. It was your idea to start with, but I can't wait to see it."

Eventually they ran out of things to say.

"Better go now," said Eddie.

"Yes," agreed Patrick, "see you at half term, maybe."

"Bye."

They both put the receivers down. Eddie suddenly felt very lonely, he really missed Patrick.

Then his mother called up from the hallway, "We're off shopping now Eddie, Ellie's coming with me. See you later."

The door shut and he was left on his own. He wandered aimlessly around the house and up to the top bedroom which overlooked the creek and the river beyond. He sat down on the terrace and watched the boats go by, all making their way up and down the grey-green river.

Just as he was thinking of making a move, the whole of the river was filled with the shape of a large sailing ship and gliding into full view was a three-masted schooner, with all the sails aloft coming into the harbour. Eddie was mesmerised for those few seconds that it was in his view. It was a wonderful sight.

Wow! he thought, *Imagine sailing in a boat as big as that, with just the sails beating against the wind and having to climb into the rigging.*

It was hard to imagine. Eddie sat bolt upright, thinking. Captain Avery would have been familiar with all the seamanship skills necessary to sail a big ship across the Atlantic. Wasn't he a sea captain who had plied from the West Indies and Boston, from Ireland and Plymouth? Could he possibly bring him back again? He must be a brilliant sailor. He could teach him to sail his small Cornish shrimper around the South West coast couldn't he? It was worth a try, wasn't it? Where was the gold medallion? Hidden in the bottom of his wardrobe still, he hoped.

Down the stairs he ran and opening his wardrobe door, he rummaged through the debris at the bottom and at last, wrapped in an old shoe box, he found what he was looking for – the gold medallion. Eddie was rather wary of it this time. His hands were a little sweaty, and he could feel his heart racing.

Think, he told himself. *He might not even come. Oh go on, give it a try,* and quickly, before he went off the idea, he held the gold medallion tightly in his hand. Very gradually he felt it becoming warmer and warmer. Eddie was determined not to let it go. He changed hands as the heat intensified. Ouch! It was very hot now. At last Eddie could hold it no longer and had to let it go. He put it on a piece of flat stone he had gathered from a beach somewhere, and waited. Nothing happened. He watched the slight smoke rising from it, proving its intense heat.

"Why won't you come? I'd so hoped you would," said a disappointed Eddie. "Something must be working because it got so hot."

He sat on the bed feeling dejected and leaned back on the pillows, watching the gold medallion, a thin grey spiral of smoke rising in the room. His eyes closed, he felt very weary and soon he was asleep.

A little later, probably twenty minutes, Eddie slowly woke up and a faint smell that he didn't recognise was in the air. He lay still, trying to focus his mind. He could hear a strange noise – a squeak, squeak, squeak, and then he knew. He was here! He opened his eyes and sat up. Captain Avery was sitting in the rocking chair with his dog beside him. This time Eddie was not frightened; he was extremely pleased.

"You're here," smiled Eddie, "And you've found your dog."

He sat over the side of the bed, and tickled the dog's ears.

"What do you mean by waking me up lad, it's the middle of the night in the spirit world," said the sea captain sternly. "It takes a long time to journey through all those years."

He paused, staring at Eddie. There was a long silence. Eddie didn't dare to speak.

"I'm grateful to you lad in my way; not many get called back. What made you do it? Come on, out with it boy," and he snapped his fingers for the dog to return to his side.

"I wondered, that is I hoped, you might be able to teach me how to sail? I've got a little boat now, and my father is away, and I saw this huge sailing ship today and well, I thought of you."

Eddie trailed off, faltering, feeling a little embarrassed, having started off so bravely.

"Ah," said Captain Avery, looking at Eddie and puffing away on his pipe. "Indeed," as he rocked backwards and forwards.

He didn't say anymore, just sat quietly rocking and stroking the dog. Eddie watched him curiously. *One problem,* he thought, *is that he can't wear those clothes out with me in the boat. Everyone will notice him. I'll have to find him something else.*

"I want to thank you lad, for finding my dog Syracuse," the Captain suddenly said to Eddie. "He's returned to me after some bad experiences, and I am grateful to you. You found our bones together, did you not?"

"I think I must have," agreed Eddie.

"This dog has voyaged the world with me. I had long yearned for his company. As you have asked me, I shall try to help you. Now, where is this craft of yours? Seaworthy is she? Caulked with good tar, trimmed and true, with fine canvas sails? Where is

our first port of call? Come boy, let's plan our first voyage. Fetch the chart and dividers, lets to it." And he stood up and waved his finger at Eddie,

"First lesson: always, always, obey the captain."

"Yes sir. Wait one moment Captain," pleaded Eddie, and sped off upstairs to where his father kept his working clothes. He pulled out a navy cotton round-necked sweater, a pair of jeans, an old red woollen pull-on hat and a leather belt. That should do. Down he went with the bundle.

"Could you possibly try these on, sir?" Eddie asked very politely. "I'm afraid that your clothes may be noticed, now that you've arrived in our time."

Captain Avery nodded to him,

"Perhaps you are right, but I cannot leave my pistols."

When he had dressed he only needed to tie his hair back, and with his beard, he looked quite a typical sailing type.

"Well lad? How do I look?"

"You look great, sir," admired Eddie. "Shall we hurry? We've only got the afternoon. My mother and sister have gone out."

Eddie, Captain Avery and Syracuse left the house and walked in the shadows down the path to the water. The sea captain kept looking all around him and shaking his head in bewilderment. How everything had changed! They made their way down the rocky slippery edge to pull the boat in.

"What, no crow's nest, top gallants, or poop deck?" laughed Captain John. "A mighty small whaler she is."

Expertly and without fuss, the tiny craft was manoeuvred into the main Channel heading out to sea. The wind was fresh and the water slightly rippled, small splashes of spray occasionally sneaked over the gunwales and wet them.

"Take note of the tide young lad, she's running out fast now,

there's rain due in a couple of hours, and the wind will freshen."
Captain Avery explained all this to Eddie and how they would
use the incoming tide to make their homeward trip easier.

"Tighten the sail now, there's more slack than we need, it's
flapping greatly and wasting our speed." Eddie did as he was
told, and soon the little boat left the river mouth behind, and ta-
cking towards the west, they hit the winds full force across Start
Bay. How Eddie enjoyed himself! He could see the lighthouse in
the distance, and far away black clouds were bunching up on the
horizon. Captain John handled the boat with brilliance, turning
and slicing through the water; he made it answer to his every
command, rudder and sail, rope and wind. He too, was thoroughly enjoying himself. They sat together, the same feelings filling
them both. The man and the boy from different centuries, sharing
a love of the sea, discovering nothing had changed during those
four hundred years. A seagull flew close to them, its wings beating hard as it skimmed across the top of the swelling sea. Eddie
knew it was Sargasso but said nothing. He was sure the bird was
anxious because he had never been this far away from the creek
before.

"This one day, reunited with the sea in a small ship with a good
crew, is dearer to me than all the years I have spent in the spirit
world," said the captain suddenly.

"I have sorely missed the taste of the salty spray, the smell of
the ocean and the freedom of a new horizon before me," and he
stroked the dog that had remained nestled in the bow of the boat.

"I thank you boy for giving me another opportunity to feel the
wind once more," and he gazed over the water taking as much of
it in as was possible in one long look.

Eddie sat silently, and eventually Captain John sat back and
told him of his life as a seafarer and of the adventures he'd had.

He spoke of Port Royal in Jamaica and how it was the English had taken it by force from the Spanish, and placed a governor of their own in charge. This governor, Henry Morgan, had been a notorious pirate in his day. They had both become very rich indeed. It was a fascinating story.

At last the black clouds forced them to turn the boat around and head back to Dartmouth. Captain John finished his storytelling and they concentrated on sailing back across the choppy sea. The two castles standing guard over the river mouth came into sight, and they rounded the headland and found calmer waters, eventually negotiating the tiny inlet of the creek.

"Shall I be able to return again?" asked Captain John sadly.

"I think you will, the medallion seems to work, doesn't it?"

"What medallion?" came the curious question.

"The one you were given in Port Royal by the governor, the one I used to get you here."

"Ah, that gold medallion," and the man rubbed his beard thoughtfully.

"I could find somewhere for you to stay, Prawn Cottage maybe. If you stay there, we won't be pestered by anyone wanting to know who you are," reasoned Eddie. "Come on, I'll take you over to see it, it's quite empty."

Captain John nodded. He'd already made up his mind he didn't want to leave. Eddie skilfully rowed across to the wooden jetty that led to the cottage. It was a tiny dolls' house built on the rocks, looking inquisitively over the river. They tied up and carefully got out, Eddie looking for the key kept in a jam jar under the jetty's first step. When they opened the creaky door, Syracuse rushed inside and woofed twice in approval. He sniffed and searched around.

"I think everything you need is here," Eddie told him, showing him the light switches.

"I've got to go back to school tomorrow, but I'll come later on."

They shook hands and Eddie left, wondering if he would be alright.

He put the boat on to the mooring and quickly sprinted home. He turned back once to see a light shining out of Prawn Cottage, and he smiled to himself. What a great afternoon it had been. He arrived home in time for tea and he and Ellie busied themselves getting ready for school the next day.

They sat in the sitting room for the evening and Eddie lit the first fire for a long time. Mary knew there was the smallest chance of a visit to Peter's ship in the Mediterranean in the autumn. She was excited and hopeful, and would give it some careful thought in her quiet moments. The three of them were thinking deeply about different things. Ellie was hoping that Ferdinand and Isabella would be very sensible for the big clean-up tomorrow. Eddie was thinking of Captain Avery and Syracuse, tucked up in Prawn Cottage. Mary was wondering where Peter was, and would she see him before Christmas? They all looked into the flames of the red fire with their own private thoughts.

Mary broke their dreaming first and got up to pull the curtains and make the drinks. She stirred their hot chocolate, popped two marshmallows in each one, and took them back to the fireside.

"Here we are, bed next I think, you've got to be up for school tomorrow. It'll be a shock to the system!"

"Oh don't remind me please," groaned Eddie gloomily, sipping his drink. Eventually they made their way to bed; Mary sat for a long while, making plans, enjoying the solitude and peace before locking up and going up to bed.

Chapter Fifteen
The Big Clean-up

There was such a to-do in the house the next morning, alarm clocks ringing, doors banging, water running, voices shouting, plates clinking, glasses tinkling, goodbyes echoing, and then... silence! Mary sipped a second cup of tea and then looking at the clock, remembered she had to be at the church at ten o'clock for the big clean-up.

It was a crisp day and Mary walked quickly to the church where an array of cars filled the narrow car park.

Goodness, she thought, *look who's turned out today for the clean-up,* as she noticed cars belonging to the vicar, church wardens, organist, four of the flower ladies from the rota, and Harry the odd job man.

Quite a crowd indeed, the more people the better, she decided, and went down the steps into the gloom. It appeared to be a frenzy of activity, with window washing, sweeping and polishing, dusting, brass cleaning, and the electric kettle was steaming merrily by the one and only electric power point.

"Good morning to you," beamed the vicar as he popped his head out of the vestry door.

"We've left the flower arranging cupboard for you Mary, thought you'd know best what to do with the junk in there. Try and be ruthless won't you?" he pleaded and nodded at her confidently.

Mrs Plunkett, the lady organist, swept down the aisle, humming furiously the tune of next week's anthem.

"Can I make you a coffee, Mary dear?" she pressed, "and I've brought a tin of my special spicy rock cakes, I think you'll like them." Her shiny round face with its circlet of curls smiled welcomingly.

Mary knew better than to refuse. Mrs Plunkett's cakes were famous in the parish, but for all the wrong reasons, as one or two unfortunate broken teeth had proved. As promised, the coffee arrived and its craggy little friend on a plate too, burnt currants protruding from the top.

"Lovely," smiled Mary, "how kind." Off Mrs Plunkett went to attend to her duties sorting out the mouldy hymnbooks from the damp cupboard where they were stored.

It was companionable work, all trying to reach a common goal: tidiness, cleanliness and order. The dust flew high in the air and was caught in the sunbeams chinking through the stained-glass windows. Smells of polish and brass cleaner suddenly over-powered the mustiness and damp odours clinging to the walls. The vicar filled his car with bulging sacks and was very satisfied as he drove each load off to eternal damnation at the local tip. Mary had opened the flower arranging cupboard and was care-fully removing, examining, and deciding what should happen to each piece.

We simply must make more room, she convinced herself. So a cardboard box was found and gradually she made her choices and the box steadily filled up. Eventually Mary got to the dark and dusty cobwebby corners of the shelves. She picked up a tiny piece of pretty lace, no bigger than a postage stamp, and looked at it curiously.

How very beautiful this little scrap is. Such tiny work; who could have made such a thing? Mary was nonplussed. She put the tiny filmy scrap of lace into her pocket to show Ellie. She swept along the shelf with a dustpan and brush, tidying and spraying with polish as she went. In the dustpan was another oddity – a teeny weeny hat with a minute feather in it.

Too small for a doll, thought Mary, and she put it into her pocket to look at later. She stepped outside the vestry with the box of rejects. Harry was going through the black door to the bell tower.

"Just going to sweep down the steps and check for birds' nests," he told her with great authority, and disappeared. The whole array of helpers were all whirring away, eager to get finished and be home for lunch. The entire church looked so different; it was just how the vicar and his wife had hoped. He beamed.

"Well done. Well done everyone," he repeated. "I love a good clear up."

But then Harry appeared, stumbling down the bell tower steps, white as a sheet, clutching his chest. Mary anxiously approached him.

"Harry, are you alright?"

"I'm hearing voices up there!" he said, "it's true I tell you, I really did. Little quiet voices, laughing and carrying on. I know I heard 'em."

He sat down and mopped his head with his hanky.

"Maybe I'm losin' me mind, Vicar," and he shook his head.

"Now now, Harry, don't talk like that," and Andrew patted him kindly on the back.

"I'll go and have a look shall I, and check it out?"

By now a little crowd of sympathetic onlookers had collected around poor old Harry, who quite frankly looked terrible.

"Scared out of me wits I was, but I heard 'em, I definitely heard 'em." He nodded emphatically to his audience.

"Does he drink?" Mrs Plunkett said very loudly to the vicar's wife.

"Shush!" hushed Prue in alarm, "He'll hear you."

"I never touch a drop except on a Friday night down the Ship and Anchor," answered Harry, most put out, glaring at Mrs Plunkett. Everyone waited for the vicar to come back from the bell tower. It went very quiet. At last Andrew appeared, wiping cobwebs from his face.

"Well Harry," he announced, "I couldn't hear anything but we've definitely got bats in the belfry." He smiled broadly at everyone.

"Hghhh! 'Twern't bats I heard," snorted Harry, "'Twas real voices, just like me and the missus havin' a bit of a barney."

"No Harry," laughed the vicar, raising his eyebrows at his wife, "I don't think so. Come along now, I'll run you home and we'll all finish off and thank the Lord for our fellowship and labours today, so willingly undertaken," and he swept Harry up by the elbow and ushered him out of the door. Harry glanced back protesting once, but was marched along by the vicar.

"Well, that's one way of getting home early," sniffed Mrs Plunkett and she bustled about angrily.

The team disbanded shortly afterwards and dispersed home after admiring each others' work, and declaring that it was a job well done. Mary packed her basket up with her cleaning materials and went to the altar to water the flowers. By the time she had finished the church was quiet; everyone had gone at last. She sat down in the front pew looking up at the stained-glass window, resting and looking at St Peter, the sea and his boat, so still and beautiful.

I must organise that trip now, she resolved. *I'll try and get confirmation of the visit from the captain's wife.*

She sat for a while in the peace and quiet and felt good about the morning's work. Then she remembered the things she had found.

Maybe I should put them back, she thought, *they might belong to somebody's children.*

So she went back and opening the flower cupboard she laid the two items – the tiny lace square and the miniature hat with the feather– on the freshly polished shelf. As she closed the door she thought she heard a sneeze, a very tiny one.

"Atisshooo!"

Then again, "Atisshooo!" and a faint voice said, "Where is my best hanky?"

Mary slammed the door, and after squeezing the padlock together, ran out of the church. She felt quite faint and eventually slowed down along the leafy lane, gathering her breath back.

I'm just being ridiculous! she thought, *I'll be carted off like Harry next!* She tried to forget all about it. By the time she got home it was a distant memory, pushed very firmly to the back of her mind.

Chapter Sixteen
Freddie makes plans and Ellie has suspicions

Freddie knew he was a day late in his welcoming get-together for the two new bats. He hated his new job with its responsibilities and meetings, endless conversations and action memos. Reluctantly he made up a little speech for the bats – now, what were their names and where had they come from? Who would he nominate as their family advisor, called by the Woodlanders their kinship cousin? It had to be someone who didn't mind the dark and who wasn't afraid of heights. What about the white owl called Oliphant? He would be perfect.

Freddie flew along the woodland path to the second ash tree on the right where Oliphant lived. The robin politely roused him with many apologies and respectfully explained the request from the buzzard. He invited him to the bell tower at dusk. Oliphant agreed, and closed the door firmly, their conversation at an end.

This shall be my first and last official task, and Freddie heaved a sigh of relief. He had made his decision, but he expected repercussions from the council at the Citadel. He flew back to the garden.

In the bell tower, Belvedere and Boadicea were busy home-making.

"What shall I give our visitors to eat?" Boadicea lisped nervously.

"I'll catch some bluebottles."

So they washed and brushed their new babies and Belvedere flew round the church looking for bluebottles as a delicacy to offer. He came back home with a small amount, just enough to share.

"Those noisy mice have gone, dear," he informed Boadicea. "They're not supposed to be up here you know. It said on our release papers we were sole occupiers."

"I think they came up here to escape those humans," his wife remarked.

"You might be right," nodded Belvedere, "I won't go down and make a fuss then. Not yet. Don't want to upset the neighbours on our first week here."

They settled down for a nap together until the appointed time for the visitation.

***

Eddie waited impatiently for the school bus that afternoon. His head was spinning; it had been a very hectic day. Now, however, he wanted to concentrate on what he was going to do with Captain Avery.

Ellie was on her school bus, wondering how Ferdinand and Isabella got on during the great clean-up. She finally arrived, and tossing her school bag over her shoulder, headed up the hill to the church in the distance.

A small green clinker dinghy came into view, with red sails and an unmistakable flag on the top. It was Sargasso, Eddie's boat. She stopped to get a better view and saw two people in the

114

boat in navy blue sweaters. One was Eddie and the other – well, she couldn't tell.

Reaching the castle she stepped inside the empty church and at once she could smell the polish and freshness the cleaning party had left behind. As she tiptoed over to the choir vestry, she could hear Isabella's tiny voice raised angrily, coming from the cupboard.

"Well I don't like bats; I've never trusted them you know, not since one of Auntie Theodora's children was lost. She never came back you know, little Clara…"

"But you don't know dear, I mean, really know for sure, do you?" interrupted Ferdinand, in his quiet soothing way.

"Well I'm not having anything to do with them, I can tell you that right now."

Ellie entered the vestry and sat on the bench.

"Hello?" she called gently.

The voices stopped and Ferdinand appeared mopping his brow with his spotted handkerchief.

"We're having a bit of a time of it, we've got some new neighbours you know." He paused as Ellie raised her eyebrows enquiringly.

"Bats," he nodded, "yes bats," he repeated. "Moved in three days ago. They've got the whole of that bell tower to themselves. Isabella's furious. She doesn't like bats, thinks they steal mice-children. I'm not so sure but I *do hate quarrels*. Just want a nice quiet life Ellie, you understand?" and he sat down glumly.

"But," he suddenly remembered, "I've found my favourite hat and Isabella's best lace kerchief from Andalusia. So lucky! It appeared on the shelf after the cleaning folk had gone. We'd gone up to the bell tower to hide – just the right advice your brother gave us, clever chap. That's when we found Belvedere and Boadicea, the new bat tenants. They're having their visitation this evening. I'm trying to keep Isabella out of the way. Don't really want her interfering and upsetting them."

Ellie was somewhat alarmed when it dawned on her that the only person who could have found Isabella and Ferdinand's things was – her mother. Ellie felt herself blushing and going all hot at the very idea of it.

Isabella appeared dressed in brown velvet made from an old cushion the vicar used to sit on.

"Has Ferdinand told you our news? Yes horrid ugly bats upstairs, they're frightfully common you know." She nodded to Ellie.

"Don't you agree?"

Ellie didn't answer, she was just glad the two little mice had not been discovered. She had another mystery to solve – the boat and Eddie's passenger.

"I'm really late home today, so I'm going now. Bats aren't so bad Isabella, they sleep all day anyway, and so they won't be noisy neighbours." She laughed rather loudly.

Ellie left the church, making her way towards the creek, where the boat was not in its place.

Eddie must still be out fishing, she thought. Then she raced up the two flights of stairs to the balcony room, and grabbed the binoculars kept on the window ledge. She watched and waited patiently and soon she was rewarded with the sight of the small boat with the sails being lowered, and two people moving about.

That's odd, thought Ellie as the boat reached the wooden jetty at Paradise Point and one of the crew got out. The person left in the boat she thought was Eddie, but it was difficult to tell at such a distance.

He'll be back in a minute then if it is him.

She went downstairs.

"Hello dear," said her mother as she entered the warm kitchen.

"Hi Mum, what's for tea?"

"Shepherd's pie tonight, and left over apple pie and cream."

"Yum," said Ellie. "Eddie should be here in a minute."

And sure enough Eddie came bursting through the back door with a bag and a bundle.

"Hi Mum, hi Ellie," he panted. "Is tea ready? Something smells good."

His mother laughed. "Shepherd's pie."

"Oh good," he grinned. "I'll just go and change and be back straight away," and he dashed off.

He was back moments later pulling a jumper over his messed-up hair. They ate the meal which was delicious, and Ellie asked innocently,

"How did the clean-up go, Mum, at the church today?"

"Oh it went very well," Mary replied with great enthusiasm. "The most unlikely people turned up to help, especially Mrs Plunkett, you remember her, from the Christmas fair? Yes it all looks so clean and tidy now, and…" She stopped suddenly. "Oh I've just remembered the strangest thing happened Ellie, I just didn't know what to make of it."

"Oh really?" enquired Ellie nervously, "What was it?"

"Well, on one of the shelves I found the tiniest little hat with a feather, and a teeny weeny lace square, like a miniature handkerchief. So sweet, but I've no idea how they got into the cupboard!" and she laughed and shook her head. "Very odd indeed. I just put them back in the end; I didn't know what else to do."

Eddie looked at Ellie and giggled. "Probably a leprechaun Mum, living in the cupboard."

Ellie exploded into nervous laughter and then glared at Eddie who kicked her under the table.

117

"I'm off to start my homework," and Ellie got up and left the room, enjoying leaving Eddie to clear up.

Mother and Eddie chattered away in the kitchen.

"Do you know that there is a chance I can go to visit your father in October, Eddie?" she told him.

She looked into his face, so that she could really see his reactions.

"I think that would be wonderful Mum, honestly. Don't worry about us, we'll be alright, you go." Eddie was perfectly calm and patted her arm, smiling. "Where are you going anyway?"

"To Lisbon. If I go," she added hastily.

"Of course you'll go." He nodded enthusiastically. "Ellie and I could stay with George and Bridget couldn't we? Maybe Patrick will come as well," and he looked very excited at this thought.

"Ellie, Ellie?" he called and raced up the stairs two at a time to her room to tell her all about it.

Mary sat down; she was pleased the news was out. She had felt a bit guilty planning a trip without the children. Perhaps it would all fall into place after all.

Up in Ellie's bedroom the children agreed that they would both like to stay at the Old Bath House if they were invited. Eddie left his sister and went to his room to be alone. He had plenty to think about.

He had rushed home from school, then down to the little pink house, and found Captain Avery and Syracuse still fast asleep. With very little persuasion they went sailing again, becoming firm friends.

Ellie was his biggest problem – he didn't want her to find out just yet. Ellie of course was on the case, but she hadn't quite worked out what Eddie was up to. It wouldn't be long before she pieced it all together. Then the secret would be out!

118

Chapter Seventeen
The bats are welcomed to the Woodland and Freddie meets a mysterious owl

Just as the light was fading, the robin flew to the door in the tree where Oliphant the white owl lived. Immediately the door was flung open and Freddie could see a large clock face with the big hand pointing to TWILIGHT, which was half way between SUNSET and DARKNESS. The robin was able to make out the other names on the clock. At the top, DAWNDAY then SUNRISE, NOONDAY, SUNSET, TWILIGHT, DARKNESS, STAR RISE and MOONLIGHT.

Oliphant appeared with his compass strapped to his wingtip.

"Alright? Ready? Take off? Go – o– o!

He flapped three times and was gone. The robin chased after him, weaving in and out of the tall trees in the woods. The owl headed due east by his compass and took a right sweep to the church bell tower. He landed on the top and the robin caught sight of a map enclosed in his feathers, folded as tightly as his wings. They came to an abrupt halt and sat together side by side.

"Speech ready? Information checked? Emergency routine? Complaints procedure?" the owl snapped out at him.

"Well, er, I think so sir," stammered the robin, "I've been through everything quite thoroughly."

"Good! Good! Good! Let's go – o – o – o – o!"

In they went through the large crack in the wall vent and found themselves in the dark rooftop dwelling. The robin could hardly see, but Oliphant, being a dark-dweller, could manage perfectly.

"Good evening friends," called Freddie, "I've brought your kinship cousin to meet you."

Then out of the darkness appeared the two bats, one with a couple of tiny babies attached to her front fur; they peered up with tiny closed eyes and sniffed the air.

"Please join us," welcomed Belvedere, and the little gathering sat down and was offered acorn cupfuls of dark wine and blue-bottles. Freddie took charge and explained the surrounding area, where the Citadel was, and how the buzzards ruled. The bats listened attentively. Oliphant then took over, giving them all the rules of the woodland and the emergency procedures.

"Understand?"

Boadicea shivered and looked frightened, but Belvedere put his wings around her and comforted her.

"My dear, we need to know these things. We are grateful, Mr Oliphant. Thank you."

"Just reading the regulations to you. No need to worry. Just doing my duty. I am after all, your kinship cousin," replied the owl in clipped tones.

"Well ... I think that's about it really," nodded the little robin, trying to be kind. "Please don't hesitate to contact us, if you have any problems."

"Thank you," said Belvedere gratefully.

"Yes, thank you both," said Boadicea, who lisped, "Some more wine or nibbles? Do finish them up."

"Thank you madam." And with that Oliphant pecked twice, and the whole lot was gone. He blinked lazily and remained still.

"We must be off then," smiled Freddie. Outside it was dark and windy.

Oliphant said, "Follow me," and off they flew due west by his compass to the Great Ash Tree and screeched to a halt outside another oval door in the huge trunk. This was the biggest tree on the old earthworks, with huge spreading branches, and a panoramic view.

"My cousin Tolivera lives here, I haven't seen him for years," announced the owl. "Coming in?"

Freddie felt he couldn't refuse, and feeling rather frightened he followed the owl through the thick door. Inside it was all dark shiny conker-wood beams and furniture, well-polished and looking beautiful.

"Well goodness me, you're a stranger!" said a voice, and Freddie saw a tawny owl with a long pipe and small glasses sitting in a winged armchair.

"Passing by, don't you know. Any supper?" asked Oliphant.

"Indeed there is, and who is this?" chuckled the owl.

"I'm Freddie, guardian of the children at Watermill Cottage, third branch on the council at the Citadel," announced the bird proudly, rather forgetting himself.

"Well, well, well! I am impressed. Will you have a glass of the Mists of Time? Go on, – – I insist...after all, it is a special occasion," pressed Tolivera.

"OK – just one."

Tolivera poured the precious steamy amber liquor into frosted glasses and they all drank together.

"What do you do, Mr Tolivera?" asked Freddie politely, as they sat in the polished chairs with the patchwork-leaf cushions.

"Communications Freddie, that's my thing. I hear and see everything. This tree gathers information. It is filmed in the branches, runs down through the sap into the trunk, and is stored in the roots. Anything that happens, I've got a record of it all. Just have to turn a tap on and the sap flows into a pool and it can be viewed. At the end of each year it is turned into my liquor, the Mists of Time. This information can only be viewed by the buzzards and anyone else they nominate. It is all very hush-hush so you keep this a secret. Understand, Freddie?" He leant forward, staring menacingly.

"Yes Mr Tolivera," gulped the robin and sat back trying to avoid his eyes. He looked around, sipping his amber liquor in silence.

"So really... you're a spy!" said Freddie suddenly, the Mists of Time having worked its way to his brain and made everything crystal clear. Oliphant gasped loudly.

Tolivera put his glass down slowly and stared at him.

"Never a spy dear boy, merely an observer," and he laughed.

Oliphant breathed again easily. He knew how powerful Tolivera was, how people disappeared mysteriously sometimes. He hadn't taken offence, fortunately.

"We mustn't stay too long, Freddie," and he got up to go.

"Stay, do. Let's eat together. Won't take long," said Tolivera, "I want to talk some more to your friend," and smiling rather drunkenly at Freddie, the old owl produced mouse steaks and chestnut chips in very quick time. "Delicious!" announced Oliphant.

"Umm yes," agreed Freddie, lying rather badly.

Freddie tried to be friendly and not tell too many secrets, but Tolivera did his best to find them out. Eventually, yawning, the two guests decided it was time to leave.

"Very nice to have met you Mr Toliphant ... umm ... Olivera ... umm, ... Tolivera," attempted Freddie. "Goodnight."

Tolivera rolled his large eyes and touched wingtips with Oliphant.

"Bye Tolly, catch you later. Good grub. Let's g – o – o – o – o!"

And soon they were off, flying through the woods and bumping into every low branch.

"Ouch! Oh my head." Eventually they made it home.

"Goodbye Freddie," called Oliphant as they reached the second ash on the right.

"Bye, Oliphant; and thank you," replied the robin.

He woke up in the morning inside the blue tit box and couldn't remember a thing about the scary Tolivera who spied on them all.

Great Ash Tree

Chapter Eighteen
Eddie loses the medallion

The summer sped on its hurried way, everybody trying to cram their outdoor activities into a few short months. Mary still had to find somewhere for the children to stay during her visit to Portugal and made up her mind to ring Bridget and George. She dialled the number timidly. George recognised her voice and smiled to himself.

"Hello Mary, how nice to hear you. Eddie's just sailed past us with a friend, actually."

"Well… I want to have a chat with you and Bridget, I've got something important to ask you."

"Have you now lass, well I think I know what it is and I'll tell you now – it's all organised, the children are staying with us."

"I don't know what to say. Oh George thank you, I'm so grateful," and Mary stopped talking, tears glinting in her eyes.

"It's fine dear, just fine. Here's Bridget."

"Hello Mary, we've invited Patrick to join them for half term. They're helping us out if anything, doing some work here in the café at a busy time. So it suits George and me."

"Oh, you and George are just… marvellous."

Saying her goodbyes, Mary felt so happy she could have skipped all the way to the tea shop to hug them.

***

Everything went along fine until the secret was discovered. Eddie had spent a great afternoon with Captain John who had taught him how to splice a rope and tie some very complicated knots. Then when the tide was right and the wind perfect, they had sailed a long way out, done a spot of fishing, caught six whiting, and then headed home. It had been the sort of day Eddie loved. They parted company at the jetty and Eddie, carrying the fish in a plastic bag, put the boat away, leaving Sargasso the seagull sitting on the mast beside the flag. He'd been with them the whole day.

As Eddie ran along the path to the slipway he saw Ellie sitting on the drain cover, waiting for him. He stopped at once, pretended to tie his trainer shoelace, and thought quickly. What was he going to say? His mind went blank. Oh well it didn't matter – too late now.

He stood up and carried on running towards his sister who waved at him.

"Hi Eddie."

He returned her wave. As he reached her she got up and said, "Who was that with you?"

"Oh, just a guy staying at Prawn Cottage, we've been out fishing together," he shrugged.

"How did you meet him?"

"Down at the creek pottering, you know, digging bait at low tide and that sort of thing. Come on Ells, race you home for tea!" and he started running up by the creek. She sprinted after him as hard as she could until they reached the driveway and ran round to the back door, arriving at exactly the same moment, bursting through the door into the brightly lit kitchen.

"Steady you two," smiled Mary. "George and Bridget saw you from the tea shop, Eddie. You had a friend with you. Who was he?"

Ellie waited with satisfaction for the reply.

"Oh, just a fishing friend, we thought we might catch a few whiting today."

"And did you?"

"Yes we did actually; they're in that plastic bag," and he pointed to the doorstep where he'd dropped it.

"Didn't he want any?"

"No, I don't think he likes them that much. Is tea nearly ready Mum, I'm so hungry."

"Yes it won't be long. Go and change your fishy clothes, then."

"I'll be very quick," he promised, and went off to wash and change.

"I saw the man Eddie was with," Ellie told her mother. "They were at the jetty on the point."

"Oh yes, Prawn Cottage," Mary nodded, "he must be staying there. They do summer lets, I know."

Ellie laid up the big table for supper and sat down to wait for Eddie. Something wasn't quite right about the whole thing. She was determined to find out.

"Can you get those fish out of that bag Ellie for me, and put them in the sink please."

Mary dished up the supper. Ellie obediently went to the bag and took out the silver-grey fish. Inside the wet carrier bag was a tiny bag on a string. She put it in her pocket. It was something interesting. The fish lay waiting to be gutted by Eddie after supper. When he arrived they began eating and Mary told them all about her phone call to George and Bridget.

"We knew all about that Mum," grinned Eddie. "Ellie and I organised that weeks ago!"

"Well I wish you'd told me," scolded Mary.

She produced the puddings and the two youngsters cheered up and the moment passed. Supper over, they cleared it up and then Mary suggested a film. Afterwards, the two youngsters went upstairs to bed. Mary got up and called after Eddie,

"Did you do the fish, Eddie?"

There was a silence, and he appeared at the top of the stairs.

"Oh no, I forgot all about it. It's still in the sink, isn't it?"

He slowly came downstairs, found some newspaper and laid it on the draining board. He got out a very sharp long knife and slit the fish up the middle, pulling the coloured, shiny innards onto the newspaper, staining it crimson. The fish were soon on a large plate, the heads and guts neatly wrapped in the newspaper parcel.

Now where's that plastic bag? I can put the newspaper back into it. Oh, I think I put it in the bin. His net bag with the precious medallion in it had been inside the sandwich bag. He groaned inwardly. Oh no! He rummaged in the bin and looked inside. The bag was empty. It was gone! But it couldn't be!

"Come on Eddie, I'm waiting to get rid of the newspapers."

"Sorry Mum." He spun around and helped pack the sodden newspaper into the bag.

"Eddie, wake up, you're in a dream. Or, better still, go to bed and get some proper sleep."

He walked out of the kitchen and upstairs. What had happened to the medallion? What would he do if he couldn't find it? He took the stairs slowly, one at a time, thinking and trying to remember his last actions. Could he have dropped it putting the boat away? Had it fallen out of the bag when he raced Ellie up the creek? He really felt like crying for the first time for months; not since his father had left. He called goodnight to Ellie but there was no answer. She was already asleep. He got undressed and into bed forgetting everything except the medallion. He couldn't sleep, and tossed and turned. Over and over he tried to remember what he had done with it. But it was no good. Eventually he dozed off into a very worried sleep. His last thoughts were of the lost gold medallion. Where on earth was it?

Chapter Nineteen
Ellie behaves badly

Eddie woke very early, cold and tired. He dressed, washed and went quietly down the stairs. He unlocked the door, and Freddie appeared like a rocket from nowhere and hopped along beside him.

"Morning Freddie," Eddie said quietly, "I could do with some help this morning," and he made his way down to the creek searching every inch with his eyes downcast. Nothing. He searched the creek edge and hauled the boat in and started looking all around. Nothing. He sat dejected in the boat. *What next?* Freddie and Sargasso watched from a distance, wishing they could find the medallion for him, but nobody knew where it was. Eddie gave up eventually and walked back home. Ellie was up when he got back.

"You're up early," she remarked, as he sat down in the kitchen looking as if he had all the cares of the world on his shoulders.

"Yes," he replied gloomily, "I couldn't sleep."

"Oh, why's that?" Ellie asked wickedly.

"I've lost the gold medallion; it was in a net bag I've been wearing around my neck. I put it in with the fish last night and can't find it now." He looked up at her dejectedly.

"Why is it so important?" she asked, sitting down to drink her tea.

"It's a long story Ellie, but I used it a few weeks ago when I was fed up, and … and I brought the captain back. I should have told you, I've been meaning to tell you, but I just wanted someone to teach me to sail. Dad's never here and Captain Avery has been showing me all about seamanship and sailing, and knots and the tides. Everything! He's alive and well and living in Prawn Cottage with his dog. Only for the summer," he added, waiting nervously for his sister's reaction. It wasn't good.

"That's who you've been sailing with, is it? Why on earth didn't you tell me?" demanded Ellie furiously. "Didn't you think I'd like to meet him, or go sailing? Why did you leave me out?" she asked angrily. "I was with you when you found him, for goodness sake!"

Eddie stared at her. "I didn't think you'd be interested. I'm sorry Ellie, perhaps I have left you out. I didn't mean to."

"I know we've got different interests sometimes, I'll agree with that, but I still like going out walking, and sailing, I haven't changed. I'd like to do things when Patrick comes to stay. You know, like we used to." She looked a bit sad.

"I suppose we have grown apart a bit, and… I'm sorry. Anyway all this doesn't help me find the gold medallion. It's a real nightmare. I don't know what I'm going to do." He put his elbows on the table and clutched his head in his hands.

Ellie couldn't decide whether to tell Eddie she'd got it or not. She felt very hurt and cross with him and she wanted to punish him

"Well, why shouldn't I have a turn with it?" she asked herself.

So she kept quiet and let Eddie suffer, which was really rather unlike Ellie. She was to go to work at eleven o'clock at the tea shop, and grabbing a banana and an apple, skipped off out of the house to say hello to Ferdinand and Isabella. At the church she pulled back the gold brocade curtains to the choir vestry and called softly,

129

"Isabella? Ferdinand? It's Ellie. Hello?"

Silence. There were no pattering tiny, scratchy feet; no tiny piercing voices, just silence.

Well that's very strange, thought Ellie, looking around for signs of them. She munched her apple slowly. *Where would they be?*

She sat down very carefully in one of the pews and watched. She removed the medallion from the bag to have a better look, and turning it over in her hand, she felt it getting warmer and warmer. Realising she had set its time travelling mechanism into action she dropped it with an "Ouch!" As she bent to pick it up, she was very surprised to see somebody sitting in the Bishop's chair at the top of the church under the stained-glass window.

It's him! she thought, *It must be him!* Slowly she made her way towards him.

"Captain Avery, is that you?" she called out, suddenly feeling a little frightened. "I'm Ellie, Eddie's sister."

He sat in the large carved chair, with a feathered black hat, pointed beard and luxurious locks, white shirt with a lace collar, a sash and long jacket, breeches, stockings, and boots which were black and shiny. There were two pistols in his belt and a sword fastened to the top of his leg. He looked at Ellie curiously.

"Aye, little maid," he answered her, "Captain John Avery at your service. Now why the devil did ye bring me here? For it is many a long and tedious sermon I've endured from the parson from that very pulpit. Come, let me look at your pretty face." He beckoned her to him. "Indeed, you have taken favour from your brother. What do you want of me, missy? Speak, hurry now," he urged her, sitting forward, his sword clattering on the sides of the chair.

"I just wanted to m-m-meet you," she stammered, feeling

exceedingly foolish.

He jumped to his feet.

"I'll not be brought hither and thither on a foolish whim young maid, let me go back at once."

He seemed a little cross. He strode down the church, boots clicking on the stones. Cautiously Ellie followed him. As he got to the back of the church a tiny squeaky voice shouted,

"Captain John! Captain John!" and she saw Isabella run out from under the door to the tower, with Ferdinand behind her. They were dressed in yellow and cream, Isabella in an embroidered gown, her arms flailing, and Ferdinand was waving his stick. Captain John stopped dead in his tracks and looked down at the floor where the two excited mice clamoured around his boots. He bent down and picked them both up.

"My two dear friends," he said in a very gentle way. "I thought never to see you again."

Ellie could not quite grasp what he meant.

"Please tell me what's happening." She sat down extremely bewildered.

"These two darlings were a gift from the Queen of Spain when that country owned islands in the Indies. I brought them across the oceans to be with me in Devon and much beloved they were," smiled Captain Avery. Isabella danced and laughed and clapped her tiny pink paws together.

"We are called for the King and Queen of Spain, you know Ellie. I've been trying to tell you of our royal connections."

Ellie was pleased, of course, at this happy reunion but remembered her work at the tea shop. She was going to be late.

"We've got to go now Captain, come on. Eddie will be looking for you," and she literally dragged him out.

"Yes, yes, I understand, farewell dear friends, we'll meet again

131

– I swear it," he called to Isabella.

"What a happy occasion – reunited once more – sweet Jesus," Captain John muttered as Ellie hurried him along. They slipped down the creek path off the main road.

"Wait for Eddie here please, will you?" she implored him.

"As you wish, little maid, as you wish," he nodded dreamily, seeming to be in a daze. She sat him down and made him promise not to move. Then raced up the creek path as fast as was possible, puffing and breathing heavily with anxiety and panic. She opened the back door, hurried upstairs to Eddie's room and burst in. He was lying on the bed, staring at the ceiling, one arm over his head.

He looked up at her. "Ellie, what's the matter?"

"Oh it's too late to explain Eddie, I'm in such a rush, but get up quickly, I've got Captain Avery down at the lime kiln, and the medallion's safe. Here it is," and she pulled it out of her pocket and put it on the bed very quickly.

"Sorry! I've got to go to the café. See you later. Hope he's all alright. Bye!" and she turned and fled down the stairs, passing her mother with a bundle of sheets.

"Hi Ellie, everything OK?" Mary looked puzzled as Eddie shot out of his room and into the bathroom, and Ellie disappeared at great speed.

"I'm late Mum, that's all," she shouted behind her. "See you later."

Eddie dashed down the stairs three at a time, almost falling at the bottom. Grabbing a coat, he yanked the door open and chased off, nearly knocking the postman to the ground as he rounded the corner.

"Steady lad," the postman called after him, "is there a fire somewhere?" and he chuckled to himself.

No, thought Eddie grimly, *it's worse than that.*

He ran along the water's edge.

"Morning, Captain." He was so relieved to see him sitting on the rolled-up canvasses.

"What the devil's going on?" asked the captain rather grumpily as he yawned.

Prawn Cottage

133

"Take me home, young sir," and he grabbed Eddie's arm, hauling himself to his feet. Without arguing Eddie fetched the boat and rowed him across the river. At the cottage, Captain John patted the dog absentmindedly and then walked unsteadily towards the bedroom, where he flopped fully clothed onto the soft bed. Eddie crept out, down to the jetty and rowed the boat to the mooring, securing the rope. Then he raced off to tell Ellie what had happened.

Back at the teashop Ellie was busy with the visitors and when she saw Eddie's face peering through the window she was surprised.

"Is it alright if I take five minutes, Bridget?" she asked, and went outside to meet Eddie on the long green bench. She felt guilt rise up in her, and she took a deep breath, to hear the news, good or bad.

"Thanks Ellie," blurted her brother. "He's alright, I found him and took him back to the cottage but he's tired and gone to sleep." Ellie sat back, relieved the captain was safe.

"I've been thinking of sending him back anyway, now the winter's coming. I shall miss him of course but we can't risk his being discovered, or worse, lost somewhere. Can we? That time travelling is a dodgy business." He looked at Ellie. She felt guilty and looked down.

"No," she agreed.

"Right, I must go back now." She got up and remembered the episode in the church.

"Oh Eddie, I forgot to tell you. Ferdinand and Isabella were Captain John's pet mice! You'd never believe it, would you? He brought them all the way back to Devon from one of his voyages."

"No!" Eddie was stunned.

His sister went back inside to finish her work, while he sat for a few moments taking in all this new knowledge. No wonder Isabella was so imperious and petulant – what a life they must have had! It explained the amazing clothes the tiny mouse had sewn. Nothing was safe – the collecting bags, the cushions, the alter cloths: she had made little garments out of them all. He went along to the church to find them and he saw Isabella coming out from under the bell tower door. She squeaked with delight when she caught sight of him.

"Captain John is with you?" she asked excitedly.

"No, he's not."

"Lord, lord I knew it!" she cried in her tiny voice, "He's left us again, the wicked man!"

She ran back across the floor to the choir vestry. Poor Eddie had to follow. Ferdinand appeared, hearing her cries, and he sat her down trying to comfort the now sobbing Isabella.

"She's made some white lace night shirts for the bat babies to wear," he told Eddie quietly. "They're mighty ugly, poor little squashed-up things. Come now, there, there, my dear. Captain John's a busy man." And he patted her back and stroked her as he spoke.

"You've got the new babies to occupy you and Boadicea has told us about the store of food by the café, crumbs and goodies you wouldn't believe possible. It's a new adventure for us. Off you go now. She'll be alright." He waved Eddie away. "Haven't had so much fun for an age. Get along now."

Eddie left obediently. Frankly, the mice were a worry he just didn't need. He was looking forward to Patrick coming again; good old sensible Patrick. It wouldn't be long now. Soon be October half term, and his mother's holiday. There was a lot going on, and he couldn't wait.

135

Chapter Twenty
The mice are discovered

Up at the Citadel preparations were being made for the autumn council meeting. Each season a special carpet was laid for the meeting. The autumn one was very beautiful – a glorious riot of coloured leaves, greens, yellows, rusts, oranges, and rich browns in various shapes, were studded all over it. During the meeting the assembled crowd sat on the magnificent carpet looking upwards to the highest branches where the Honourable Members of the Council sat.

The pine tree was surrounded by hawthorns, dense ivy bushes, treacherous brambles and stinging nettles, which deterred unwanted humans. Beside the clump of trees, marking the edge of the Woodlanders' kingdom, there was a five bar gate – the Freedom gate. Anyone passing through it lost the protection of the woodland and was exposed to the weather and the fury of the sea. No one was a prisoner, but once they chose to open the gate there was absolutely no coming back, it was final. Many had done it, rebelling against the rules; they had left the territory and were never seen again. Some, it had been reported, were just a pile of bones on the coastal path; others – well – had just disappeared, reputed to have fallen and drowned or frozen to death. For many, beyond the gate still held a tantalising fascination but deep in their hearts they didn't have the courage to leave, preferring the routine security the woodland offered.

The band of squirrels that dashed among the treetops was responsible for providing seasonal refreshments at the meetings. Autumn was their favourite season, with piles of acorns, beech, chestnuts, and hazelnuts to offer. Juicy blackberries, rosehips, sloes and wild cherries were kept damp and ripe under cool leaves. The whole woodland was alive with activity, the squirrels working day and night to finish their work in time for the main event of the Woodlanders' diary, the autumn council meeting. It would be held very soon, just before Hibernation. What would be the main topic? Nobody knew. Would Freddie cause a sensation?

***

The time was drawing nearer to Mary's visit to Peter in Lisbon and all the arrangements had fallen into place. She knew how much the children were looking forward to staying at George and Bridget's and very excited at the prospect of being reunited with dear Patrick, who wrote each week from his school and telephoned at weekends.

Eddie was desperate to share the excitement of the sea captain with Patrick. If the autumn weather stayed calm, they could set sail again and catch the last of the soft breezes before the stormy grey skies of winter blew in from the east, forcing them to haul the boat out of the river and store it until the spring.

When Captain Avery had gone Prawn Cottage would be empty again, perched on its rock, its grey shutters closed. As the winter winds whipped up waves, spray, laden with salt, would crash over the tiny house and rusty marks appear, running down the walls like bloodstained tears.

Eddie spent a lot of time upstairs messing around with his new inventions. His calendar told him when the next full moon would be, and he resolved that if it was clear on that night, he would show his experiments to the sea captain. He noticed that there was an interesting happening on the night of the next full moon: there was to be an eclipse, a total eclipse of the moon. The shadow of the earth would blot out the light for about three minutes.

Well that will be quite exciting, thought Eddie, *Patrick will be here then too. Brilliant.* And he happily started making his plans. What of Ellie? Should she be included in this late-night adventure? Yes, Eddie decided, especially after her outburst over the medallion. The three of them would all be in it together. He would try and make it up to her.

The day of Patrick's arrival finally came. George had kindly offered to take them in the car with him to collect his godson. Mary was off to the hairdressers' in town and to do a few last minute bits of shopping. Eddie took Ellie into the kitchen and said quickly,

"There's just one thing Ellie – I'm going to tell Patrick about Captain John."

She was surprised and thought for a moment. "Yes, but that means he's got to know about Ferdinand and Isabella as well." She looked up at him seriously.

"Well I suppose it does," agreed Eddie slowly. "But he might as well know everything. I don't think he will tell. Captain Avery might not be around for too much longer anyway. Let's go and have a hot chocolate. Mum's going out in a minute. Come on."

Mary came downstairs to see them.

"I'm off now, bye dears." And the door closed behind her.

Walking along towards the café, the path was littered with beautiful golden leaves in great piles. Ellie loved the autumn: scuffing through the leaves, enjoying the crunching, the colours and shapes around her. Eddie linked arms with her as excitement mounted in his heart. He was looking forward to an eventful time with Patrick and hopefully an adventure or two. They arrived together at the tea shop, and Bridget, wiping her hands on a large striped tea cloth, came up the steps from the kitchen, face beaming, to greet them.

"Hello my dears, can I get you something?"

"We're going to have two hot chocolates, please Bridget," Ellie replied, and the warm-hearted lady bustled off to get their order. George brought their drinks out, huge frothing mugs with piles of cream, with chocolate chips and hazelnut curls tucked onto the saucers. He sat down beside them squeezing his bulky frame into a chair behind the table.

"I'll come round for you at four o'clock to fetch Patrick. Anyone late gets left behind, no second chance." His eyes twinkled at them.

"Don't worry," laughed Eddie, "We're ready now," and licked the foaming chocolaty cream from his lips.

"What time does your mother leave?" enquired George.

"She's being picked up at ten in the morning the day after tomorrow. She's gone to the hairdressers'. She is really excited, and that chocolate was wonderful," sighed Ellie, saying thank you to Bridget, who had come to join them at the table.

"Funny thing, I'm sure we had a full box of Belgian chocolate chips last time I looked. There's not many left now. Can you remember Ellie, when I last ordered a box?"

Ellie put her head to one side and thought, frowning.

"Well, we didn't use up much in the summer and you had two full boxes then."

"Let's go and have another look," suggested Bridget. Down in the lower cupboard there was just one box of chocolate chips, almost empty.

"Here's the other box, Bridget," Ellie called. She had discovered it right at the back.

"It doesn't feel very heavy," and she got hold of it and lifted it out. Chocolate chips rained down onto the floor. Bridget saw the problem at once.

"There's a hole in it, right at the back." She pointed to a small ragged aperture in the cardboard box.

"Oh no," Ellie said out loud, thinking *mice* rather fearfully.

"We've got mice," said Bridget grimly. "They've been helping themselves to my best Belgian chocolate chips, the little devils. George, George!" she called. "Come here a minute will you?"

Ellie was so afraid of what George would do that she stood in horror in the kitchen trying not to show how dreadful she felt. George examined the box and then looked right inside the cupboard with a torch, kneeling down on the tiled floor.

"Yes, I can see the problem," he pronounced. "There's a gap here where one of the water pipes runs along."

Bridget and Ellie looked at one another.

"I'll just go outside and have a look out there," and the big man went outside to explore.

"What's wrong?" asked Eddie as George came out of the kitchen.

"Mice!" was the answer and Eddie raised his eyebrows.

"Oh dear." He got up to go with George, not daring to look back at Ellie.

George followed the rock wall around outside and noticed that where the waste pipe came out there was some mortar missing, dislodged no doubt by driving wind and rain followed by hot sun and dry spells. Eddie watched him, knowing that this man would have no truck with mice.

"This is where they're getting in." He pointed it out to Eddie: "Up the pipes, into the wall, the cupboard, the box, and bingo! A feast of chocolate, the little blighters. They love it you know. People put it in their mousetraps instead of cheese."

Eddie shuddered.

"Well, not much time today to fix it lad, eh? I'll just put a mousetrap in the cupboard. That will sort them out for now."

"Sh-sh-should think so," stammered Eddie.

140

Examination complete, they went back to tell Bridget what they had discovered.

"Oh no, mice!" She grimaced, "and to think they've been all over my cupboards. Makes me feel quite queasy. Ugh!" And she sat down, lavender-scented hanky to her nose.

"What are you going to do?" asked Ellie very quietly, looking at Eddie, who stood by impassively.

"Oh, a mousetrap will sort, em out for today," said George cheerily. "Tomorrow I'll block up the masonry outside. Don't you worry about it. I'll see you later on, four o'clock precisely."

Bridget waved quietly to them, still sniffing her hanky. Ellie gave a last desperate look back. As soon as they had rounded the corner she burst into tears.

"I can't bear it. We have got to tell them. They might be killed, Eddie! Come on, we must find them!"

Eddie knew exactly who had been into the cupboard and pilfered the chocolate chips. It was of course Isabella, in her quest to store up her larder for the inevitable winter famine that overtook the bleak countryside. No self-respecting winter survivor left his gathering and garnering too late. By December's wan light and sombre days all store cupboards should be full to bursting.

On Boadicea's advice, the mice had discovered that the tea shop provided a huge choice of food previously unknown to them, and Isabella had plenty of containers in her cupboard, all kindly provided by the flower arrangers of St. Petrox. Pieces of cake, scones and sandwich crusts were scrupulously gathered from under the outside tables and stored. To prove the point, Ferdinand's yellow silk waistcoat was exceedingly tight now and several of the pearl buttons were undone.

Ellie went to try the church door. "It's the winter opening times, isn't it? Will it be open?"

141

Chapter Twenty-one
A warning for Ferdinand

Eddie and Ellie stood in a soft, light drizzle that had started. They fumbled with the difficult door and eventually it swung open. Reaching the uneven floor of the choir vestry they pulled aside the heavy gold brocade curtain. All was still, the air smelling of polish, old wood and musty books.

"Ferdinand, Isabella?" called Ellie. Silence met her gentle voice. She looked at Eddie in despair. "Where are they?" She tried, again louder this time.

Eddie searched desperately around the church. High on the altar were two autumn arrangements which his mother had done, full of blackberries, rose hips and Chinese lanterns. Ellie joined him and together they systematically checked each pew. Then Eddie stopped, listened and beckoned to Ellie, smiling and pointing at something. Curled up in the folds of the vicar's favourite red cushion was the sleeping and snoring Ferdinand. He was enveloped in the soft velvet cloud, his face serene and happy in sleep, tell-tale stains of blackberry juice on his green waistcoat straining across his fluffy chest. He had been found, but where was Isabella?

Ellie called his name. Gradually he stretched and opened his eyes.

"Ellie my dear. Eddie, what brings you here?" He yawned and twitched his whiskers.

"Where is Isabella?" urged Ellie.

"Isabella?" He paused for another yawn as the children danced with impatience. He scratched his head "Um, she's gone to visit the bat babies."

"Have you been in the café, Ferdinand? You know, up the pipe and into the box of chocolate chips?" questioned Ellie.

"How do you know about our secrets?"

Ferdinand was shocked. He paused. "I can't get into the hole now," he admitted, patting his tummy.

"Well she mustn't go back there again, do you understand Ferdinand? Not ever. They have laid a mousetrap for you."

The little mouse clutched his chest and shrieked.

"A mousetrap? Oh my! My Uncle Horatio died such a death. Horrible." He shook his head. "Horrible."

"You do realise how bad it could be, don't you?" insisted Ellie.

"Well, I do now," agreed the worried little mouse, wringing his paws together.

"Tell her the minute she gets back," added Ellie firmly

"Thank you, thank you."

"Right, we'd better be off then," agreed the youngsters.

"Goodbye."

They left by the side door, carefully locking the door behind them.

"Thank goodness for that!" breathed Ellie.

"Yes," agreed Eddie.

Doubts welled up in his mind; doubts he dare not voice to Ellie. He shivered as they walked back home in the rain, the light fading. They had done as much as they could and the day was moving on quickly now.

"Come on Ellie, we must hurry, there's loads to do and worst of all we've had no lunch."

They sped home and set to work in earnest. Eddie made huge toasted cheese and marmite sandwiches which he liked just a little burnt, and mugs of steaming tea. The mouse situation was pushed to the back of their minds as they concentrated on everyone's differing departures.

"We'll pop back with Patrick tomorrow, Mum, shall we?" asked Eddie, sitting back in his chair, full up and relaxed.

"Yes, that would be nice. Come and have some soup. Bridget has kindly asked me to join you all for supper tomorrow. Well my dears, the other ladies are coming in a minute for tea. These naval wives are so organised, every last detail is covered. We only need a uniform and we could take over the ship!"

Eddie and Ellie nearly choked on their tea as they all laughed together.

"What time are they coming?" asked Ellie.

"Four-fifteen precisely," laughed Mary, "you'll have left, hopefully, by then."

Ellie and Eddie collected their luggage into the hallway and sat down to wait for George. At last the car drew up in the driveway and Ellie called out,

"He's here Mum, George is here."

"Right Mary, we'll see you tomorrow evening, best bib and tucker, I expect you've plenty to do still." He smiled at her. Kissing both her children, she watched them climb into the back seat looking extremely happy and excited, and in a moment they were gone.

Mary closed the front door and went back into the strangely empty house and put the kettle on. As she looked out of the window the little robin was eating her cake crumbs.

"Hello little robin," she murmured through the window, "how could I possibly feel lonely?"

She watched him for a few minutes, until the bell outside clanged and she hurried to open the door. This was it, she was almost on her way and the children were off to collect their greatest friend. Would they be alright without her?

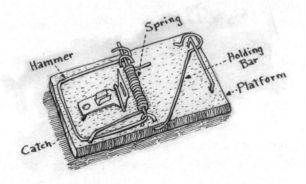

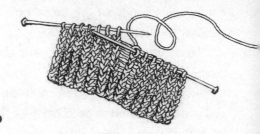

Chapter Twenty-two
Patrick returns

During the journey to Totnes station Eddie and Ellie looked out of the window, many thoughts swirling around inside their heads like oily water. They parked by the white fencing. Across the railway line there was an old signal box café which reputedly sold the best cooked breakfast for miles around. Train-spotters thought themselves in heaven, with a big plate of bacon and eggs, a mug of tea and an uninterrupted expanse of track to look down on.

George pointed to it.

"Shall we?"

They crossed the bridge and went into the steamy warm café.

They sat by the window and soon the cheery waitress talked them into having thick slices of gingerbread, sticky and dark with plump raisins. It was five-ten and soon the first sounds of the train would echo round the bend.

Ellie leant forward, and looking George in the eyes she said quietly, "Did you put the mousetrap in the cupboard, George?" and fixing him with her intent gaze.

"Yes indeed, I put two in," he nodded, pleased with himself.

"Oh."

She remained silent. Eddie squeezed her hand.

With the whistle of the approaching train they quickly left their table, sprinted back across the access over the track and found a spot on the opposite platform. As the train creaked to a halt, suddenly doors flew open, luggage appeared and the empty platform became full of hasty travellers anxious to leave the carriages.

"I can't see him," said Ellie anxiously, scanning the oncoming procession. When the crowd thinned they spotted him, unhurried, helping a rather large elderly lady with a huge shopping trolley. Patrick looked up and saw them, raising his eyebrows to signal his amusement at his slow progress. A man in a black polo-necked sweater suddenly appeared, and taking over the trolley from Patrick said, "Thank you so much for helping my mother. Hello Mother," and pecked her powdered cheek. The old lady was wearing a large squashy velvet beret and a voluminous black cape, pinned on the shoulder with a huge silver Celtic brooch.

"Late again, Paul," she chided. She turned gratefully to Patrick and beamed her most winning smile.

"I am so grateful to you Patrick for your help. We've had a good journey haven't we? You've been such an interesting companion. Goodbye now, Enjoy your holiday!" and she squeezed his hands and shuffled off with her son, berating him again for being late.

"Well I didn't expect this," Patrick said, pleased to see all three of them. "It's great to see you again, it really is," and he adjusted the heavy backpack on his shoulders. "I met Mrs Finch-Ingram on the way from London. She had been buying antiques in London and that shopping trolley of hers is stuffed full of Chinese pieces. She lives somewhere near you I think. Anyway, tell me all the news."

He linked arms, one of Eddie's and one of Ellie's as George

led the way to the car. The journey home seemed much shorter and soon they were speeding down College Way for their first glimpse of the River Dart.

"It's just great to be back," Patrick said as he saw the river and the pretty town, his Scottish burr very apparent. He sat back contented, breathing a long sigh of weary satisfaction. He had been counting the days off slowly, one by one, on his dormitory calendar.

"What's the plan?" he asked, and "When shall I see you again?" as the car slowed down outside the Old Bath House and manoeuvred into the parking bay.

"But, we're all staying here – didn't you know? Mum's going out to see Dad in Portugal, she leaves tomorrow," Eddie told him. George chuckled in the front.

"You are joking!" Patrick was astonished.

"Didn't you tell him?" Ellie tapped George on the shoulder. "How could you?"

George got out of the car, still laughing. He went round to the boot for the luggage, enjoying the huge surprise that he had planned for Patrick. Soon all their belongings were safely indoors and they closed the door to the world outside, the darkness and the drizzle.

Inside it was almost like Christmas – bright and cosy. Bridget had a warm fire going in the big fireplace and the table was laid; a waft of delicious supper came from the kitchen. Through the windows the river murmured by, glinting in the light, black as ink.

"Right – get yourselves unpacked and sorted and come back in here for seven o'clock for a celebratory drink before supper."

George rubbed his hands together in front of the fire and sat down in his favourite armchair to rest and recover. They followed Bridget downstairs to the bedrooms. Each room had river views, big fluffy pillows and soft downy covers.

"We always believe in very comfortable beds," she told them. "Hurry up now, don't keep George waiting for his special whisky." And she left them to it – billowing white dressing gowns, and toiletries, televisions and tea trays welcomed them

"Wow! This is just brilliant!" Eddie was overwhelmed with the hospitability.

"It's always like this," said Patrick.

Ellie appeared at the door. "It's like a hotel," she said, "I love it. I've got my own bathroom as well." She had brushed her hair and changed into a new blue sweater, her cheeks were pink and she was excited. She had forgotten about the mice at last.

But Eddie hadn't.

Eddie was hatching a plan for later on that evening. The three youngsters joined George and Bridget in the long sitting room upstairs. A tray with sparkling grape juices, colas and lemonades welcomed them. A crystal bowl of ice, and tall glasses stood in rows, with ornate stirring sticks and cocktail cherries of bright red and green. It looked wonderful. Small bowls of tiny cheese-biscuits and nuts were scattered around the room. Feeling very grown up, they helped themselves to their favourite drinks and gathered up a few nibbles as well.

George sat with a crystal-cut glass of pale brown whisky which he sniffed with appreciation.

"Your parents sent me a box of this, Patrick; it is a special fifteen year-old malt whisky from the Isles. I shall accept it graciously." He toasted them all by raising his glass, and called for Bridget to join them.

"Well, this is nice," she said breathlessly, beaming at all her borrowed brood "Happy holidays." And she raised her glass and they all joined in laughing and sipping the delicious cold drinks.

"I can't believe I am here," said Patrick sitting back in the huge sofa. Eventually, Bridget invited them to the table to sit down. She brought steaming plates of chicken pie with buttered vegetables and they all tucked in. George refilled their glasses and they ate the lovely food. Chocolate mousses followed. After supper George and the boys cleared away and went downstairs to the bedrooms to discuss lights. Ellie washed up while Bridget sat down with her knitting. She was working on a jumper for Patrick, to keep him warm in the cold Scottish winter. Her fast needles clicked away, the wool slowly coiling out of her knitting bag.

"Can you knit, Ellie?" she asked, relaxed and comfortable after her busy day.

"No, I can't."

Bridget smiled at her, clicking away in a seemingly effortless manner.

"Would you like to learn?"

"I don't know, it looks so difficult," and she frowned.

"It's just practice, like everything else. I could show you if you'd like." Ellie sat on the floor beside Bridget watching the wool slowly creeping out of the bag.

Ellie browsed through the patterns of hats.

"Do you think I could ever knit one of these?"

"Don't see why not." Bridget continued to knit.

"Shall I get a pair of needles?" Ellie got up and found several pairs.

"Choose the biggest pair, and get a ball of wool from the big bag."

Bridget finished her row, put her needles through the wool and packed it away into the bag. Ellie was well and truly hooked by now – she smiled a tiny smile of satisfaction to herself.

"Well now, sit here beside me and watch carefully."

So the lesson started, both becoming engrossed in the compli-cated world of knitting.

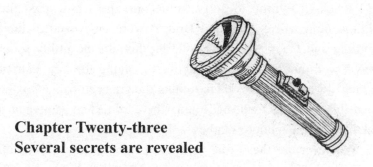

Chapter Twenty-three
Several secrets are revealed

George and the two boys arranged and re-arranged the gadgetry required to produce the Moonmirror and the crystal signaller. Patrick pored over the details, handing bits to Eddie, who told him exactly what was required. George was glad they had drawn diagrams; it seemed a long time since they had stood on the turret, making their own kind of magic.

"In a few days time there is a full moon and believe it or not, there is also an eclipse that night," Eddie told them.

George yawned, "Well I'm off for a nightcap and to bed." He patted them both on the shoulder. "Nice to see you again lad," he said to Patrick, and left them to it.

As soon as he had gone upstairs Eddie sat Patrick down on the bed and said,

"I've got work for you." Patrick looked confused.

"What do you mean?"

"We've got a little mission to accomplish tonight, but we need the key to the café first. Where does George keep it?"

Patrick thought carefully.

"They've got a small safe in the utility room and I think spare keys are on a board above it in there. It's worth a look."

"Yes, go and see and bring a roll of something green called oasis fix from the flower arranging box," Eddie instructed him.

Patrick, frowning, quietly tiptoed up the stairs, past the sitting room where Ellie and Bridget were engrossed in their knitting and George dozed beside the fire. In the utility room was a wall-mounted safe and above that hung the key. Patrick snatched it off its hook. Then, finding the green stuff in a box he made his way back to the bedroom, where Eddie had gathered his torch and some outdoor clothes.

"Whatever are these for? You had better tell me, this is all sounding a bit mysterious. I've got the key," and grinning, he held it up on the string.

"Great."

Eddie didn't know where to start. It did all sound a bit unbelievable. He breathed deeply and began:

"Ellie discovered two little white mice living in the flower arranger's cupboard at the church." Patrick raised his eyebrows. "And they've really come from another century; somehow they have got stuck in time."

Patrick opened his mouth.

"Yes, and they dress in the most incredible old fashioned clothes which she – that is Isabella – makes from the church furnishings. Isabella has discovered a hole into the wall of the tea shop and she's been getting into the cupboard and taking the chocolate chips."

Patrick's eyes widened. He looked stunned.

"But, George has discovered it and before we could tell her, he's put two mousetraps down and I have to check she's not been caught yet and fill up the hole. That's all."

Patrick frowned and held out his hands to emphasise his points.

"Let me see if I've got this right. You have met two mice who

152

live in a cupboard in the church, from another century. One, called Isabella, may be trapped in a mousetrap in a cupboard in the café and we are going to rescue her in the middle of the night?"

Eddie nodded looking very awkward indeed. Patrick sat still, looking out of the window at the trees and river and the dark sky in silence. Suddenly he jumped up,

"Well what are we waiting for?" And he pulled the startled Eddie up to his feet. Eddie started to explain again.

"Don't bother! It's fantastically impossible, but if you say so I'll go along with it." He laughed nervously.

"I'll just check upstairs," and Eddie went back to see what time everyone was going to bed. Ellie came out of the sitting room yawning.

"Hi Eddie, guess what? I've been learning to knit!"

"Good," said her brother smiling, "you can knit a scarf for me then."

"Well I just might," tossing her head in reply.

"Goodnight. See you tomorrow."

"Night night." She yawned again and half stumbled into her bedroom firmly closing the door.

"We'd better go and say goodnight or it will look a bit strange," and the boys made their way upstairs yet again.

"Ah boys, all sorted then?" George asked.

Eddie just grinned.

"Well now, I'll lock up and send Bridget off to a well earned rest. We'll see you in the morning, anytime will do. Goodnight."

"Goodnight," chorused the boys together.

From the bedroom window the sky looked black and forbidding; it was windy, dark and wet. Somehow it held excitement however, and the boys were keyed up and ready for an adventure. They waited for the final sounds of Bridget and George's preparations for bed to cease.

The plan was quite simple. Leave the house by the patio door, checking that they could get back in, possibly having to wedge the door a little open. Then, enter the tea shop with the key and search the cupboard for any unhappy events that may have occurred. The next step depended on what they found. Do whatever was necessary, and return by the same method. Easy!

Collecting the green putty and the key, they opened the sliding door and crept around the side of the house and up the garden path leading to the road. It was breezy and chilly as they passed the church door and rounded the narrow path leading to the café. Patrick paused and grabbed Eddie's arm.

"Shhhh. Listen."

They stopped and stood still. A high pitched squeaking noise sounded in the air above them. Looking up they could both see a small black shape flittering like a large butterfly.

"It's a bat," whispered Eddie. It was Belvedere, circling around and then returning with a high pitched squeak.

"Come on. Don't worry about it, let's get inside."

Quietly they opened the door of the tea shop and shone the torch around.

"Which cupboard is it?"

"I don't know, but it must be in the back, roughly in line with the waste pipe where it joins in from the wall."

They both crouched down and began opening the white doors and shining the torch inside.

"Anything?"

"Not yet."

"Next to the sink maybe."

Eddie opened the white door and shone the torch. Yes, he could see the hole. Nobody was in either of the mouse traps either. In the darkness they heard a car heading their way. Then headlights appeared shining onto the windows.

"Quick, torches off, lay down." Eddie hissed and they both tucked themselves behind the door breathing rapidly. A police car drew up, slowly cruising to a halt. The occupants rolled the windows down and the boys could hear the radio transmitting messages. One of the policemen got out and lit a cigarette, looking over the wall out to sea.

"Don't fancy being out there tonight," he commented watching the waves rolling over and crashing on the rocks. The other man agreed.

"Nothing much ever happens out here," said one to the other, "still, got to look haven't we? Come on Brian let's go," and he got into the car, extinguishing his cigarette. They slowly did a three point turn and drove off, leaving the castle in darkness again.

"Phew! That was scary." The boys relaxed and breathed again. "Thank goodness we didn't put the light on in the café."

It didn't take long to push some of the green sticky putty into the hole and seal it up.

"Good. At least Ellie won't be organising some sort of mouse funeral tomorrow," laughed Eddie. "She would, you know."

Patrick smiled at him admiring his brotherly concern.

Locking the door securely, they scurried home, back through the patio door. Throwing off their clothes, they got into their beds and huddled up under the duvets. It had been a worthwhile exercise. Happy now, Eddie slept soundly until morning. Patrick however lay awake for a while going over it all in his mind; some of the strangest things he had ever heard. Nothing like this ever happened at Burnside College. How glad he was to be back with Eddie and Ellie. More adventures to come with the trials of the Moonmirror. Great! He didn't want half term to ever end.

Chapter Twenty-four
A sailing trip to meet Captain John

The two boys slept late into the morning. George and Bridget opened the tea shop as usual at ten o'clock, so when Ellie finally got up she was met with a very quiet house. Unwilling to wake the boys up in case she annoyed them, she made her way to the café. She was filled with dread, nervously waiting to hear the fate of her beloved mice. Bridget and George were drinking tea.

"Hello young lady, sleep well?" they greeted her.

"Well now, do you fancy a nice big toasted tea cake?" tempted Bridget.

"I think I do," and soon she was drinking hot chocolate and munching her giant tea cake oozing butter. She smiled at last. George went outside for quite some time, going backwards and forwards with a bucket and a trowel. Ellie took no notice, too engrossed in her breakfast. Bridget replenished the drinks in the chilled cabinet and came back.

"Funny thing Ellie, both those mousetraps were empty this morning," she told her.

Ellie looked up at her, suddenly realising the importance of this information.

How wonderful, she thought, *they're both safe.*

"George is filling up the hole in the wall right now. They won't be back again in a hurry I can tell you," and she gave a little nod of satisfaction and pursed her lips together. She was happy now, no more mice. Ellie was even happier! She now knew her little friends were safe and sound. They smiled at one another for completely different reasons.

Back at the Old Bath House the boys were discussing the evening's outcome.

"Are you going to tell her?" asked Patrick.

"No fears!" Eddie flicked his eyes up, "she'll go mad that we didn't wake her up and take her with us."

"Then why didn't we?"

"Frankly she couldn't have coped with it. What if we'd found her dead? Or both of them? No, Ellie was better off in bed believe me."

Patrick realised how very much Eddie cared about his sister and obviously didn't want to upset her. He felt very fond of him and his good heart.

"Shall we get the boat out today?" he asked cautiously," I think the weather forecast is quite favourable."

Eddie thought about it and tried to decide what to do.

"We've got supper tonight at seven o'clock, Mum's coming round. I suppose we could. We'll go down and bale her out, get her ready in case we go this afternoon."

Patrick nodded in agreement, his mouth full of the last slice of toast.

Ellie could hear the boys talking when she arrived home jubilant. Voices were coming from downstairs. Then Eddie appeared.

"Coming sailing this afternoon?" he asked her.

"No, I don't think so thank you. I'm going to stay with Mum – but I will definitely come the next time," she replied, letting them go with good grace.

Eddie and Patrick bailed out loads of rainwater from the boat and then wandered up the narrow road together to the cottage. Mother had lunch ready for them all. She was thrilled to see Patrick again and gave him a big hug.

"Oh you've got thin you poor boy! Don't they feed you at that school of yours? Come on, eat up your soup while it's hot. Tell me all your news."

The soup was gobbled up and they had chocolate chip ice cream to follow. Eddie and Patrick asked her permission to go sailing and Mary sent them off to enjoy their afternoon. Both boys grinned and waved goodbye as they ran off down to the creek, excited and happy.

Ellie and her mother drank coffee and chatted, enjoying being on their own. Ellie did her hair in braids for the dinner party, and put some tiny butterfly hairclips in too, and then they did their nails and talked clothes for the holidays.

At the creek the boys rigged up the sails and stowed the outboard engine, taking no chances this time. Looking over at Prawn Cottage, Eddie made up his mind to tell Patrick about Captain John.

"Patrick," he started, "I just want to talk to you about something else."

"Well, wait till we get through here and I've got the sails just right – mind your head!" he shouted as the boom swung round. Then they settled down with a Jupiter bar each and Eddie tried again.

"You know the mice and all that stuff, I know it all seems a bit crazy, but there's more, lots more. I think I'd better introduce you to somebody."

"You mean it's a person this time?"

Eddie undid the zip on his sailing jacket and fished out the gold medallion held around his neck on a string.

"I did notice that last night but I thought it was a lucky charm or St Christopher. What is it?"

"Ellie and I found it in the garden one day with an old pistol and a pile of bones."

"Oh yes… and?" Patrick waited for the rest of the story that he knew was coming. He steeled himself.

"I cleaned it up and when I held it in my hand it got hotter and hotter. I woke up and he was there in my room! Rocking in the rocking chair and smoking a pipe!"

"A real person?"

"Yes. He was dressed in funny clothes and he was quite cross at first. Anyway it turned out that he had been a sea captain living in Jamaica. He got very rich and sailed home and set up house here in a thatched cottage, right where our house is now. I think somehow he lost all his money and retired here with his dog and an old servant."

"Duck!" shouted Patrick and smoothly they changed course again. "Yes, go on."

"He loves it here, and has been living in the pink cottage for a while, teaching me how to sail."

"What?"

"Well you'd gone home, Dad's away and George was too busy… So what was I to do? He's a great sailor; we've had some really good days. Oh and the most amazing thing of all is that those two mice were his."

"Surely not! How come?"

"They were a present from the Queen of Spain. He brought them home as pets and somehow after Captain Avery died, they have been in the church locked in a time warp. Ellie discovered them one afternoon."

"Hey we're going to collide in a minute, mate!" yelled Patrick as the ferry loomed large in front of them. Then, "So am I going to meet this old ghost of yours?"

Eddie looked at his watch. He couldn't be late for supper the evening before his mother went away.

Patrick tried again. "Let's go. I'm dying to meet him. Come on."

"Alright, but if you really want to know how to sail he'll show you, just you wait," Eddie told him gleefully.

They turned the boat round, lowered the sails and gently, with the help of the oars, came back upstream and slid into the bank of the river in the leafy undergrowth below Paradise Point gardens.

After securing the boat the boys crept around the side of the cottage.

They knocked gently on the old brass dolphin door knocker but finding door already open, went inside. Patrick found himself in what looked like an old ships' cabin. Panelled walls of old timber, ships' lights, rope-work chairs and a ships' wheel table, bits of salvaged remains from the seashore, porthole windows and candle lamps. Captain John himself stood up, an impressive tall figure with black curls restrained in a pony tail, a navy Breton sweater and blue jeans tucked into leather boots.

His carved clay pipe gave off clouds of heavily scented smoke, wreathing up into the skylight window. He was a very handsome man indeed with a neat beard and blue eyes, his face tanned and a little lined. Smiling at Patrick he held out a firm hand.

"Welcome, another shipmate Eddie? Has he brought his papers, and can he handle a pistol should we meet the enemy?" He laughed heartily.

Patrick stepped forward. "How do you do sir, Patrick Mc Nab," he replied in his gentle Scottish voice.

"My pleasure," replied Captain John.

The boy noticed hanging on the back of the door a long frock coat and a leather belt with a sword and dagger in their covers. Two beautiful pistols were lying on the special wheel table, powder horn, ramrod and shot all carefully placed beside.

Syracuse, the black dog, trotted over to have a good sniff and

160

say hello. The boys patted him appreciatively.

"Be seated, be seated," urged the captain waving his hand, and the two boys obeyed obediently. "Are we set for fair weather?"

"I hope so. In a way that's why we've come today, Captain John," Eddie told him, stroking the dog. "We'd love to have a day out sailing tomorrow. Any chance?" and he raised his eyebrows questioningly.

"Yes, yes, it would be my pleasure young man."

Eddie got out the chart for the captain to plan their voyage of discovery for tomorrow. He looked at his watch. Soon be time to go.

"Now let's see," as they leaned over the large chart, "which port of call? You choose."

Patrick and Eddie decided to go to Salcombe, and they set the time for a rendezvous at the creek at seven-thirty in the morning. The tide was in then.

"And your pretty sister, shall she join us tomorrow?" asked Captain John.

"Oh alright," agreed Eddie reluctantly.

"All's settled then. Crew will muster at seven of the clock, inspection and loading to follow." Captain John laughed.

The boys got up and shook hands with the captain and left the cottage to return to the boat bobbing on its mooring rope at the foot of the ladder.

"I told you."

Eddie couldn't wait to hear Patrick's appraisal of their extraordinary friend.

"He's really something, a proper sailor and navigator – none of your modern nonsense. I really liked him Eddie. I think he's great." Patrick nodded appreciatively. "I can't wait until tomorrow."

They stood on the rocks and pulled the boat back into the river. The seagull watched from the roof of the old quay. They were back.

161

Chapter Twenty-five
Mary goes on holiday and a sailing picnic is planned

Patrick and Eddie raced quickly back to the Old Bath House to get ready for dinner. The fire was laid up by Eddie and the logs brought in by Patrick, as the house filled up with delicious smells.

"We must ask Ellie to come with us tomorrow, she'll really like that," they agreed. Patrick and Eddie were both alight with happiness; life was good at the moment, they almost felt like brothers. Patrick put a match to the fire and watched it crackle and the flames brightened up the darkening room. Eddie wandered into the kitchen.

"Anything else to do, Bridget?"

"No dear, thank you, it's all about ready now. Just the finishing touches to do."

"What are we eating? It smells delicious."

"Roast duck with orange sauce, it's an old favourite, especially if you crisp up the skin just right." She smiled rather secretively.

The two boys changed down in their bedroom and checked the weather forecast on the television. It sounded chilly, chance of showers, sea state moderate, and wind north-westerly veering to westerly force four. They found George by the fire looking rather dapper in a tartan bow tie, white shirt, and a red v-necked sweater. Patrick looked admiringly at his very smart godfather.

"Something to drink lads? Your mother and Ellie will be here in a minute I expect Eddie."

The two boys asked for colas and George obliged. They sat

around eating peanuts and crisps and Bridget joined them for a glass of sherry.

"This is my treat," and she sipped her favourite tipple.

"Bridget, do you think we could make a picnic for tomorrow? We're hoping to go sailing in the morning, if you don't mind. Ellie's coming too, only we haven't asked her yet. Will it be alright, George?" Eddie looked at him, seeking his approval.

"I don't see why not, might be a touch chilly out there so wrap up well. Might come myself actually, yes, good idea."

Fear struck both their hearts. Before they could muster any excuses Bridget interrupted,

"No dear you can't go, you've got the dentist at one o clock – don't you remember? In Totnes? You're meeting Jim Bell for coffee."

"Oh yes, course I am," was the grumpy reply from George. "Sorry lads, have to be another day now won't it?"

Sighing great sighs of relief inwardly, both the boys protested together.

"What a shame."

"Oh sorry George."

Eddie was hoping they could all go out soon, but not with Captain John. Definitely not!

The doorbell rang and Patrick leapt up to answer it. Standing on the doorstep stood Mary and Ellie, well wrapped up against the cold, damp night air.

"Come in it's great to see you, give me your coats." Patrick was the perfect host. Ellie looked her best, with her braided hair, wearing red top and black trousers, and Mary was elegant in a grey trouser suit. She held a sweet-smelling posy of small white roses for Bridget, while Ellie clutched her favourite Belgian chocolates, wrapped in pink tissue paper and a purple ribbon.

163

The evening proved to be a very happy one and the duck was superb. After supper the grown-ups chatted while Eddie and Patrick cleared up and prepared their picnic at the same time. Bridget, George and Mary settled down to drink coffee. Ellie joined the boys in the kitchen. She leant against the fridge eyeing up their activities. She knew they were up to something.

"What's going on?" she asked, feeling resentment and anger rising inside her.

"We're going sailing for the day tomorrow," announced Patrick buttering bread.

"Oh really?"

"Yes, I'm doing this picnic to save us time in the morning. There's four to feed and we're leaving early."

"Oh." She pursed her lips crossly.

"So, set your alarm for six-thirty because Captain John hates us to be late."

Eddie winked at Patrick and they both spun round to face her, and burst out laughing.

"You beasts!" she yelled, and added, "I thought you'd left me out again."

"Captain John requested your company himself actually," admitted Patrick.

Ellie helped them finish the picnic, excited and pleased.

Mary decided to go home quite early so Eddie and Ellie volunteered to walk back with her. George, Patrick and Bridget waved her goodbye, assuring her that she wasn't to worry, and they would keep in touch by telephone.

The three shadowy figures walked along by the shiny black river in the quiet darkness. They arrived at the doorstep of their home, and Mother gave them each in turn a big hug and smoothed their faces with her hands.

"Have a wonderful time with Patrick and take good care of yourselves. I shall miss you both. Dad and I will ring you as soon as I arrive, so don't worry. Be good and I'll see you very soon." She kissed then both again. "Off you go now."

Ellie and Eddie felt very strange walking away from her in the dark.

"Bye Mum," they called and they turned to see her silhouetted in the doorway. She waved to them with a smile.

Eddie took Ellie's arm. They felt curiously lonely and were very glad to have each other.

"She'll be fine, and we'll be fine," Eddie told her confidently. "Let's hurry back to George's – it's cold."

Bridget was waiting for them.

"We're just having a hot drink before bed."

She ushered them in and soon they were back by the fire drinking hot chocolate with Patrick and George.

"Got your engine sorted, plenty of fuel and the oars?" gently reminded the old man, knowing how disastrous these trips could be without good preparation, especially if the weather is not kind. "You all have a good day, keep your wits about you, and stick to the rules! I hope you will feel sorry for me at the dentist," and he pulled a face.

"Stop it George," scolded Bridget. "We don't want you up half the night with toothache do we? I'm sure he is the one who has eaten my Belgian chocolate chips in the café – not the mice at all," she laughed.

"You've filled up the hole in the wall and boarded in the back of the cupboard haven't you?" questioned Eddie, "So let's hope nothing like it happens again," he said cheerfully. "Bed time I think, early start tomorrow," and he leapt up from his seat on the sofa.

"Coming now Patrick?" and he pulled him up by his arm, very anxious to escape.

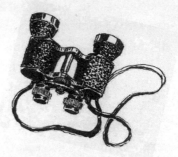

Chapter Twenty-six
A day to remember

The morning dawned with an icy blue light as the three children prepared themselves for their day out with layers of cotton tee shirts and woolly jumpers topped off with sailing waterproofs. Patrick and Eddie ran through their list and checked off each item. They nodded to each other,

"Think we've got everything, don't you?"

Ellie remembered their picnic and carrying the sturdy canvas bag, torches and thermos flasks they shut the door quietly. It was a cold morning and they were very glad of their warm clothes.

They reached the mooring edge and at last, fully loaded, carefully climbed into the boat and cast off the line. Eddie rowed gently across the river and steered to the foot of the jetty, where Captain John and Syracuse were now waiting.

"And a fair morning it is too!" he greeted them. "My compliments Miss Ellie," bowing to her. He stepped in with perfect balance and lifted his precious companion over the gunwale.

"We meet again, sir," he acknowledged Patrick with a nod.

They settled down to rigging up the two sails and Patrick sorted out the outboard engine, and they re-arranged themselves to even the weight and make sure the boom could swing without knocking the dog out. Eventually Captain Avery gave the signal and Patrick pulled the cord, started the engine and off they went out into the main Channel and out towards the sea. They very soon passed the Old Bath House and Eddie pointed out to Captain John where they were staying.

George was an acute observer, and fetched his binoculars and trained them on the little green boat, now heading towards the castle.

"Why, I believe there's someone else in that boat with those kids – whoever can it be?" and he strained to see the fast-disappearing craft as it chugged out to sea. He put the glasses down dejectedly.

It could have been me with them, he thought, *instead of going to the dentist.*

He told Bridget what he had seen as he ate his breakfast.

"Well of course they've got other friends George, you know that. Try not to mind – you can go another day, can't you?" she shook her head. Men!

Sargasso, the seagull and namesake of the precious boat, skimmed over the silky green water following them.

"Enough of this noxious odour and clattering now lads," as Captain John waved his arm towards the spreading ocean before him, "Let us sail out into the far reaches and battle with the ocean and the wind."

"I think he wants us to turn the engine off," whispered Patrick.

Ellie giggled and smothered it into a cough. The little boat left the protection of the river mouth at this point and entered the wide sweep of the bay, passing Blackstone Point.

The engine was obediently silenced, and the sails took their turn, propelling the fully laden Cornish shrimper through the choppy water. The wind blew into the canvas and they picked up a mighty speed. Little wavelets slapped against the sides causing tiny splashes of seawater. They all took turns helming and shortening ropes, changing places and calling to one another. Their captain instructed and led them as the excitement and exhilaration of speeding across the ocean, freely and silently, took hold of them all and held them in its spell. The difference in the centuries meant nothing now, here in the coastal waters, with the four people enjoying the power of the wind and water – just as it always had been.

They sailed away on their magical journey, passing the lighthouse landmark, across Start Bay and rounding Prawle Point. The wind eased and they coaxed the breeze into the sails as they started steering her into the Salcombe Estuary, beautiful and wide. Windblown and hungry, they moored up in the harbour and opened the picnic boxes and gratefully drank from the thermos flasks, lounging in the boat.

"That was an amusing little voyage, was it not?" asked Captain John, puffing away on his clay pipe and enjoying the whole new spectacle of twentieth-century Salcombe.

"Wonderful," agreed the boys. "She flies along with a good wind doesn't she?" said Eddie proudly.

"Aye lad, she surely does," agreed the captain, smiling.

"Are we rested, crew? Time to make way I'd say." Captain John instructed Ellie to prepare for sea and cast off the lines, and Patrick started the engine to get them out into the Channel to find the wind.

"It has its uses, this contraption called an engine," admitted the captain, "although I detest the smell and the confounded noise." The youngsters smiled. They were beginning to convert him. Modern inventions had their place.

"We must make land again before darkness falls," advised the captain, as they left the estuary, out into the widening expanse of ocean. They settled down again, Ellie hugging the dog to keep her warm. The temperature was dropping as darkening clouds approached. The wind raised itself and soon the sails were stretched and creaking, with the strong gusts increasing their speed. A few heavy spots of rain dropped out of the sky, the surface of the water changed to grey and small white crests appeared on the wavelets.

"No faint hearts here!" announced the captain. "Tis but a ripple," and he grinned at the boys and patted Ellie on the head. They all felt very confident and glad the bold seafarer was in charge.

It was a short but frightening shower. Hailstones lashed onto the sea, the wind blew in howling gusts and the water lapped over the sides from time to time. Eddie was the chief baler, Patrick steadied the tiller and Captain John managed the sails. Ellie shouted when the boom swung. Eddie switched on his masthead light for a bit of security, and seeing brighter skies behind the storm knew it would soon be over – and soon it was. Ellie distributed hot drinks and chocolate, and although wet and a bit cold, they began the task of sailing home smoothly and efficiently.

Land passed them on their left-hand side and as they approached the Dart estuary, two black objects appeared in the water just round the corner from Blackpool Sands.

"Look! Look!" pointed Ellie in excitement, "over there!" and as they stared and strained their eyes to see, the bobbing black things developed faces with big eyes and long noses. It was Solomon and Bathsheba.

"The seals, it's the seals! Oh do look Captain John!" cried Ellie.

"A pair of seals, no great danger my dear." He shook his head and laughed. "They'll not capsize us child – don't fret," he pacified her.

The seals disappeared under the water, diving and swimming around the boat, their shiny glistening coats looking smooth and black.

The seagull flew off to join the seals and they had conversations and swapped stories in their own way. Bathsheba told him of a restless spirit among the Seafarers, a feeling of an impending happening – nobody knew when or where. They were all watching for the signs. Sargasso listened and then the seals swam off back to their sheltered cove beneath the Trip Trap bridge with a flick of their tails.

"They've gone." Ellie sighed in disappointment and sat back against the boat.

Captain John nodded and smiled. The wonders of the deep were well known to him; he'd seen them all. However, one thing intrigued him now, more than all these – Eddie's solar-powered masthead light.

"Tell me young Edmond if you will, why the oil in this lamp never burns out? It vexes me much." He pointed to the light fastened to the top of the mast.

"Oh that? Well it's solar powered, from the light of the sun." Captain John looked puzzled.

"You explain Patrick," urged Eddie, knowing the difficulties of explaining the advances of more than three hundred years of scientific progress.

In his patient way, Patrick slowly described power. He kept it simple, factual, and easily understood. Captain John said very little but sat thinking. Everything he had seen since he arrived by some sort of Universe Reverse travel had amazed him. He had tried to follow the logic of it all, the telephone, television, engines, warships – such an enormous amount to come to terms with – but accept it he must, because the evidence of it was all here for him to see.

Hardly daring to overload the poor confused captain, Eddie blundered on

"Well sir, that's not all! We've – that is George, Patrick and me – we think we've invented something else! Something new; a light with the moon as its source, and a flashing light of colours from a crystal. Yes really! What do you think of that?" He laughed, proud and pleased. Captain John was quite ready to accept another new idea.

"I suppose it's all possible young man. You know so much and I so little." He spread out his hands. "I am only a spectator from another time."

Patrick and Eddie looked at one another,

"Shall we show him?" whispered Patrick, "it's the full moon tomorrow. You know, the eclipse."

"OK, why not?" agreed Eddie. "We could show you if you like

171

sir. Tomorrow night is a full moon – perfect conditions we hope. We would be honoured."

The boys looked anxiously for his reaction.

"It would be a great pleasure to me, and a new chapter in my education," answered Captain John. "Consider me part of the crew sir. Now let's get this vessel into harbour before the darkness falls. All hands ready!"

So they glided down the river, reaching the shelter of the wide quiet waters, delighting in the calm after the excitement of the open sea. Disembarking at the creek, Captain John made a sweeping bow,

"Until tomorrow then, collect me after dark if you will," and yawning, he took Syracuse and wasted no more time in conversation. They hurried into the tiny cottage and disappeared.

The three children unpacked the boat and pulled it back into the middle of the river on the running mooring. Sargasso sat quietly in the shelter of the kiln and shuffled into a comfy position to sleep. It had been a long flight. Eddie stroked his head and whispered goodbye. Quite exhausted by the fresh air and activity, they trudged home wearily to George and Bridget's.

"Ah ha, sailors back from the sea," greeted George as he opened the front door to the weary travellers. "You look tired, come in," taking some of their bags from them.

"Had a good day? There were some squally showers weren't there? I could see it clouding over from the window."

They were very glad to be back, and shedding their salt-encrusted jackets and trousers, they unpeeled the layers of clothes, suddenly exhausted.

"I'm off for a bath," announced Ellie and disappeared downstairs.

"Tea anyone?" Bridget called from the sitting room where she was surrounded by balls of wool and knitting.

"Not just now thanks," replied Patrick popping his head round the door. "Just need a soak in the bath, see you in a while Bridget," and he and Eddie went downstairs too.

Later, refreshed and changed, they joined George and Bridget around the big dining table for supper, their faces glowing pink with the wind and fresh air as they tucked into liver and bacon, sausages and mash. It disappeared in no time. Revived, they chatted together about the day, and George suddenly said, "There were four of you in the boat, weren't there?"

Eddie took control at once, having rehearsed many times the explanation of Captain Avery's presence.

"Yes, actually there were. We took John, a friend with us who I met at the creek. He's staying in a house down there for a short while and loves sailing."

They were so very tired after supper and by ten o'clock were all yawning uncontrollably; one by one they crept off to bed. Eddie was the last.

"Goodnight," he called from the doorway, "Thanks for everything."

"He's a good lad," said George after a long silence. "If I'd had a lad I'd have liked him to have been just like that. You know what I mean?" He looked at Bridget rather sadly.

"I do dear, I do." She added no more for there was no more to say. *We're lucky to be able to share them; they're lovely kids,* she thought. She knitted on, a long striped scarf appearing at the end of her needles.

"Still, I would like to go sailing with them all again. Next time I'll go instead of that John fellow," decided George firmly and sipped his special treat, the wonderful malt whisky.

173

Chapter Twenty-seven
Plans to show off the Moonmirror

It was at breakfast the following day that Ellie discovered three long white envelopes their mother had given to George before she left. Soon they were ripped open.

"Twenty pounds each! Lovely," beamed Eddie.

They were very pleased; pocket-money was hard to come by, especially when Dads weren't around. They decided to go into town that morning to spend it. Patrick sat and thought very carefully what he was going to buy.

"Well, I'm rather taken with having a compass of my own. Do you think I'll get one in the chandlers'?"

"That's a really nice idea," approved Ellie.

"I've always wanted one of those Swiss Army knives that do everything; they've got them in the window of the sports shop," Eddie told them.

"Ellie?" inquired Patrick, "Only you now, what do you think?"

"Knitting needles probably," added Eddie laughing.

"No it is not!" glared his sister, "I don't really know to be honest. I'll have to wait and see."

They got dressed happily, left a note for Bridget and George, then feeling rich and with the anticipation of spending their collective money, they trekked off down the road.

The town was quiet, with mostly locals shopping and meeting for coffee. Ellie loved it without the visitors, they always seemed to take up so much room, hustling and bustling in the streets. They set about the task of shopping. Eddie found his knife, and Patrick his compass in a local chandlers, and Ellie bought a hat with ears, some pretty gloves, a torch and a leather waist- bag with a long strap.

"Well, I think Mother would approve, don't you?"

Eventually they sauntered back up the long hill leading to Southtown and Warfleet, meandered along the castle road, having looked to make sure the boat was safe, and checked that the shutters were closed on Prawn Cottage.

"He's probably still asleep." said Patrick.

"Hope so."

"I just don't know what we are going to do about George and Captain John tonight, I can't decide. What do you think Patrick?"

Patrick said nothing but thought deeply. There had to be a solution to this problem.

"Just let me think for a while, I'll come up with something."

They walked the rest of the way in silence. Eventually Patrick spoke.

„I think I've got it." They all stopped dead in their tracks.

"Well?" Eddie and Ellie demanded.

"If we are going to use these inventions as some sort of signalling device then we need to signal to somebody, otherwise we won't know if they're working. Why don't we send Captain John out in the boat with one of us, and Eddie and George or whoever is doing the signalling, can stay on the tower?"

"And he knows we've got a friend who sails with us because he saw him yesterday. Brilliant! That is perfect." Eddie was delighted.

"We'll have to try to keep them apart however," Patrick warned.

"I'd like to go with Captain Avery," said Ellie suddenly, "I'd rather be in the boat." She adored the captain and his dog.

"Are you sure?" questioned Eddie doubtfully, "you might be out there for an hour, maybe two?"

"I think so," Ellie replied firmly.

"OK then, that's it. George, Patrick and I will go on the tower and try to get the Moonmirror and the crystal signaller to work, and you and Captain John can stay in the boat and make notes. That sounds really good. Patrick –you're a star." And he squeezed him by the shoulders good naturedly. "Well done."

Ellie was thrilled.

"What's the weather forecast?" Patrick asked. "Must check that when we get back."

"I'm glad George is coming tonight, it's only fair." Eddie felt better, it was all working out.

When they got home to the Old Bath House Eddie and Patrick sat down with a notebook to plan the evening's events. They put on the television to catch the forecast and listened eagerly to the news of the eclipse of the moon, visible that night from a few places in the south-west of England.

Ellie got her knitting out to do some more of the scarf she had begun; red and soft, it was growing slowly. She hadn't decided who she was going to give it to yet, but somebody was going to be very lucky. From the kitchen smells of toast wafted and she went to investigate. There were tell-tale signs that Eddie had been at work.

"Any left for me?" she called hopefully.

"They're in the oven," was the reply. Ellie got a tea cloth and opened the door; a warm plateful of sandwiches sat temptingly in the middle. She carried the loaded plate into the sitting room and sat down on one of the plump squashy sofas.

"Wonderful!" she sighed, munching away happily. "Does George know about tonight yet?"

"Not yet, we'd better go and tell him. We'll nip round to the café." nodded Eddie.

Ellie returned to her knitting, watching as the red wool gradually crept out of the ball and onto the needles, and turned itself into quite a nice scarf.

"I think I might give this to Captain Avery," she decided. "I'm sure he needs one," and she sat concentrating trying not to drop stitches or pull the wool too tightly. Bridget arrived home and came to see what Ellie was doing.

"Oh how nice, you're knitting." She sat down heavily in the chair. "Ah, that's better. How is it coming on?"

Patrick and Eddie had reached the café. People were beginning to go home and the car park was almost deserted.

"We thought we might try out our experiment tonight George, would you like to come too? It's an eclipse of the moon, and it should be really interesting," Eddie said.

"Well, that sounds a good idea." He beamed at them, smiling. "What time do you think?"

"The eclipse is at nine-fifty and it gets dark by about six-thirty so we could set up in the last of the daylight. It would make it easier wouldn't it?"

"Right, we'll get geared up for six then. I shall look forward to it. Thanks lads, see you at supper then." And he hurried up his daily closing-down routine of sweeping and mopping.

"How are we going to fetch Captain John?" puzzled Eddie.

"He will have to go out in the boat with Ellie and be there

waiting for us to start. She'll have to leave with us and then nip down to the cottage for him. George won't know who it is in the dark if he sees them."

They chased off. Eddie felt he always seemed to be watching the clock nowadays. Freddie the robin appeared, bobbing and chirping and following them along the path.

"Hi Freddie, I expect you've been wondering where we are, we've not been at the cottage for a while, have we?" Eddie told him guiltily.

The crumbs on the window sill had all gone now and the house was dark and empty. Freddie didn't like it. He followed them back and sat in the porch. The boys went inside and found Ellie and Bridget deep in a sea of knitting.

"Hey, where's my jumper?" Patrick asked jokingly. "I thought it would be nearly finished by now."

"Just come into the kitchen for a minute Ellie, I want to tell you something." Eddie beckoned to her. She reluctantly removed knitting needles, wool, pattern and bag off her knees and got up. Immediately Patrick sat down. He had the task of breaking the news to his godmother about this evening, while Eddie told Ellie about their slight change of plan. He tried to explain to Bridget about the lunar eclipse and she knitted on, listening, digesting everything he was saying.

"If you're worried dear that I shall mind you all going off and leaving me I can assure you that I have no desire to stand outside on a cold night –even for a lunar eclipse, which will last all of, what? Three minutes?"

Patrick nodded.

"I've got plans to make my Christmas puddings tonight. They'll all be boiling on the stove when you return, you'll see." And she patted his hand and looked over her glasses at him. "It's kind of you to worry about me, but go ahead and enjoy your evening." She smiled and continued knitting.

"Thanks Bridget."

When George came home they took themselves off to dress properly for an evening outside.

"This is like Bonfire Night," said Eddie, as they zipped up tops and put on several layers of socks.

"I've divided up the equipment into three cardboard boxes," explained Patrick carefully, "one for each light gadget and one extra with spares and things we might need. So that's a box each to carry. We must set our watches to the right time. There are a few clouds about you know, I hope they won't spoil it. So, Captain John and Ellie will go out to the buoy and wait around for our signal. I'm afraid it might be a bit boring for them."

Ellie was primed to go for Captain John, and George was engrossed in the excitement of another night of mental acrobatics.

"Nearly ready everyone?" called George from upstairs, and the three youngsters met by their bedroom doors.

"Do you know exactly what to do, Ellie?" Eddie asked quickly. She nodded enthusiastically.

"Patrick?" He nodded too.

"I hope I do," grinned Eddie, "I don't want to mess this up. Come on then."

They went upstairs to rendezvous with George.

"Have a lovely evening," Bridget beamed at them.

"Oh, we will!" they chorused and trooped up to the road, where the daylight was beginning to turn blue and the stillness of evening was creeping over everything. Eddie nodded to Ellie, her signal to leave them, and she turned in the opposite direction towards the creek. She had a very important mission to accomplish all on her own.

179

Chapter Twenty-eight
The evening of the lunar eclipse

George, Eddie and Patrick, each carrying a cardboard box in their arms made their way towards the tea shop, discussing their first experiment as they walked along, the boys distracting him from Ellie's disappearance. George opened the door and they walked through the café to the small door which led to the turret room. Squeezing up the narrow stone steps, huffing and puffing, they eventually arrived at the top where it opened out into a castellated battlement overlooking the harbour entrance.

"Right, let's get started." George rubbed his hands together enthusiastically. "What's first?"

"Shall we try the Moonmirror?" Eddie replied.

"Good idea."

Eddie and Patrick carefully lifted all the items required out of the cardboard box marked Moonmirror.

"This is well organised I must say," admired George, "Well done boys." He knelt down to help. And so the fragile mechanism, based theoretically not on a solar battery but a lunar one, was carefully put together, with the aid of a diagram drawn some time ago by Eddie after their first attempts. They talked it through as they constructed the light, each adding a few thoughts, making a slight modification here and there, until eventually it was ready.

The light mechanism had a curved tinfoil back with a magnifying glass to intensify the rays. The powerful light then charged the batteries and what it finally emitted was a wonderful blue-white light similar to the pale light of the moon. It was by no means as powerful as solar light, but it was a strong searching beam – or so they hoped, as they waited anxiously for the moon to illuminate the sky. They could see a white moon rising in the fading blue of the sky to their left. Eddie found his hands were shaking with anticipation and nerves. Patrick was strong and steady with quiet confidence. He looked around at the view out to sea, wondering about Ellie.

She was carefully executing the well-discussed plan. She had two extra helpers – Freddie and Sargasso. As she had done so many times with her brother, she untied the rope and pulled the little green boat towards her. Stepping very carefully from the slippery rocks, she slowly got into the right position and putting the oars into the rowlocks, she quietly rowed across the river to Captain Avery's jetty. Freddie sat on the front encouraging her and Sargasso sat on the mast keeping watch. Captain John was waiting for her, but – what a surprise! He was not dressed in their father's old sailing clothes, but in the full regalia of a seventeenth century Buccaneer, and magnificent he looked too: long boots, silver-buttoned black frock coat with a blue sash tied across it, wide black hat with a feather, swords and pistols and ammunition strapped to him, every inch a fighting man.

"Why, Mistress Ellie." He took his hat off and bowed to her.

"Good evening Captain Avery," she replied in the politest of tones, sensing this was an occasion.

"At what hour shall we make way?" he asked her, holding Syracuse close to him by the back of his elaborate collar.

"Not long now, it's beginning to get dark isn't it?"

"Aye it is," he replied with a faraway look in his eye. "I feel restless this night."

"Oh," said Ellie "In what way?"

He turned to her, "I've a longing in me to return to the sea with my pirate band, to sail the oceans of Madagascar. I'm tired now of this quiet life. I've a mind for adventure along the Guinea coast of Africa in my old ship, the *Fancy*." His eyes glazed over and he looked far into the distance.

"He can't return now!" thought Ellie frantically, *"It's not possible!"*

"Come on now Captain," she gently pleaded. "I think we should leave don't you?"

He stared at her blankly.

"Is that you Sarah Adams, my old quartermaster's wife? Is that you, my Sarah?"

Ellie felt frightened; he was looking at her in a strange way.

"No Captain I'm not Sarah, I'm Ellie. Captain John, Why can't you hear me?" He shook his head and it seemed to clear away the mistiness from his eyes.

"What? What did ye say maid?"

"I'm Ellie. Get into the boat now please." She spoke firmly to him, smiled and held out her hand. He took it and climbed in. Syracuse nuzzled in between them. The Captain seemed to have recovered himself now. Ellie kept quickly glancing at him, but he rowed them carefully out into the river and put up the little sails. They passed the Old Bath House and the café, the sea and sky darkening around them.

"There they are." Ellie pointed out the three black figures on the top of the tower. "We're to tie up to the second buoy out at sea, the blue one." She pointed to the bobbing triangle.

"Right lass, whatever you say," replied the captain. Eventually, bouncing through the slight swell they slowed the boat, looping the rope around the top of the huge metal marker. Ellie sat, uneasily watching Captain John. She rummaged about in her bag and found two chocolate éclairs. She handed him one. He studied it curiously, untwisting the blue and gold paper.

"Well eat it then," she told him. He put it in his mouth and chewed it slowly.

"Look!" Ellie pointed to the sky as the bright, pale moon broke through a patch of scudding thinning cloud. In the blue-black sky surrounded by stars, it was breathtakingly beautiful. The reflection cast a pathway across the sea of rippled silver and white. "They should be starting the signalling soon." The boat gently rocked in the middle of the dark sea and the two waited silently.

It began falteringly at first, a winking small light from the top of the tower. Gradually the intensity grew, interrupted once or twice, until an arc of silver-white brilliance shone out over the water and they had to shield their eyes. Eddie, Patrick and George were clearly visible from the tower; they could hear the three laughing excitedly. It had worked! The light was moved slightly so the two in the boat wouldn't be blinded, and the surface of the sea was lit up like day, showing the surprised seagulls, who had been trying to sleep, bobbing on the water. On the turret there were shouts and clapping as they congratulated each other wildly, dancing round and round, shouting, "It works! It really works!"

The moon disappeared again behind a thick black-centred cloud, with its brightness just visible around its puffy edges. Consequently the signalling Moonmirror went out too, fading fast.

"It's not charged enough yet, we haven't had enough moonlight. What a pity," murmured Eddie looking anxiously at the sky. George and Patrick were confident that it would shine again.

"Wasn't that wonderful?" breathed Ellie from her seat in the boat.

Captain John sat still in amazement. He shook his head. "Wondrous, truly wondrous. Such learning and knowledge in menfolk so tender in years. It is an achievement to behold." He couldn't find enough words to praise the phenomenon he had just witnessed.

George was overjoyed too.

"I'll just nip down and get us a drink while we wait for the moon to come out again. Won't be a tick," and he squeezed down the stone steps into the kitchen and busied about with the kettle and three mugs and a big jar of hot chocolate. He hummed to himself, thrilled and excited, pleased with all their efforts. Carefully balancing the three mugs in his fingers he took them back up to the darkness, accustoming his eyes, blinking and squinting.

"Here we are," and they took a seat on the rooftop on plastic bin sacks.

"Oh that's good," they agreed as they sipped the chocolaty drinks.

Suddenly George cried out and put his mug down hastily, burning his fingers. "Oh my tooth! Oh! Oh!" He clutched his face with both his hands, continuing to moan loudly. He stood up and hopped about, obviously in pain. Eddie was very concerned.

"It's the hot drink I expect."

George could hardly speak.

"Oh dear, my tooth! My tooth!" He kept repeating, shaking his head in agony.

"I'll take you home," offered Patrick getting up at once. "Come on George, you can ring the hospital." He sympathetically put his arm round the poor man and helped him down the steps. George didn't argue, he felt too ill, and soon Eddie was alone on the rooftop as he watched the two figures slip out of view behind him.

"Poor old George," he thought out loud, "What a pity, I'll just have to manage by myself. I can't waste this opportunity," as he resolved to carry on with the next experiment. Ellie of course had no idea George had gone home, and was enjoying rocking in the boat in the intermittent moonlight, Captain John relating more stories of life in Jamaica and on the high seas.

"But tell me how you came to our cottage," she pressed him." You did live there, didn't you, with Syracuse?" She rubbed the dog's back and cuddled him towards her.

"I did lass, with Bartholomew my faithful servant – not a better man lived on this earth. We took the cottage, thatched it was then, a pretty little sort of place with a duck pond by the side. Our seafaring days were nearly over and we tucked ourselves away from prying eyes."

"Oh, and why was that?"

He remained silent looking out at the darkness, his face sad and sombre.

"I had resolved to think of it no more, to put it into the past, best forgotten, but…" He hesitated and put out his hand to Ellie. "I am ashamed of some of the deeds I have done in my life, of greed and thieving, of murder and destruction." He hung his head and Ellie was upset to see him so, and hear his words. "You cannot understand," he continued, "A life far removed, among men, some the best and some the worst to be had in all the world. We lived in thrilling times, with riches and dreams won and lost in a single day. I cannot make amends, it is done now. Too late, all too late." He bowed his head again sorrowfully.

Ellie was dismayed at his disclosures. She had thought him so very fine. She looked towards the tower; all was dark and she felt concerned. *What is Eddie doing?*

It had been silent and without light for some time. Captain John seemed to gather his composure again and retied their mooring line as the tide altered.

Eddie had put the Moonmirror to one side, leaving it exactly constructed in its successful combination to recharge as the moon revealed itself. He then got the crystal signaller box with its many components. He needed the moon to appear again to strike the crystal prism and reflect the beautiful but transitory colours of the spectrum. The light was needed as the initial source of power and using the cut glass, water and the crystal, it was refracted and twinkled and rainbowed second by second. At last he heard Patrick's return; the door opened and he hurried up the stone steps to the gallery outside.

"What's happened?" Eddie asked him anxiously.

"Oh he's been taken quite bad, Bridget's trying to get a duty dentist to see him as soon as possible, she's found some oil of cloves and painkillers. So —he'll not be back tonight, I can tell you."

They stood together glumly.

"What a shame, and it's the eclipse in eight minutes." Eddie looked out to the buoy.

"Can you still see Ellie and Captain John? Are they all right?" He checked his watch and peered into the darkness.

"I can't see them at all, but shall we have a go at the next one now – before the eclipse?"

As they consulted each other and organised their equipment, they were lucky enough to see the thick clouds separate as the wind picked up again, and out of the midnight blue sky the pale and complete moon emerged luminous and large.

"Great! Just what we want." Patrick was overjoyed at their good fortune.

Ellie and Captain John, gently lulled almost to sleep in the rippling movement of the boat, were immediately alerted by a red pinprick of light, so short it was hardly possible to see it, then it changed to pale yellow, green, blue, back to red, and it twinkled like the fairy lights on a Christmas tree.

"Oh that's so pretty." Ellie was excited. The shafts of light were thrown onto the surface of the water, brilliant shards of piercing colour, almost blinding.

Captain John was captivated.

Ellie reached in her bag and extracted her tiny torch. "The time! I must check it. It's soon to be the eclipse," and pointing the small light at her watch she could see there were four minutes to go. "Keep your fingers crossed that the clouds keep away, I do so want to see this," she told her puzzled companion, and she altered her position in the boat to view the moon better.

Patrick and Eddie were beside themselves with joy and excitement at their success. The little crystal signaller had been brilliant. It seemed to take charge of itself as the light hit the prism and ran backwards and forwards through the spectrum. Some colours were better seen than others.

All at once the Moonmirror, charged up again by the moon's light, discharged its powerful beam and Ellie and Captain John were once more illuminated where they sat.

They all waved furiously at each other. Eddie looked anxiously at the sky. Would the clouds keep away for the eclipse? A huge cloak of threatening gloom was appearing to their left, over the Kingswear hill. They started the countdown, staring up at the moon in silence, keeping still and full of expectation as they waited. The dog shivered and his back legs shook. He whined mournfully; uneasy, sensing the tension. Captain John stroked him whispering words of comfort, consoling him, but the dog continued to whine, an uneasy atmosphere enveloping him, one familiar and unwelcome from the spirit world. He could feel the waves of it intensifying as they vibrated through the air.

A tiny splinter of a black arc distorted the perfect round shape of the moon. Gradually as the seconds moved with the light, it became a shadow, a crescent, obscuring steadily more and more of the moon's face. The dark trespasser moved on almost invisibly; it marched across the surface of that perfect circle of light. Then a thin misty cloud wafted across, dimming the brightness. The onlookers, both in the boat and on the turret, watched helplessly, riveted in silence, as the interplanetary ballet took place, their positions in the solar system realigning. The moon's face was almost covered now; just a thin wedge of light curved around the edge, the obscured area still visible in an aura around the black

circle of the earth's shadow. Unluckily, the bank of cloud reached the moon's surface just as the final arc of light was fading. It glided over the entire lunar eclipse, blocking everything from view and plunging the night sky into an oppressive darkness. In the distance thunder rumbled, far, far away across the black ocean.

In the little boat Ellie shivered and the dog howled like a banshee. Captain Avery felt damp and cold, and fingers of anxiety crept into his head. "I don't like this, lass," he whispered to her. "Something's happened. I don't feel right. Syracuse feels it keenly too, poor creature," and he pulled the agitated dog to him.

On the battlements, Eddie and Patrick were plunged into a heavy blackness, thick and cold.

"I can't see a thing," complained Eddie.

"It'll soon come out the other side, and if the clouds go over, we'll see it again," reassured Patrick. Nothing happened. The air was still and clung to them making cold shivers run inside their clothes, a chilling fog enveloping them. Strange noises began to filter through the air, hardly audible at first. They said nothing to each other, but each listening and then hearing a horse whinnying, another stamping, clanking of metal, the rumble of a cart …, and then the voices started. A short shout, a reply. Laughter, a name called, the sound of feet on stones. Eddie and Patrick looked at each other uneasily.

"What's going on?" they whispered to each other, afraid for the first time. They could smell something too. A waft of a vegetable, meaty smell, horse manure, wet wool, people, animals and food.

"I don't like this at all." Patrick's face was closed and his mouth firmly set.

"It sounds to me as if it's from below. People. Things are happening. What can it be?" Eddie questioned. He was now becoming very frightened. In the dark fog they stepped through the turret door, Eddie having the presence of mind to lock the door behind him.

"We don't want anyone sneaking up here spoiling our stuff, do we?" he told Patrick grimly. They slowly and fearfully trod down the old staircase leading into the café.

Except that it wasn't the café, it was totally changed. They had stepped into the guardroom of the old castle. One soldier was on duty, dressed in what looked like the re-enactment costume of a fighting man from a very long time ago. He jumped up at once.

"Hey, who goes there? A couple of fine lads I'd say. What say ye boys, mischief bound I'll reckon." He grinned a toothy black grin.

"Edwin?" he called. "Edwin, two for you I'd say!" he shouted outside. Eddie and Patrick were totally aghast and stunned at what they could see. They seemed to have entered a very different world. They were slap bang in the middle of a huge soldier's encampment. A candle flickered in a holder in the wall and on a roughly made table a flintlock pistol lay, with a handle of fine wood and a hammerhead action. Propped up around the walls were some very old guns, 5 to 6 feet long.

"What are we doing here?" anxiously whispered the boys, clutching each others' arms in disbelief. A fat woman waddled in wrapped up in layers of woollen clothes, a rather dirty white flat bonnet on her head, turned back at the sides. She carried a wooden bowl full of stew and a lump of bread.

"Not more mouths to feed," she grumbled, placing the bowl on the table, her face shiny with grease and sweat from cooking over the fire that could clearly be seen glowing outside. She smelt of smoke, cooking fat and other unpleasantness.

"Shall we try to get out of here?" whispered Patrick to Eddie urgently. "I don't fancy staying whatever's happened." He nodded his head towards the small wooden door where once the café entrance had been. The soldier, distracted by the food, ate hungrily. They both hugged the wall with their backs and gradually side stepped round towards the door, nimbly and slowly.

"Run!" signalled Patrick, and the two boys ran straight out of the door into the unknown.

The troops of the Royalist Army had been encamped at the castle since 1643 when they had laid siege to the town for many wet and damp weeks. Dominating both sides of Warfleet Valley, and with superior artillery, Prince Maurice had engulfed the castle from Gallants Bower and taken Paradise Tower. Three years had passed in occupation of the town and the army settlement was well established, surrounding the church, the castle, and the fortifications on the top of Gallants Bower. The Royalists were firmly entrenched in Dartmouth town. It was into this bustling camp that Eddie and Patrick had stumbled – the eclipse of the moon the means of returning them to the seventeenth century; a faltering in the mechanism of the interplanetary systems, never known before. A large astral body had interrupted the orbit of the moon and had reversed the time for a while. They were well and truly stuck. The year? 1646.

PART TWO

Chapter Twenty-nine
Ellie hides at the old manor house

On the river Captain John and Ellie surveyed the scene before them with astonishment. It was still very dark, the moon refusing to reappear and thick clouds covering the night sky. They could see flickering fires; the silhouette of the castle had changed dramatically. Walls had appeared and the whole area seemed much larger and somehow more enclosed. They could hear men's voices travelling over the water, and the place seemed very much alive.

"What's happened?" Ellie asked the sea captain, who strained his eyes in the gloom.

"I cannot say lass, something is amiss. The air is filled with danger, I can smell it." He began to untie the mooring line. He knew from his instincts to get away into sheltered waters; they were vulnerable and exposed, tied to the rusting buoy.

"Come on little maid," he instructed her, "let's head for a safer harbour, we're sitting ducks here. Up now! Away with us!" and they spurred into action. Captain John removed his spyglass from the large pocket in his frock coat and scanned the castle battlements.

"Tis strange, very strange, it vexes me," he murmured to himself. He could see little in the darkness but figures moving around.

"Make no noise lass, one oar each, slow and steady now. Pull deeply as you can, child." He smiled encouragingly at her.

"Where shall we go?" Ellie asked, a little bewildered. "What about Eddie and Patrick? We can't just leave them."

"Hush child, they're lads, they'll prove themselves to be quick thinking and ready for whatever befalls them. They'll be home before you, I'll wager." He chuckled reassuringly to her. "This black fog'll put an end to their tinkering. We'll abandon our plans for this night, eh? Let's to it lass."

He turned the boat, trying to match their strokes as they began to slowly head back towards the castle. Captain John kept constant watch on the battlements. He felt invigorated, full of energy and anticipation. Excitement surged through him just like in the old days. He didn't know what had happened to him, but it felt good, so good.

One thought went through his mind. He was convinced they should conceal themselves, and he pointed to the opposite bank, on the Kingswear Castle side of the river. This castle was also occupied. Ellie nodded and in the darkness they manoeuvred their small craft to the rocky shoreline's shadowy edges. Sargasso the seagull, faithful as ever, sat on the prow of the boat before them as hundreds of years of history sped by. Captain John's instincts had been right. The river edge of the fortification had a duty guard strategically placed on the grassy verge, huddled in front of a blazing fire. On the hour struck by the bell, a patrol walked the perimeter checking the landward and seaward sides.

The two sailors eased the boat through the water which was surging and swishing into the rocky crevices. By the firelight they could see a previously unknown theatre playing out before their eyes– men, women, dogs, horses, tents and shelters, sounds and sights so very foreign to them; but perhaps not to Captain John, for he had been accelerated back to his own century. Ellie looked on with a terrified curiosity, as she struggled to maintain her oar strokes.

"That's how the castle was a long time ago, isn't it? Are they making a film or something? It looks so real, don't you think

Captain John?"

"Aye lass, too real," was his only reply, as he too pulled his oar, steadily inching down the river at a slow but silent pace.

"Where are we going?" Ellie asked, her voice a little breathless with the exertion. She was getting hot.

"Why, to Warfleet Quay where else? My good friend Cedric Mortlock will give us shelter."

"Oh," replied Ellie, "I don't think I know him."

After a long time they rounded the small inlet and rowed into the quiet waters. There were no lights and no boats to be seen. They tied the boat up to an old iron ring in the wall at the old quay and Captain John helped Ellie climb the ladder up to the quayside garden.

"I'm exhausted," she complained, "I'll have to sit down for a minute, please!" and she sank down onto the damp grass. Captain John went back to help his dog up the difficult access.

Poor little maid, she has done well, thought the captain and patted her back. "Come now, rest for a minute, we must seek good Sir Cedric, I must have news of him." He pointed to the pretty manor house behind them, sitting comfortably sheltered by the water's edge.

"But I don't know where I am," complained the confused and tired Ellie. "Where are the lime kilns and the holiday cottages? Why does it all look so different? And what is this house doing here anyway? It wasn't here yesterday."

Captain Avery knew exactly where he was. It was entirely how he had last remembered it. Somehow he and Ellie had arrived back at his final resting place, and he was utterly convinced that should he walk up the lane he would find the small hamlet of Warfleet waiting for him at the top of the creek. He smiled to himself; the anticipation of going home was irresistible. After letting Ellie rest for as long as he dared, he helped her up gently.

"Come now," he coaxed.

Together they approached the dark house, but keen-eyed Captain John had seen a candle flicker across the window. The windows were low and mullioned. It was a beautiful Devon manor house set in a lovely garden. They approached the door and looking carefully around, knocked loudly.

"Open up, 'tis John Avery!" Eventually the big studded-oak door opened a small chink.

"Is that you Captain? Can it be?" came the soft and frightened female voice.

"Aye it is, Captain John Avery, who's there? Speak up, we'll not eat ye!"

The door opened a little bit more and a frightened face appeared surrounded by blonde curls and a white starched cotton head-cover.

"Why Sarah, what's amiss here?" questioned the captain, the frightened girl holding the candle up to see outside.

"Oh sir, they've all gone. Sir Cedric to Plymouth with all the men and the house in ruins, all been taken, everything save a few sticks of furniture. Look, come and see," and she beckoned him inside. Ellie followed and they looked around the looted house, which looked sadly dejected and violated.

"I can barely manage to eat sir, just a few hens and one cow left. The soldiers took everything. I have to hide us all, in case they come back and take what little I've got. There's a whole garrison of them at the castle to feed."

A small fire burned in the big chimney with a few meagre logs smouldering. The room felt damp and cold. Ellie shivered, but the dog sat down by the hearth.

"You're welcome to what there is Captain, and you Miss." She bobbed a curtsey.

"Let's make a good fire Sarah, warm us up and I'll think on it." He helped her pile up logs from outside, stored in a lean-to. Ellie sat on an old wooden stool and tried to decide what had happened to her.

I'm in a time warp. She realised she must be back in the olden days, Captain Avery's time. *I'm probably right in the middle of the Civil War by the looks of it. I hope I can get back. And what has happened to poor Eddie and Patrick? They were on top of the lookout tower."* She began to feel very worried and frightened. What would happen next?

"Where is William Adams, pray Sarah?" asked Captain John as he warmed himself by the now blazing fire.

"Gone to Plymouth with Sir Cedric sir. Who's to know if he'll ever come back," she remarked sadly, "what with all that fighting and all."

"He will triumph I tell you Sarah. Don't sadden yourself; he was the best quartermaster who I ever sailed with. I'll be glad to see him again. I'm sure he's a good husband to you lass."

Sarah fetched some eggs and milk and a very hard country loaf. Together they made a meal of what they could. It was simple fare but sustaining. The three of them sat together. Sarah closed the shutters tightly and gave them a coarse woollen blanket each. "It's all I've got sir," she apologised.

"I'm going out to look for those boys in a while," the captain announced.

"I'll come with you," Ellie said at once.

"No," came the firm reply. "I think not, lass. You are safer inside with good Sarah Adams. Syracuse is here, no one shall get in with him to guard you."

He looked at the sky and reckoned he had one, maybe two hours at the most, before dawn. He had to find the boys before

199

daybreak or he would be discovered. There was no time to waste.

From past experiences of skirmishes ashore with raiding parties in foreign lands, he knew his white face was the giveaway. So he pulled a charred log from the grate to let it cool down and begged a heavy cloak from Sarah. He could cover up entirely with this and with a blackened face felt confident he could conceal himself from the soldiers as he made his way back to the camp. He instructed the two young women to stay well hidden, and to put no more logs on the fire, as the smoke would give away their presence. He would return soon and they would decide on their next move then. He rubbed the charcoal onto his face and hands as the girls looked on; only the whites of his eyes and his teeth showed now. He left his pistol and musket behind, taking only a deadly looking knife with a curved blade, ornate and much engraved.

"From a Mogul in the East," he explained, grinning. Waving his farewells to the two rather apprehensive girls he left them guarded by his dog to search for the boys. Almost four hundred years separated the lives of the two left behind. Could they bridge this gap? They both had need of shelter, warmth, food and water, clothes and a comfortable bed – not such a surprise after all, because very little had changed.

Captain John made his plan as he went. He needed to see as much of the camp as he could without being discovered. Either he had to get very high up to look down into the fortifications, or bluff his way into the camp by the main entrance. He knew the fort at the top of the hill was also occupied, so he chose the middle ground. He would hide in the woods below the fort and look down with his spyglass to try and see. Perhaps he was not too late to save the boys from capture. He would try with every ounce of his being to find them. He had to, for Ellie's sake.

Chapter Thirty
Eddie and Patrick are imprisoned

Eddie and Patrick had run straight into two hefty pike men changing places on the hour. Each wore a thick buff coat, white shirts, brown breeches, cream stockings and heavy buckled shoes.

"You young beggars, not so fast." One soldier caught Eddie and the other Patrick.

"Let go of me!" Eddie wriggled, desperately trying to get out of his grip.

"Young spies d'ye reckon Edwin? They've had their locks shorn off." The other man cuffed Patrick's head.

"For Parliament are ye lad, with your round head? A puking Puritan, eh?" He hit Patrick again on the head.

"Leave him alone you coward!" shouted Eddie.

"Fighting talk from a mewling boy," laughed Edwin and pushed Eddie to the ground.

"Tie 'em up," ordered the other soldier.

"Aye Nathan I will, gladly. Still, ye brats!" Despite their struggles the boys had their hands tied, then both feet, leaving a length of rope between them so that it was possible to walk.

"Take 'em up to the captain, he'll squeeze their tongues I reckon," laughed Nathan the pike-man. Another foot soldier was called over and he tied their rope to a small chestnut mare, which he led across the central field and up a narrow path overlooking the sea.

"We'll be alright Eddie," called Patrick, as they stumbled together up the hill, sliding in the mud, almost being dragged by the steady plodding pony. The path led up into the woods. The sea was crashing on the rocks far below, and glancing out towards the horizon Eddie could make out the first glimmerings of daylight. He knew where he was, above Castle Cove and Sugary Cove, on his way up to Gallants Bower and the old fortified earthworks. He'd walked it a hundred times with his mother and Ellie. How had they ended up back in the seventeenth century, in the middle of the Civil War? he wondered, thinking all the time as he struggled, half walking, half stumbling, upwards through the steep path.

It must have been the eclipse, it was the only answer. The unthinkable had happened. Somehow as the shadow of the earth covered the moon, time had stopped, and then spun backwards leaving them back in sixteen-something. He knew some history of the Civil War. He must find out what year it was, it could prove to be very significant. His arms, which were pulled behind his back ached, the ropes burned his wrists and it was very hard to walk. He was short of breath and felt giddy.

"I'm not giving up," he told himself. "Keep going, come on, it will soon be daylight, and at least they didn't kill us." He gritted his teeth and plodded on. Patrick was in front of him, slipping and sliding just the same. At one stage he turned around and laughed at him.

"We'll make it laddie! Whoops!" He twisted on the rope and fell onto his face in the mud.

"Here, what's going on?" complained the soldier leading the faltering pony. "You're in for a beating if you don't step up a bit! Look lively you scum!" he shouted angrily.

Along a flatter area they caught their breath, and then emerged out of the heavy woodland into an open, gorse-edged grassy hill. Fires could be seen glowing, and they heard murmuring voices and horses whinnying and snorting.

"We're here," whispered Eddie. "This is it," as they were led through the middle of the first earth wall, which was very steep and muddy and then dropped down into a wide sheltered grassy plain, surrounded by earthed-up walls, a lookout point on two corners. A huge fire burned in the middle; rough tents and shelters surrounding it. They were dragged to a small stone-built sentry box, very small and smelly, with an iron grille set in the door. Pushed inside, the boys sprawled over each other and the door bolt shot across behind them.

"We'll be back!" shouted the soldier. "Don't go away!" and he chuckled to himself.

"It's nearly daylight, we'll soon see what's going on," reassured Patrick to Eddie as they lay in the dark.

"We're in the Civil War I reckon, don't you?"

"It seems like it," agreed Patrick. "How it's happened I just don't know."

"I do. It's got to be the eclipse. What do you think has happened to Captain John and Ellie? I'm so worried about her." Despair flooded his muddy face, his hair sticking up untidily.

"I shouldn't worry too much Eddie. Think about it: she's with Captain John and he's been transported back to his own time, so he's going to love it. He'll be right in his element. Everything's familiar, knowing this area. Maybe the timing's not exactly right –he spent a lot of time overseas – but still, it's got to have its advantages, don't you think?" He tried to sit up but fell over, hurting his shoulder on the ground and groaning.

"We've got to get our hands free somehow. It's impossible like this. Have you got your Swiss Army knife by any chance Eddie? I think now's the time to use it, if you don't mind me saying."

Eddie, who wholeheartedly agreed, found that he couldn't check his pockets, of course, with his hands tied behind his back.

"I think it's in here, in my jeans pocket, but you'll have to get it for me. It will be hard to open it with your hands tied up, because you won't be able to see it."

He wriggled over to Patrick who tried each pocket but it just wasn't there.

"Blast! I can't seem to find it, sorry."

" It was there I'm sure of it." Eddie was furious. "It must have fallen out somewhere. Blast and damn!"

"How are we going to escape now?"

"Maybe Captain Avery and Ellie will still be in the boat, or perhaps they'll be looking for us."

"I don't know. I just don't know anymore. This is all so unreal; but it is happening to us. They hang spies you know." He sniffed mournfully.

"Shut up Eddie! Don't say anymore, it's no good thinking like that." Patrick bit his lip and concentrating, said "Just let's sit and rest and think a bit."

Eddie heard an owl hooting very loudly in the trees behind him. It was a reassuring and comforting noise in the turmoil. It reminded him of home.

"We will do this Patrick, we will," he resolved.

Captain John was having a fruitless search. He had entered the woods from opposite One Gun Point and stealthily crept his way towards the castle. As he got closer he went higher and higher but still could not see over the walls of the camp. They were too high – forty feet they towered, making an impregnable impasse. He decided to risk all and try to reach the camp from the river by boat. He went back as carefully as he had come, returning to Quay House full of disappointment. Ellie and Sarah were sleeping, huddled together on a straw pallet before the fire. He tapped gently on the window twice. Sarah, with a terrified look, woke up and slowly went to look out.

"Ah 'tis you sir," and smiling with relief she opened the door to him. Ellie woke up too, waiting to see the two boys troop in behind Captain John, but it was not to be. Nobody followed him in, and Sarah closed the door.

"You haven't got Eddie or Patrick!" Ellie shouted accusingly. "Where are they?" She burst into floods of tears, covering her face with her hands. She sat sobbing, shaking her head and repeating, "Oh no! Oh no!"

Captain John felt humiliated. He had neither found nor rescued the two boys. He strode over to Ellie in his long and muddied boots and put his arms around her.

"I'm so sorry little maid, it just wasn't possible, but have courage, we will find them, never fear. Come, drink some ale, you'll feel better." He beckoned to Sarah who was heating a poker in the fire, ready to heat the spiced brew kept in the huge jug. She plunged it into the ale and then poured it into a beaker, giving Ellie the hot spicy honeyed drink. She sat silently sipping it. It tasted strange, but rather nice. They sat together and talked of what they would do next. Ellie sniffed and wiped her face with her hand, she listened but was inconsolable. The whole turn of events had confused and upset her. She wanted to go home and she wanted her mother. This was not how it was meant to be. She seemed to be a prisoner trapped in history, and she didn't like it. If only she could find Eddie, everything would somehow feel better.

She tried to pay attention to what Captain John was saying. Daylight crept in through the windows, and she wandered over to look out. The creek waters lapped gently beneath the quay. The limekilns had gone, so too the boats, the bridge and the road. In their place she could see some little low farm buildings and a couple of cottages. Water gushed down the creek; it looked very pretty indeed.

I've always wondered what it looked like long ago. She felt in her leather bag still fastened around her waist; her sweets and torch were both still there. Eddie must still have his precious knife then and Patrick his compass, because they had all put them in their pockets before they left the Old Bath House – *That wouldn't be there either,* thought Ellie.

Where had Bridget and George gone? It was all so hard to understand. She could see their dear little green boat however; that had not evaporated away, and yes there was a seagull sitting on it. Could it possibly be Sargasso? He had been on the boat with them that night, she was sure. She dared to wonder. A feeling of hope swept over her and she opened the door and stepped outside. Sarah went to prevent her, but Captain John restrained her.

"Let her go, all will be well."

Outside, Ellie stood in the grassy garden and waited, looking towards the boat. At once the seagull flew to her feet and croaked his seagull noise, nodding his head up and down and pecking her feet. She bent down to stroke his head.

"Can it be you Sargasso? Is it possible? How have you stayed with us? Can you help me find Eddie? Please?" Sargasso croaked again, tilted his head and looked at her knowingly. He took off, his great wings flapping, and flew steadily through the creek, turning in the direction of the sea. Ellie watched him go, hope filling her.

"Maybe he'll find them." She shivered, it was a chilly damp morning and as she turned to go back inside, a little brown robin barred her way. She almost stood on it. His black beady eyes blinked at her, and he chirruped a sweet greeting.

"Freddie," she whispered, "you too? It's impossible. I'm so happy to see you!" and she started to cry again. The little bird flew up to her shoulder and pecked her hair.

"It is you, isn't it?" She wanted to believe it so badly. "We've lost Eddie and Patrick," she sniffed. "Can you help Sargasso to find them? Please dear Freddie, please?"

The bird chirruped another cheerful song and flew off too, higher and higher into the trees, and was gone. Ellie went back into the house delighted and much happier, beaming at the curious couple waiting for her.

"It's going to be alright. They've gone to find them."

Sarah nodded sympathetically and brought her back to the fireside. Captain John indicated his boots and the good Sarah Adams helped him pull them off.

He lay back in the one wooden armchair and dozed off to sleep. Sarah gently covered him with one of the blankets. The two girls set about tidying the ravaged house, fetched water and had a chilly wash. Ellie swept the floor and Sarah shook the straw mattress. They made some rough country bread with the meagre flour left and cooked it over the fire on a flat griddle. The fire smoked and made them cough. Then Sarah took Ellie outside and showed her the privy. Ellie nodded, understanding only too well. They picked vegetables and washed and chopped them, filling a black iron pot.

"No meat I'm afraid," apologised the country girl.

Ellie was now enjoying herself in a strange sort of way. The sound of horse's hooves startled them. They ran to the end window of the house where, above them on the road, both could see riders.

"Dear God in heaven save us!" and Sarah crossed herself in terror. They waited, hardly daring to breathe, huddled together in the darkest corner. A face appeared at the window and Ellie whimpered in fear. The man peered in curiously.

"Sarah? Sarah Adams? 'Tis your husband Will, are ye there lass? Open up." Sarah saw the face of her good husband Will Adams and ran to the door in joy.

"Oh Will! Will, my husband!" She tore open the door and they fell into each other's arms.

"Come now wife, inside, I have great news!" and he extricated himself from her embrace. "Plymouth is free! We never gave in! Cromwell is coming and the siege is lifted! The Royalists are on the run. Lord Thomas Fairfax and his New Model Army are on the way. Sir Cedric and his men will join them and we'll soon take back the town, I promise you! Great news Sarah, is it not?" He picked her up and swung her round laughing. She squealed in pleasure and suddenly Will noticed the sleeping man in the chair. He put Sarah down and drew his sword.

"On your feet sir, if ye have ravaged my wife I'll slit your throat and drink your blood. Get up man!" He prodded his chest with the point of his blade.

"No Will, no!" Sarah shook his arm. "Its Captain Avery, Captain John of the good ship *Fancy*. See?" and she pulled the blanket off and Captain John woke up, confused and disorientated.

"What? What the devil?" He reached for a pistol but in surprise he recognised the face of his attacker.

"Will? Will Adams? Put down your sword man, 'tis I, John Avery!" and they both laughed loudly, put down their arms and embraced, clapping each other loudly on the back.

"I thought never to see ye again!" sniffed Will Adams, overjoyed to see his old captain again.

"What brings ye here, sir? Tell me all. Ale, bring ale, Sarah." Sarah scurried around to fetch a jug for the two delighted men.

Will Adams told them stories of the siege of Plymouth. Of how they had fiercely resisted the army led by Prince Maurice, who was the nephew of King Charles. He had gone to Plymouth with Sir Cedric and two hundred of his men. Will looked around the house.

"What's happened here Sarah? The house is sacked and all the fine furnishings gone. What of the warehouse yonder?"

Sarah shook her head. "All gone, Will dear, all gone."

"The plundering devils! What of the ships and the guns? Surely something's left?" quizzed Will in disbelief.

"No my husband, the soldiers have been here, all is lost. Poor Sir Cedric."

"A fine homecoming he'll have, and him fighting for justice and Parliament." Will shook his head. "Murdering devils! Well, within a few hours the first foot soldiers will be here, the cavalry not far behind them, then musketeers and pike men, and all here to oust the garrison. I cannot wait. But first I must make my way to Dartmouth town to tell our loyal friends that help is on the way, and to watch and wait this day. But I'll be back Sarah, I'll be back." Kissing her again, he clapped Captain John on the back and left in a great hurry. He returned a moment later.

"I forgot to give you this Sarah," and he opened his jacket and pulled out a rabbit.

"Fresh meat lass. Enjoy it, I'll eat on my return."

Sarah had the rabbit skinned and in the pot in five minutes flat.

Chapter Thirty-one
Interrogation, and the hunt for the boys begins

Daylight did not help the situation. Before Eddie and Patrick could execute any of their escape plans, they heard voices outside their stony prison. Patrick and Eddie waited, their heart pounding as the door bolt was tampered with and the door flung open.

"Here they are, Captain," the big burly soldier with the black and missing teeth told his superior officer who had arrived at the sentry box. He was a little better dressed than the others, in an armoured breastplate, front and back, and a long, loose red jacket with a bandolier of powder measures slung around him. In addition he was wearing a large felt hat with an out-of-place bright sash and feather.

The young officer wore a pointed beard and moustache, looking imposing and arrogant.

"Get up at once," he snapped. "Why they're only boys!" he ridiculed, "Strange ones at that. Puritans I'll grant ye by their shorn heads, but little danger surely," he laughed. "What's your name boy?" He prodded Eddie.

"Edmond, sir."

"And yours?" Patrick was next.

"Patrick, sir."

"Where do ye hail from? Speak up, I've little time."

"From Warfleet sir, down in the valley."

"And are ye both spies?"

He leaned forward and stared into their faces, looking harshly at them.

"Of course not sir. We were out snaring rabbits and came into the camp from curiosity only." Patrick spoke bravely.

"Please sir, what is the date and the year?" asked Eddie, very carefully and politely.

"Are ye loose in the head boy, that ye do not know what day we live in?" answered the surprised Captain Francis. "What a pair of dolts! It is January the eighteenth, sixteen hundred and forty-six, and as cold and damp a day as ever I spent in the service of the King. Will that do ye? Lock 'em up Edwards, till I make up my mind. I've an idea they're both simpletons, but who's to know?"

He turned to leave.

"Please sir, one minute," called Eddie, as Captain Francis turned around exasperated.

"This day will go down in history sir. Be on your guard." He spoke slowly and with feeling. "I know it to be true, sir."

"Oh do ye boy," sneered the captain. "Maybe you're a spy after all. Lock them up and give them no food." He strode off angrily.

This day will go down in history? Whatever did he mean? Stupid driveling idiot.

But the words echoed in his head and drove him into an irritable bad temper. Eventually he shouted to "Double the Guard!" and the men were a little surprised at the ill-humoured Captain who seemed out of sorts and edgy.

The robin had flown to the old church, which he had found turned into the garrison store. So many men were hard to feed – sacks of flour, oats, kegs of ale, water, salted and dried meats and honey were piled up. A constant stream of unwilling local farmers arrived who were forced to bring cartloads of vegetables and eggs, chickens and ducks, from their smallholdings and farms as far away as Kingsbridge. Some of the soldiers were an unruly bunch and often made forages into the town to steal food. They forced ale-house keepers to supply them, threatening and mistreating them. It was a difficult time for the townsfolk.

Taking a good look at the situation, the robin decided to fly in through the bell tower and speak to the bats before finding Ferdinand and Isabella. It seemed miraculous, but the Time

Reverse process had catapulted these creatures back along with the children.

The little robin found Belvedere and his family sound asleep, but felt compelled to wake them, wishing for an unembroidered account of what was happening, rather than the hysterical and exaggerated story he would get from Isabella. Ferdinand, of course, would never get a word in. He gently tapped with his beak to arouse them, and soon Belvedere appeared.

"My dear fellow, how good to see you. Now what is the matter? Tell me all." He turned himself up the right way to speak to Freddie.

"We've lost Eddie; well, two boys to be precise. Have you seen them anywhere among the soldiers?"

"To be honest, I haven't." Belvedere sadly shook his head. "But I can go and look for them. I'll be able to hear their voices from a long way off, if I tune into their human frequency. Would you like me to go now? If you would stay with Boadicea in case she needs a hand?" The kind and willing bat smiled his rather devilish grin, teeth showing.

"Yes, yes, I'd be so grateful." The robin felt immensely relieved.

"Not a problem, back in five minutes," and the little furry creature unfurled his leathery serrated wings and soared off up to the top of the tower and disappeared.

Sargasso had also gone on a hunt for the two boys. He had flown over the whole area, circling and calling. He could look down and see practically everything; but it was so changed, so many people and animals, noise and activity. Walls had appeared, the car park had gone, the café disappeared, fires and tents and comings and goings. It was hard to tell what was happening in this changed world.

He could see no sign of the two boys and he decided to be

bolder. He landed down in the main camp, and hopped around, looking anxiously everywhere. A seagull with only one leg was a curiosity, an object of ridicule. Dogs barked at him and somebody cruelly threw a stone, which he narrowly avoided. There were groups of women cooking and mending, and one of them threw a scrap of mouldy bread at him. He had no time to eat, he must find Eddie.

Disappointed, he flew to the top of the hill, where the Second Garrison was camped out above Dartmouth, cold and windy. The earth had been heaped up to provide some shelter and six corner lookout points stood up proudly with views of the entire area. A small wall of dry stone had been built as an extra boundary and dense trees surrounded two sides. They were not far from the Citadel, the large pines further up the valley towards Little Dartmouth where the buzzards lived.

He landed again, searching every corner, but he could not find them. He was dejected and disappointed. The soldiers chased him and he was forced to fly off. He went back to sit on the tower of St Petrox church, and watch and think. They had last been seen at the castle, but that was all changed and was an unfamiliar chaos. As he sat watching the strange scenes below, he noticed a black bird circling, fluttering like a butterfly. Sargasso followed its staccato journey, intrigued. *That's not a butterfly, that's a bat! Yes it's a bat, how odd, and in the daylight too. It must be Belvedere, I suppose. He's keeping strange hours."* He continued to watch, fascinated.

The bat completed its radar search of the castle encampment but could pick up no signals from any of the buildings or clusters of makeshift dwellings. It was obvious that Eddie and Patrick were not among their numbers. Undeterred, Belvedere swooped and flittered his way up the steep hillside, furiously beating his tiny leathered-skin wings. As he reached the hilltop fortifications a small sound pierced his sensitive ears. He followed it as it gently increased in intensity and soon he could hear human voices muffled, coming from below him. He reduced his altitude and pinpointed the spot – a small stone building tucked into the sheltered back wall of the grassy encampment. That's where they were! Locked inside. Belvedere swooped low, and although his eyesight was poor, he could report he had found them. Delighted with himself, he flew round the back of the camp, down through the woods, and returned to the bell tower via the vents in the wall. He had succeeded!

Freddie and Boadicea eagerly watched him fly in. He was very tired, it had been a difficult upward flight for so small a creature whose wings did not have the strength of a bird's.

"Just one moment, I'll be all right. I'll tell you all." He caught his breath back.

The robin was fit to burst with excitement and blinked furiously as the seconds ticked by.

"I've found them! I know exactly where they are!" Freddie and Boadicea jumped for joy.

"They're up at the top fortification, locked in a tiny hut. It's the only building up there. I can't see much as you know, but I heard them talking. However there are a lot of soldiers up there and its walls are patrolled and there are sentries on every corner. It will be quite a feat to help them escape. We shall need some assistance," he told them seriously. The robin was undeterred. He would fly up there immediately and assess the situation.

On the tower, Sargasso had observed Belvedere's return. He was of course too large to fit through the vents. He waited for news anxiously. Soon Freddie flew out and he greeted the seagull and told him the wonderful story of the bat's intriguing powers.

215

Sargasso was relieved that his precious Eddie was safe, but concerned that the two boys were in such a difficult place to be rescued. They hardly knew which way to turn.

"I've already looked up there," the seagull told the robin, "but I couldn't see them."

"Let's go and have another look. Come on." And the two birds, one so large and one so small, flew up to the top of Gallants Bower together. They scanned rapidly for the small stone hut; once they had located it, both landed a short distance away, trying not to attract attention.

"You go first," nodded Sargasso. Obediently the brave robin hopped to the door, which was firmly bolted – but the grille was open. Freddie perched on the edge and peered inside.

The two boys were huddled together trying to release their hands, without much success. They sat back to back, encouraging each other, tired and hungry.

"It's so difficult because I can't see," complained Eddie, frustrated. Freddie hopped through the bars and landed at Eddie's feet, cheeping and pecking him with his beak.

"Hey, what are you doing here little bird? Hello little fellow, you're brave coming in here." The bird hopped up onto his leg and pecked again.

"Is that your robin Eddie, Faithful Freddie?"

"Oh it can't be, unless it's over three hundred years old. Don't be daft." The robin hopped around to Patrick and chirped away, pecking him gently.

"Well it's very friendly, are you sure?"

"It's impossible Patrick, don't be so stupid," Eddie said angrily.

"Well, I'm sure it is."

Freddie looked at the knots tying their hands and feet. He

couldn't possibly unpick those. He flew out of the iron window to Sargasso.

"It's no good, they are well and truly tied up and there's the bolt to undo outside as well. We just can't do it with our beaks. We need hands, just for once in our lives."

"What shall we do now?"

"We could go and tell the buzzards, see if they've got any powers to help us."

They sat hidden behind the hut, thinking very hard.

Unknown to them, high in the tallest ash tree, which was just behind them, spreading out huge and wide, Tolivera the owl was observing all. He took no sides and remained impartial, the Happenings all being recorded in the Mists of Time. He had kept the buzzards fully informed, but the woodland kingdom took no part in the struggles of human beings. The revivals from the spirit world of the soldiers and their conflict had been predicted, and waves of unrest had been felt for weeks in the surrounding hills. There were evil spirits abroad who had murdered their fellow brethren in a bloody war; only humans murdered each other in such a way.

The loss of the children, and their sadness at being parted, was all noted by the Princes of the Skies. Fate would dictate the outcome. They could not, and would not, interfere. The cycles of life and death had their own rhythms; to break these was disastrous. Their plight was watched with interest and the outcome, whatever it should be, accepted. The robin and the seagull must bear their anguish as best they could.

As they racked their little brains for a way out for Eddie and Patrick, Freddie noticed a small grey squirrel chasing along a high branch in the bleak leafless trees, his tiny claws scratching on the surface of the bark. He watched mesmerised; he didn't care for squirrels, cheeky nasty things like rats with long bushy tails. The robin suddenly flapped his wings and jumped up in the air, startling Sargasso.

"Yes! I know what to do!"

"What?" asked the seagull, puzzled.

"Ferdinand and Isabella! They've got paws with tiny hands – they'll do it! They must still be in the church, don't you think? It's hardly changed over the years. Come on! No time to lose! They can nibble through the ropes and open the bolt, I'm sure."

"They'll never be able to run all the way up this hill – he's too fat for a start."

"No I agree, but you can carry them up on your back, you've got such big powerful wings."

"Yes I have," agreed Sargasso modestly.

"Well then, come on, what are we waiting for?" The little robin was full of enthusiasm. He was sure they could do it. Flying down the hill together, they felt hope at last that perhaps Eddie and Patrick might be freed and soon reunited with the lonely Ellie.

The little church had been transformed. Worship had taken second place. Ferdinand and Isabella were no longer alone, horses clopped in and out, and straw bales were everywhere, but best of all, sacks of delicious grain spilled out leaving more food scattered than either of the two mice had dreamed of.

Despite the intrusion by the soldiers, their followers and animals, life was very exciting because of course they too had been transported back into their own time. New dangers lurked however; cats appeared to terrorise Isabella, Ferdinand had lost weight as he had to run everywhere for fear of being trodden on by a horse's hoof or a large boot, crushed by a cartwheel or eaten by a cat. They lived dangerously, emerging from their quiet lives for the first time in several centuries.

Chapter Thirty-two
Will rounds up the crew of the good ship *Fancy*

Will Adams got a huge surprise when he reached the Dart-mouth's town quay. There were numerous ships tied up in the river and plenty of disgruntled sailors filling the taverns and alehouses of Lower Street. Many of the fleet had sailed from Newfoundland and had been unaware of the blockade of the town. Consequently these ships were trapped in Dartmouth, unable to move their cargoes of Newfoundland salt cod and tobacco. These unfortunate vessels had also to pay customs duties to the gover-nor, a gentleman called Edward Seymour. The Civil War had pre-sented him with great responsibilities, not least of which was to maintain law and order in the town, quite a task with so many soldiers and sailors spilling over in great numbers.

As Will made his way to the home of his friend Hugh Pollard he stopped dead in his tracks. There, lying at anchor in the river was the sweetest sight ever to cross his eyes. The good ship *Fancy* turned prettily on her mooring.

Well, well, well! he smiled to himself, *I thought it was you, my beauty. Wait till I tell Captain John that you're waiting in town for him, just ripe for the picking.*

He reached Hugh's house full of excitement and was ushered in quietly by a servant girl. The two men embraced each other and exchanged news in hushed whispers.

"They'll be here by nightfall Hugh, I'll take an oath on it. Marching now from Plymouth. Yes!" He nodded at Hugh's ama-zed expression. "Fairfax and Sir Cedric. Make ready your men;

219

they'll attack down the valley from Stoke Fleming to overthrow the castle garrison. Oh, I've dreamed of this day when the final score is settled. The town will be ours tomorrow."

Hugh Pollard was highly agitated. "Well, what news! Can ye be certain Will? To show one's colours, uncertain of victory could be very dangerous, very dangerous indeed." He rubbed his chin constantly.

Will tried again to persuade him. "Trust me this once Hugh, it's God's truth, but I cannot linger. I've left my wife Sarah at Quay House, what's left of it, 'tis a sorry sight, sacked and ravaged by the King's men." He spoke grimly, but was anxious to leave undiscovered.

"I'm off now Hugh, I wish you Godspeed. I hope to be here tomorrow, free men, drinking good claret with ye eh? Stolen from those damned Royalists!"

He laughed and slipped out of the ground floor window. He went back for another look at the *Fancy,* a three master, sails all tied aloft, proud and idle, her ships' figurehead of a saucy lass, her chest bared, her carved wooden dress fluted and frilled.

"We'll be back for thee lass," he promised her. He dived into one of the worst alehouses, full of noise and smoke and smells and laughter to see if, by chance, any of her old crew was there, lolling in a stupor as was their habit when ashore. Sure enough the first person he saw was Juno McCormack, closely followed by Tom Edis. They didn't recognise him, they were so drunk and half- asleep

That's two, he told himself, moving on down the street. The next one proved to have no one he knew drinking inside, and he left swiftly to try again. The last one was more successful. Six of his old shipmates were sat playing dice together, sipping ale and swearing.

That's eight, he counted gleefully, careful that they didn't see him. They were a ragged but reliable bunch. *Ten altogether, with me and the captain and Sarah of course. I reckon we could sail her with just ten men – out of here, anyway.* It was more than he'd hoped for. He couldn't wait to get back, and untying his horse from the Coach House yard, he rode quickly back to Warfleet.

Captain Avery was having a difficult time pacifying Ellie and convincing her that if she was patient for just a little longer, he would be able to rescue the boys. When Will returned they would

221

eat and devise a plan. Sarah tried to keep Ellie busy, taking her round the garden to pick herbs, milk the cow and collect the eggs, which proved to be an essential part of domestic life now.

Will burst in, finding Captain John cleaning his pistols with a rag and oil.

"Will!" He was thrilled to see his old Quarter master again, and greeted him warmly.

"Well, how did ye find the town?"

"Awash with drunken sailors and strutting musketeers," replied Will laughing. "They're nothing but a disorderly rabble – we'll soon be hoisting our colours over the town, it'll be a short battle, I'm convinced. Thomas Fairfax commands much respect from the men, and he has an iron resolve. The New Army he created with Cromwell will triumph; they're trained men, disciplined and efficient. It will be a glorious and daring victory. You'll see, Captain."

"I can hardly wait," drawled the captain lazily, polishing his pistols to a gleaming and deadly shine.

"The best news of all…," Will could hardly contain himself in his excitement, as he had kept this until the last

"Yes?" looked up Captain John, alerted by Wills excitement.

"Is that the *Fancy* is lying at anchor in the town."

"Nay Will, ye jest!" gasped the Sea Captain, gripping the table and standing up at once, "Truly? Don't mock me man."

"Sir 'tis as true as I'm standing here. She's been blockaded in here these several months, cargo wasted. Those at the castle have chained the harbour entrance and she cannot leave."

Captain John listened intently.

"Best of all sir, I took a search of the taverns and at least ten of the *Fancy's* old crew are idling away, ready to be rounded up again I'll be bound. Juno McCormack and Thomas Edis are two good men. The others, well, they'll man the ship well enough to take her into fresh waters. What think ye of it, sir? Shall we sail the *Fancy* one more time?"

"Capt'n?" He waited for the reply but in his heart he knew the answer already.

"Aye Will, I think we shall. It's too much to resist … it's meant to be … it must be, her sitting here waiting for us. But I've a lot to think about, I've unfinished business here, and the men will be caught in the thick of chaos in the town this day, if ye don't inform them of our intentions to, um … shall we say *borrow the Fancy?*"

Will laughed loudly and deeply.

"Aye sir, leave that to me. I'll make them ready. Have ye a purse on ye sir? 'Tis always a sweeter persuasion."

"No Will, if ye give them gold 'twill all be pissed away by nightfall. Give them the promise only. Now, let us eat. Call the wenches, I've a plan to hatch yet."

Will called Sarah and Ellie and they sat together eating the rabbit stew which had simmered in the pot for several hours. The two men explained to Ellie of their intention to fetch a ship from the harbour.

"She was in my command once you see," Captain John told her.

"She's no crew and a wasted cargo, and no captain. We're going to sail her out of the river and anchor her off the castle. From there we'll find Eddie and Patrick, I swear it to ye lass. There'll be a change of colours over the tower this night." He winked at her knowingly.

But Ellie didn't understand what he meant, and she didn't care. All she wanted was Eddie back, and of course, Patrick. She was sad and rather quiet. Sarah, who was a sweet kindly girl, comforted her.

"Come now. You'll have your Eddie soon, the Captain will see to it. Hasn't he promised? He always keeps his word doesn't he Will?"

"Aye lass, he does," agreed Will, finishing his plate of stew with satisfaction.

"You haven't lost your touch wife, that's the best stew I've had these three years."

Sarah laughed, and Ellie looked up in surprise.

"Where have you been then?"

"Why fighting the Royalists in Plymouth. We've not yielded, they've laid siege on the town, tried all manner of trickery, but we've held out against them and now today, the hour is coming. God bless Oliver Cromwell!"

Ellie stared at him, puzzled. She hadn't been much good at history, and perhaps it was just as well, because if she'd known what was going to happen, as Eddie did, she wouldn't have had so much courage.

Will kissed his wife and hugged her farewell.

"I've one last thing to see to, and the Captain and I will be off to fetch the Fancy. Stay well hidden both of ye, and I'll see ye in an hour or two."

"Well don't stay away as long as ye did last time," scolded Sarah. "All you think about is fighting! I want a bairn for my empty cradle Will Adams, so come back soon," and they both laughed heartily. Sarah, resigned to Will's departure, began to prepare the rabbit skin for curing, and set about pegging it onto four sticks on the ground, while Ellie watched fascinated.

So Will left once more, to set the whisper round the crew of the regrouping of the Fancy's men, and of the disorder expected in the town. It would prove to be a convenient diversion for the ship's disappearance from the quayside. He hadn't felt so excited and light-hearted since the old days of adventure on the high seas with Captain John and the crew of the good ship *Fancy*.

Chapter Thirty-three
Escape is planned and the mice are recruited to help

Eddie knew they had very little time. If his memory was correct, today was the day when the New Model Army swept over Devon, recaptured the castle, and set the town free. Wasn't it all over the walls of the castle now, set in pictures by English Heritage? And hadn't he and Patrick read them when they visited the old part of the castle last holiday? He was almost convinced. He voiced his fears aloud to his dozing companion.

"Patrick! Patrick! Wake up!" He nudged him gently.

"What?" replied his sleepy friend.

"We've got to think of something. We'll be caught in the battle that's coming later on. Wake up, please." He bumped him again with his back.

"OK, OK, I'm awake. What battle?" He was tired and dazed.

"From what I remember the army, led by Lord Thomas Fairfax will arrive today from Plymouth. There's going to be an almighty fight up here. We'll be caught in the middle of it if we can't get out."

Patrick tried to think. He yawned and he was cold.

Eddie voiced his worst fears. "Don't you see, if we can't get out they'll take us for Royalists and either take us prisoner again, or kill us. We've simply got to get that door open somehow. Now think Patrick, think!"

***

The small robin with the brave heart gathered all his courage to face the formidable Isabella.

After all, he kept telling himself, *she's only a mouse!*

He flew down to the church, where the door was wide open

225

and inside was thronged with camp followers fetching food for the never-ending drudge of preparing meals. Sneaking in quietly, Freddie found the mice's favourite hideaway and tapped with his beak on the ornately carved panel. He waited, his heart beating fast. Very slowly and quietly the little hinged door opened and a tiny nose with whiskers peeped out.

"Who is it?" called a shrill voice.

"It's me, Freddie, Freddie the robin, open the door please."

The doors inched open a fraction more.

"What do you want?" she demanded.

"I need your help Isabella, to free Eddie. He's been captured by the soldiers," he hissed quietly.

"Come, come Isabella, open the door!" and Ferdinand pushed her out of the way and dragged Freddie in, quickly closing the door behind him.

"Thank you," the tiny bird gasped gratefully, "I really do desperately need your help."

"Fetch wine and wafers, Wife," ordered Ferdinand with great authority. "I can see this is a crisis. Tell us all dear friend, Eddie's in danger did ye say? Come! Sit! Begin!"

Isabella went off, flouncing sulkily, to fetch the refreshments they pilfered from the vestry. Freddie told Ferdinand the distressing news of Eddie's capture, and that he and his friend were imprisoned at the top of Gallants Bower, unharmed, but unable to escape without some outside help. He and Sargasso had devised a plan, which involved both he and Isabella, who they hoped could open the bolt and nibble through the ropes. The gentle seagull would transport both mice up the hillside, so they could begin the urgent task of rescuing the boys.

"We just can't think of another way," said Freddie sadly, shaking his head." You've got to help. Please, please say yes," and tiny bird tears filled his eyes.

"No question of it! I'd trail to the other end of the world for that boy – he saved Isabella's life you know," he told Freddie confidentially. 'Course she doesn't know. She'll come with us if I have to carry her myself, you can depend on it." And he patted the little robin's wing.

"I must tell Sargasso at once, he's waiting outside. Just let me go for a moment." Freddie hopped out of the door in a rush to tell him the good news.

"Wait here," Freddie told the seagull.

He hopped back into the church and was soon with Ferdinand and Isabella again.

"You'll have to cover yourselves up," warned Freddie, "Because you're very noticeable with your white fur."

"We could take a mud bath," winked Ferdinand at the bird.

"Indeed we could not!" spluttered Isabella. "I'll look out some very dark clothes. Come husband," she beckoned to him.

"Please hurry," begged Freddie anxiously. "Bring your walking stick Ferdinand, it may be useful." In a very short time the two mice emerged, swathed in black like a couple of desert sheiks.

"We must stay close to the shadows, we don't want to be spotted by any of the soldiers, and mind the horses too. Follow me." Obediently the two mice followed the robin out of the church. Sargasso was keeping watch for them round the side of the building where it was quiet and looked over the battlements to the river. Very carefully the little mice climbed onto the back of the seated seagull and settled themselves down between his wings.

"Hold on tightly – close your eyes if you're frightened," he told them. "Let's go. I'll take off as slowly as I can, one, two, three, go-o-o-o!"

With his wings outspread, a couple of flaps later, his one orange foot trailing behind him, the beautiful white and grey bird soared gently and smoothly up into the air, with the tiny passengers clinging on, their black head covers blowing in the breeze. Up they went, high above the castle, the walls and the people bustling about below. Ferdinand opened his eyes nervously and saw the rolling waves and white crashing foam, the black rocks and the grassy clifftops spread out underneath him.

"Look Isabella! Look!" But she was too frightened to open her eyes.

"It's wonderful my dear," he whispered to her, "open your eyes, do."

Very slowly she opened one of her eyes and then the other. Amazement spread over her face.

"I'm flying! Everything looks so small," and holding Ferdinand's hand, she watched in wonder as the world flew beneath them. The robin followed behind, his little brown wings beating fast.

Nearly there, he told himself panting. *Nearly there.*

Sargasso wisely chose to land his passengers in an unobtrusive place where his arrival would be least noticed. He dropped down some way behind the camp in a leafy covered patch on the edge of the wood. His one good leg took his weight and he bounced into an upright position. The two mice jolted forwards and down they went, rolling over in the gold and brown mattress. Sargasso folded his wings up neatly.

"Are you alright?" he asked.

"Never better," nodded Ferdinand, "The most thrilling ride of our lives, wasn't it my dear?"

"Why, yes," she replied, astonishing herself.

Freddie hopped beside them. The four unlikely members of the rescue team had a final briefing on exactly how they were going to carry out the plan.

"It will take a long time to nibble through the ropes," agreed Ferdinand, "but we can rest and take turns."

Both the mice would fit beneath the doorway. Sargasso's only but vital role was to keep watch and attack anyone who tried to obstruct the escape. Freddie could fly in through the bars and keep an eye on the mice, reporting back to the seagull.

"Ready everyone?" They all nodded. "Let's go."

The brave little mice scampered close to the ground, directed by the robin, and found the sentry box easily. They scrabbled and wriggled under the dark heavy door, rubbing earth from their eyes and whiskers when they arrived on the other side.

Patrick and Eddie sat in a dejected heap. They weren't feeling too well by now. They hadn't been fed and were cold and damp from the frosty air, falling asleep against each other for warmth. The knife had been lost so had proved useless. They were still bound with uncomfortable wet ropes, hands and feet. Hypothermia was slowly beginning to creep over them, making their brains sluggish and ideas of escape impossible. The two mice had arrived just in time. They ran across the muddy floor to the sleeping boys and without waking them, began chewing through the stout bindings. Nibble, nibble, nibble, their sharp little teeth began the task. The robin sat on the window bar and watched, urging them on, hoping they would succeed.

We must have patience, he told himself, *they are so very small.* He watched the mice, feeling a strong wave of emotion sweep over him. His beloved Eddie would soon be free.

High on the windy Citadel the buzzards had distanced themselves from what was going on. It had been a great many years since the Universe Reverse Process had taken place. The humans dictated everything; their power was much greater than the Woodlanders' and whatever happened was always of their making.

Tolivera, overlooking the hilltop fort from the Great Ash Tree, had seen the recent events, all the memories good and bad, dissolved in the Mists of Time. The buzzards could not help but know of Eddie's plight, and the other stranger boy who was with him. They watched and waited impassively. It was all very disconcerting. The aloof Citadel dwellers aware of impending dangers gave no sign to their subjects. Not yet.

Chapter Thirty-four
The arrival of the soldiers is imminent

The bid to recapture the *Fancy* was drawing to its final conclusion. Will Adams had secretly crept back to the town and visited his old crew, patiently searching the taverns again. Making himself known to the eight men, he explained the plan as quietly as he could. It had been difficult to stir them; lazy and bored, they had wasted themselves away, trapped in the small town for months. Will had an understanding of their plight and was not harsh with them. Two of the more sober ones reassured him they would all be at the mustering point on the edge of Bayards Cove at the appointed time.

"We'll not let you down, Will," Thomas Edis promised. "I can't wait to rid myself of this place and smell good fresh sea air again."

Will seemed pretty certain their promises were true and was sure the captain would be well pleased with his efforts. One thing bothered him. What of Sarah his beloved wife, who he had left for three years? He had only just returned to her and already she was in her twenties with no child. He resolved to take her with him on the *Fancy;* women were unlucky on ships, all seagoing men thought this, but he was determined to take her, even if he had to dress her as a boy.

Will returned to Quay House, quietly entering by a rear door from the kitchen garden. He crept up to Sarah who was bread-making, and put his arms around her, kissing her neck.

"Will Adams, ye made me jump and gave me a fright," she scolded him laughing, and spun round to kiss him.

"Where's the Captain?" Will looked around the empty house.

"He's in the garden with the young miss. She's a strange one, eh Will?"

Captain Avery was struggling to cope with Ellie.

"Don't fret so, dear child, soon this will all be over. You'll think kindly on us when you return to your time. Not many have travelled through the spirit world Ellie, it is an unsettling experience."

She shrugged her shoulders. She was fed up now, and wanted to go home very badly. When would all this end? She was close to tears.

Then she had heard a strange noise. It was very faint and in the distance; a thudding noise, regularly beating; a murmur of voices. She looked up to the top of the valley, and there on the horizon she could see, snaking along the hills, a black moving line, banging and thudding and talking. It was the drumbeat of the Infantry marching down from Plymouth – flags waving above their heads, helmets catching the dull light, blinking silver. Ellie gasped in horror.

"The soldiers are coming! The soldiers are coming! Can't you hear them?" She grabbed Captain Avery's arm.

"Come and listen," and she pulled him outside. He could hear it and he nodded,

"'Tis them alright, we've got to get the *Fancy* and sail her out of town before the fighting starts. There's the chance they'll burn her just for a lark. I'm off to get my ship, we'll call for you two maids. Be ready to board when we come alongside here," and he grabbed Will Adams, the two setting off in great haste.

"Sir Cedric is coming back and what he'll say when he sees this place ruined I don't know. Still, 'tis a roof over his head, there's many would long for it. Nothing that money can't mend

232

I'm sure. Now, Will says I'm to dress like you, breeches and hat, so the crew don't throw us overboard for bad luck. Come now," and she linked arms with Ellie, and they set to work organising themselves for sea.

Chapter Thirty-five
Freedom but help from the Woodland is needed to escape

In the closing light of the winter afternoon, the tired little mice struggled to break through the rope holding the two prisoners. Both the boys were alert now, amazed at the birds and mice helping them out of the impending danger. Ping! Ping! Ping! The final threads twisted and severed from each other, as Patrick and Eddie fell against the floor. Both hands and feet were at last unleashed.

"Now for the bolt!" instructed the robin, hardly giving the mice a moment to rest. Isabella and Ferdinand scampered under the door and up the side to the large iron bolt. Ferdinand tried to wedge his walking stick under the handle of the bolt to lever it up straight. They pushed and wiggled it, puffing and panting and finally it lifted into the straight position. Ferdinand, holding the walking stick firmly, dared not to move a muscle.

"Steady, steady," called the robin. "Hold it there. Now Isabella, pull the bolt back while Ferdinand keeps it still. Come on now, pull hard. One big effort! One, two, three!" and Isabella pulled with all her might until the bolt suddenly shot across, causing her to fall backwards and tumble head over heels down onto the muddy grass. Ferdinand's stick also fell down, and the robin and the mouse ran to her side to try to revive her.

"Speak to me Isabella, please!" pleaded the distraught Ferdinand.

Isabella opened one eye. "Did we do it?" she cried out breath-lessly.

"We sure did." Freddie was triumphant.

"Quick, hide! There's someone coming! Sit down Eddie," said Patrick. The two mice and the robin hid behind the sentry box, where Sargasso was also hidden, as two soldiers and the captain approached.

"Oh no, the bolt's open," groaned Eddie, but before they reached the door, a shadow came from above with outstretched wings and dive-bombed the surprised soldiers. Sargasso pecked their hair and went for their eyes, and holding their flailing arms above their heads to shield themselves, the men tried to fend him off. It proved to be a lucky diversion, for gradually the noise of distant drumming, horses, footsteps and shouting reached their ears. They stood still, listening. The sentries sounded the alert at the same time, seeing the terrifying sight of an army on the march, advancing along the hill from the west. The Captain turned white and issued hurried instructions to his men.

"Reinforce the West Wall! All muskets primed and ready! Take cover and alert the castle garrison! We're under attack!"

He momentarily forgot the two boys. Sargasso loaded up his passengers once again, and after consultation with the robin, decided to take them to Quay House, worried that the church and castle would soon be under fire. They would be safe there with Ellie. The mice clung on with hardly the energy to move, while Sargasso flew his precious cargo out of danger. He glimpsed below him several hundreds of men and horses making their way to battle, determined to regain control of their town. He was frightened as he resolutely turned towards his destination.

The two boys unwound the rest of the ropes to free them-selves. Pushing the door open, they crawled up the bank behind

235

their prison, rolling down the other side to the leafy hollows, then crawling behind the nearest thick clusters of tree ivy to hide.

"We'll have to split up, it will confuse them if we are followed," whispered Eddie.

"Let's make for the coast. The woods will be full of soldiers and we're bound to get caught. I don't quite know what we're going to do, but let's try it, shall we?"

He looked at the dirty, dishevelled and exhausted Patrick, nodding for him to agree.

"OK," was all he could manage.

The woodland behind was full of paths all leading in different directions, but they had the advantage – they knew each one. The

Sentry box

sound of the drums was getting nearer and nearer. It was chilling to hear. The thump, thump, thump of marching feet began to echo and shouts got louder. The camp was in uproar above them; people running, calling, horses and supplies being moved, orders yelled, and fear spreading. Captain Francis remembered the words the boy prisoner had spoken to him. "This day will go down in history, sir." How had he known? What manner of boy was this? More importantly, who would win the battle which was now becoming a reality with every second? Maybe the boy knew that too.

"Edwin! Nathan!" he yelled above the noise, "Get here to me!" and the two stout infantrymen, hearing his call, trundled up the bank to his tent.

"Fetch those two dolts we locked up, I want a word with them. Then, after I've finished with them, you can cut out their tongues and string them up." Brutality had become part of the way of life for soldiers in the Civil War; it had brought out the worst in mankind: power, and the misuse of it.

By the time the two men had reached the sentry box the door was swinging open on its hinges. They ran inside cursing and swearing, looking around in disbelief. "They've gone!" they shouted. "Alert the guard! Captain! Captain! Sir, them spies have flown!"

In great anger and determined to catch the two escapees, Nathan and Edwin demanded permission to search for them. Grabbing their helmets and breastplates and some lethal-looking weapons, they were ready.

Captain Francis urged them on, "Bring them back alive mind, I want to talk to them. You can have them later!" he warned his bloodthirsty men, who grinned and nodded.

The robin, who had lodged himself in the ash tree to make sure that Eddie was safe, shook in horror. He could see the boys hidden in the thicket, still making plans. They were about to go their separate ways, but would clearly be seen by the two determined and cruel men who would stop at nothing until they caught them.

The bird felt terror creep into his soul. This was the end. He couldn't save him now – or could he? As Eddie and Patrick clasped each others' hands in a final farewell, with promises of courage and luck, they stooped down low and ran in different directions, trying to keep to the woody cover of the edges of the trees. It was winter however, and no leaves concealed their movements as the trees were thin and bare.

The robin flew like an arrow to the highest point of the Citadel, rousing the buzzards, and showing no fear, for he felt none, he pleaded on Eddie's behalf. He half shouted at them, so great was his anguish.

"You can't let him die, I won't let you! He doesn't deserve it! We've got to overcome this, it's the Spirit of Evil here in our wood! There's going to be killing and bloodshed! Where is your power? Use it now, show your strength if you have any! Where is your courage?"

The robin puffed out his breast and drew himself up to his full size, his eyes sparkling. He was brimming with bravery and vigour, and yet – he was so very small, compared to the greatness of the mighty buzzards, who could have torn him apart with their talons in seconds, crushed and eaten him. Who was this lowly creature daring to call them into question? They stared down at him, only slightly moved by his emotional outburst.

As in all good stories luck was on Freddie's side, and at that precise moment the first foot soldiers, pike men and musketeers arrived within firing range. A loud cry of "Make Ready! Present! Give Fire!" was issued. One shot glanced off a huge tree not far from the buzzards, swiftly followed by another, and a loud crack was heard above their heads. They jumped violently.

238

"Who dares to invade our territory?" the enraged male buzzard demanded.

"This cannot be! Robin, you are right! Release the Power! The time has come!" and he screamed the words of authority over the entire woodland kingdom.

The black rooks fetched the Striking Stone kept buried for many years, and they held it out for the huge bird. Spreading out his wings he struck the Stone three times with his sharp and deadly talons and sparks emitted from the surface in a crackling bright explosion of light. It caught the bark of the pine tree, illuminating it, and the sparks flew from one branch to another, passing to each tree, bush and branch all around the perimeter of the Woodlanders' territory, initiating the incredible Power to all within its boundaries. It was a wonderful sight, like the brightness from a hundred sparklers held on Bonfire Night. The rooks were terrified; nobody had seen the Release of Power before.

At the same time the garrison soldiers, taken by surprise at the swift advance of the loyal soldiers from Plymouth, had gathered their forces, taken control of the situation, lined up in their defensive position and lifted up their spirits for a fight. They took the order to fire from their captain and the battle commenced. The Royalists retaliated, with every man determined to fight to the last, whatever the outcome.

As the power the buzzards had commanded spread, amazing things started to happen; the energy released in the woodland worked its way through the entire population of living things. The trees groaned in their old age as the power flooded them, and slowly and agonisingly they lifted up their roots, and long sinewy outgrowths raised them up several inches, blocking the paths and the woodland byways. Everywhere was now criss-crossed with sharp obstacles, making progress through them extremely difficult.

The trees were old and stiff, and the effort required was a huge one.

The wind shifted to the west and increased its strength, and as the power intensified, the trees swayed together in a wild rhythm, the wind rushing and rumbling through the branches like a faraway train, noisy and wild, rising and peaking in shrieks. The sloe trees guarding the Citadel on both sides crossed their thorns over the pathway and became impenetrable, and the gorse bushes on the top of the hill shuffled together into a thick and thorny barrier. The winter sun broke through the clouds and beamed a ghostly pink and yellow light, casting strong shadows, and an eerie glow appeared in the western sky.

"Look to the boy and the stranger boy," cried the buzzard, who took off from his lofty tree and covered the light of the sun with his great wings.

"We shall save them! Invoke the ancient call to the Woodlanders and the Seafarers! Let the Spirit of the Sea hear us! Let the Skywingers join us too, for it was laid down in the Triumvirate long ago… They are all our allies in times of trouble. Make the sound. Now!"

Every bird and animal found a southerly direction and faced the sea, and in unison called the same double cry of two notes, one high and one low, each in his own voice, and the sound travelled like a horn blast over the land and over the sea and echoed further and further, getting quieter and quieter, until it finally petered out somewhere across the Channel.

Not a living creature failed to hear its haunting notes. Great shoals of fish in the deep, seals and dolphins far away in the cold waters stopped swimming to listen. The two whales embedded in stone at Sugary Cove began to wake. They had been beached there and turned into rocks, waiting for the right time and the summons from the sea. The water washed over them as the tide grew higher, and the white spray stronger, and slowly they regained their living bodies and joined the call from the Spirit of the Sea.

He answered the buzzard's ancient cry and instructed his Seafarers to follow. The sea began churning with returning aquatic creatures, drawn to the coast of Devon by an irresistible tug of nature.

Meanwhile Eddie and Patrick ran for their lives, each in an opposite direction. Both were spotted by the two grisly bloodthirsty soldiers, who called out, excited and thrilled to see their prey.

"There they go!" yelled Edwin. "Let's get them! Give chase Nathan!" and roaring a war cry horrible to hear, they charged over the earthworks into the woods.

Patrick had chosen the lower route which encircled the castle side of the fort, and he followed the path around the front of the camp and down the way he had been dragged up by the horse. Nathan galloped behind him, his heavy armour and pot helmet hampering his speed. The tree roots, groaning, lifted themselves up in one last effort, and managed to trip him up after Patrick had raced through safely. Nathan fell heavily, cursing.

Then small woodland birds flew down and attacked his face, pecking him and drawing blood. He shrieked in pain and rage, flailing his arms about above him. Patrick ran out of the wood at the bottom of the twisty slippery path and found the way down to Sugary Cove. Nathan had clumsily risen to his feet now, and charged on, glimpsing his quarry in the distance. The whales had already left, gliding out to deeper waters as the boy ran for his life, down, down towards the rocky shore.

At the top of the hill the soldiers engaged each other, but the Parliamentarians heavily outnumbered the small contingent of men at the fort. The New Model Army swarmed over the hill, spreading out. As Eddie fled along the top path with Edwin in

241

pursuit he was running towards the advancing army. Soon he would meet them face to face. The sloe bushes parted to let him pass, and then clamped their thorny branches closed so that the soldier, not far behind, was unable to follow him. He shouted in rage. Eddie found himself at the foot of the Citadel, resting breathlessly among the dense undergrowth of brambles, nettle spires, and tree ivy which rose up to hide him, as the men from Plymouth passed by on the grassy hill. He saw the Freedom gate in front of him, and getting up, he climbed over it, ran out of the woodland territory and into the world where none of them could save him.

He was spotted at once by the soldiers who immediately thought he was an escaping deserter from the castle. Edwin had by now hacked his way through the sloe bushes, and wild with anger forced his way out and over the hill, where he came face to face with the invading force. He fought with a soldier in deadly combat, and then another, before escaping down the steep hillside, charging after Eddie who had got away.

"Let him go," shrugged one of the oncoming hoard, indicating Edwin. "He's wounded anyway and can't get far."

Unknown to Edwin, a gash on his leg was bleeding profusely, and he leaked a red and bloody stream onto the grass. He felt giddy and sick but carried on, his determination to catch Eddie a kind of madness. He felt no pain, and he wasn't going to stop until he had cut down the boy who he had hated from his first sighting of him.

Patrick had run himself into a blind ending, chasing down the steps to the beach where he had given no thought to his escape. He was confronted by a roaring sea, crashing waves, and surging foam. He could go no further without certain death, and behind him the huge and enraged body of evil powered down the steps, determined to wring his neck. He was caught on the shores of no return.

Chapter Thirty-six
The *Fancy* sets sail and takes on board two souls
from the sea

Captain Avery and Will Adams sent Tom Edis to round up the men, now eagerly waiting on the quayside at Bayards Cove, one hour from first hearing the news. There was an outbreak of fighting at the top of the hill by St Clements' church, and shouts and cries could be heard spilling down into the town. The news spread like wildfire,

"The soldiers are here! Come to take back the town from the Royalists!"

Quickly and without further delay, it was important to board the ship, and the small bunch of men with all their scanty belongings wrapped in rags made their way to the jetty, weapons at the ready. Captain Avery nimbly ran up the gangplank, overpowered the one remaining member on guard and told his men to search the ship. Once he had the all-clear, he issued his orders and manning the ropes, cast off from the quayside, and letting go the sails, they turned the capstan to draw up the heavy anchor. Grinding, she slowly winched in, and as soon as they were ready the order to make sail was issued, and the smallest man was sent up aloft to keep a lookout. The Master Mate took charge of the chart and the crew swung her round in the river and the *Fancy* was free! Nobody in the town seemed to notice, they were so preoccupied with the turn of events of the day. It was hard work to sail the ship with only ten men, but slowly she made her way down the river.

Will had instructed Sarah to be ready as soon as possible and Ellie, sensibly realising the large ship could not manoeuvre into the creek, fetched the small green boat. Sarah wrapped some bread and cheese in a cloth, and corked some ale in an earthenware bottle. A tapping at the door sent Ellie looking out of the window, but she couldn't see anybody.

"Be very careful Miss," warned Sarah. Ellie opened the door just a chink and saw the seagull with his two weary passengers still clinging to his back.

"Oh my goodness!" she gasped, as the seagull waddled in and the two mice slid down onto the floor, utterly exhausted. Unable to explain the extraordinary situation to Sarah, Ellie decided not to bother; all too difficult under the circumstances. Wide eyed, Sarah shrank back into the darkest depths of the room, shaking her head in disbelief.

"They're free now Ellie," Sargasso told her with delight, breaking his pledge of silence. "I think they got away. All bedlam's broken out everywhere! I heard the Spirit of the Sea, and the buzzards have released the Power. I don't know what will happen now, but I'll have to go –you see we are all called. I am a Seafarer and have work to do. I must guide our friends from the oceans. Take care of the mice, they have worked so very hard – both of them," he added meaningfully.

Sarah by now was in shock and had to sit down. She thought herself ill or dreaming. Ellie picked up both the mice very tenderly, and placed them on a sack in the corner and covered them with her coat.

"I'll let them sleep now," she told the seagull who was anxious to be off. Sargasso knew he must hurry and join his fellow Seafarers who were waiting for him. He had more work to do for the Spirit of the Sea. He left by the same door, cawed farewell, and flew off high up into the sky which was darkening rapidly now.

"Keep a look out for the *Fancy,* Sarah please," Ellie told her, deciding to take charge and be firm with her. Sarah, looking very scared, got up from the table.

"Yes Miss," she stammered. "Are you a witch?" and burst into tears.

"No, of course not you silly girl! Get your things and be ready, come on. Go and look for Will and the *Fancy*. Go on, everything is alright, I promise."

Sarah obeyed, sniffing loudly. She had no sooner got to the window than she called out,

"I see her! She's just coming up the river!"

"Right." Ellie wrapped the mice in her coat, pulled on her hat, and ushered Sarah out of the house, down the iron ladder and into the little green boat. Ellie rowed out to meet the *Fancy* and the crew helped them on board, and tied the boat behind the large ship on a rope.

"Cabin boys eh, Captain? We need a couple that's for sure," laughed Juno McCormack, smacking Ellie's behind and not realising they were girls.

"Umm, get below lads, to my cabin," ordered Captain John quickly, "I'll speak to ye later. Hurry up now, look lively."

The two girls climbed down a hatchway and hid in Captain John's cabin. Ellie carefully placed her coat on the bed with the sleeping mice cocooned inside, blissfully asleep and unaware of anything.

The ship sailed slowly towards the river mouth and the castle. Captain Avery was relying on the fact that both the castles would be too busy fighting off the enemy to bother to pull up the heavy chain which spanned the entrance and could capsize a ship. The whole of the ship's company was alerted to the noise and cries, shots and smoke, which came from the two castle garrisons. The fight was on in earnest.

"We left the town just in time, sir," remarked Will. "Listen to that, poor beggars, they don't stand a chance. Our colours will be flying above the castle before nightfall." He was greatly satisfied. What are your orders, Capt'n?"

"I wish the *Fancy* to anchor off, just out of range of the cannons."

"What, here sir?" a puzzled reply came.

"Yes. I've got a debt to pay, unfinished business, you might say."

"Aye aye, sir," said loyal trusting Will, and he set about telling the crew their duties. There were only two hours of daylight left at the very most, and a waning moon to see by.

Ellie sat wondering and worrying about Eddie; she had missed him so. What had happened to the boys? The ship slowed down, and she peeped out to see where they were – right in the middle of the bay, but well out of range of the gunfire. The wind seemed to be increasing, as they reached the open waters of the sea, and she felt a rocking motion as waves lifted them up and down. Captain John appeared in the doorway, looking tired and anxious. He beckoned to her. Sarah had fallen asleep on the built-in cot-type bed, alongside the two mice wrapped in the coat. Ellie put her finger to her mouth,

"Shhh, don't wake her." She tiptoed out of the cabin and made her way to the deck. Captain John pointed to the shore, and Ellie could see clashing swords, men running in all directions, smoke and flames and she could hear screams, shouts and horses whinnying. It seemed very frightening, and her heart sank.

"What do you think has happened to Eddie?" she asked in a very small voice. She didn't really want to hear the answer.

Captain John squared up to her, put his hands on both her shoulders, looked into her eyes, and said quietly, "I cannot tell lass, maybe we should prepare for the worst."

Ellie shook her head, "No, no! I won't listen! You said you'd save them! Go and do it!"

He looked away ashamed, watching the horrors of war as a bystander, helpless. He fixed his gaze on the twin castles and the river. For once in his life he didn't know what to do. He prayed for help, from his heart. "Dear God show me what to do! I don't want the lads to die! Give me a sign!" They both stood in silence, unable to move. Then Ellie pointed to the castle.

"Look! Look!" and as they watched, over the castellated top of the battlements of Dartmouth Castle, a blue flag was being hoisted. Slowly it reached the top of the flagpole and spread itself out in the stormy wind. It was the colours of the Parliament Army, with a church on it!

"They've taken the castle!" gasped Captain John. "They've surrendered!" At Kingswear Castle, accompanied by a loud cheer, the same flag unfurled itself, flapping its bright colours in the breeze.

"Launch the cutter!" shouted the Captain, springing into action, "Will, Tom, Juno, come with me!" They prepared to leave the ship. "Ned Burrows, you're in charge," he barked at the Master Mate,

"Aye aye, sir," was his ardent reply, grinning with pleasure.

It was no easy matter. The wind and the tide were rising fast and a storm seemed to be brewing from every direction. Flights of birds circled in the distance high above the hillside in great black flocks as the small craft was tossed in the bouncing waves. The men found it hard to row.

"Where to, sir?" asked Will, trying to steer in the choppy waters.

"Wherever we can make shore," was the answer.

Shoals of fishes never seen in the coastal waters before arrived in unceasing, constantly changing swirling groups, and dolphins jumped and dived in great numbers. The two huge whales circled some way off the shore, waiting and watching, their bodies undulating black and shiny. The seals from under the Trip Trap bridge went to join them, to guide their way.

Eddie ran down the hill towards the sea, climbed over the stile, and stumbled down the narrow rocky steps to the coastal edge, with its clefts and grassy tussocks, where spumes of white spray exploded over the rocks with great crashes. He was exhausted and breathless. He stopped for a minute, and looking out to the raging ocean he saw the big ship anchored in the bay beyond him. He stretched out both his arms and called out desperately, "Won't somebody help me? Please!"

The Spirit of the Sea was ready to answer his pleadings. As the lumbering and now-tiring Edwin doggedly followed Eddie to the shoreline, Sargasso flew down leading a formation of seagulls and sea birds who dive-bombed him. Next, a battalion of black cormorants shot through the air like missiles fired, striking the soldier in the chest with their beaks and knocking him sprawling into the rocky crannies.

"Godsooth, I'll never get that devil's spawn!" he cried out, winded, suffering more attacks by the birds, trying to defend himself with his sword.

The whales, instructed by Sargasso, turned and faced the shore, looking for the boy who was by now limping towards the Trip Trap bridge, hardly moving from exhaustion. Edging towards the rocks, the whales raised their tails and beat the water with them, causing huge green tidal waves to swell and move slowly towards the shoreline. Eddie struggled to cross the bridge just before a tumultuous shower of green water flooded and swamped everything. He clung on to the bridge, and Edwin tried to follow but was washed back into the huge surges of water. He disappeared in a frenzy of oaths and cries, under the gushing foaming waves.

Eddie watched, horrified, gripping on for dear life. The two seals popped up in the rocky inlet, with their kind faces and big eyes.

"Come to us," they called to Eddie, "Come to us, us, us."

In the midst of the hissing and crashing water, Eddie climbed down the gully, and putting one tired leg over a seal's back, he sat on the grey slippery creature, swimming with its mate out into the sea to meet the whales, who had ceased churning their tails.

"Thank you! Thank you!" Eddie gasped as he shivered and shook, holding on as best he could. Sargasso watching above him was delighted and thrilled at his rescue.

At the water's edge of Sugary Cove, Patrick looked around him. There was no escape. *I'd rather drown trying to get away than be killed by him.*

Without a second thought, he launched himself into the plunging waves which crashed over his head. Nathan screamed in rage, but he wasn't going to follow. He watched in furious frustration at the boy being swept out to sea. He had so nearly caught him. "Well, he'll perish in the water that's for sure," he thought with great satisfaction.

Moments later a great shoal of silver fish emerged from the water, knocking him off his feet and pushing him into the roaring and foaming green waters. He did not reappear; he had been suffocated by the mass of fish which prevented him surfacing.

Patrick's head came up and he struggled bravely in the crashing water. He was a good swimmer, but it was impossible in the heavy seas which engulfed him. The Spirit of the Sea called to the dolphins, and they raced to the edge of the cove, leaping in excitement. The lead dolphin, Doryana, dived underneath Patrick, lifting him high out of the water so that he could breathe again. He coughed and spluttered, and then, realising what was

happening, clambered somehow onto the dolphin's back and was carried away, the others following.

Seeing that both the boys had been delivered from certain death and were safe with the Seafarers, the Spirit of the Sea called his subjects back, and bid the waves and the wind to be calm once more. Both boys saw the small cutter ahead, and pointed to the dolphins and the seals. They shouted to each other, laughing in delight, as they flew through the water on the backs of their incredible rescuers.

The small boat with the brave sailors had almost capsized, the crew believing their last hour had come. They were unable to reach land and had wallowed hopelessly in the peaks and troughs of the wild swell. Now the wind had dropped, calmness seemed to spread over the surface and they felt themselves at last in charge of the boat once more. Looking now towards the shore they were filled with fear as the huge shape of an advancing whale could be seen. Gripping each other, certain of drowning in its wake, they saw another one outlined on the sea.

"Sweet Jesus, help us and save us!" called out Captain John. "Hold on men, do not jump! Stay where you are!"

His voice boomed at them and they obeyed in fright. Slowly the whales glided towards them and came closer, as the sea state became glassy and smooth. Then Captain Avery spotted the boy crouching down on the back of the seal, beside the giant creatures from the deep.

"Praise the Lord!" he cried, "It's the boy."

Tears flooded his eyes and streamed down his face. The crew were transfixed in utter bewilderment, believing themselves to be at death's door. Their Captain rallied, and Eddie was transferred to the boat, and patting the back of the black and grey seal, he whispered his thanks humbly and quietly. The two accompanying whales arched their backs and swimming at incredible speed out to deeper parts of the ocean, blew great spouts of water as if to say goodbye, and disappeared out onto the horizon.

The fun wasn't over yet, as the school of dolphins approached the cutter next, carrying the other boy. Patrick was discharged into waiting arms and pulled on board, lifted up the boarding ladder in his exhaustion. The dolphins clicked to each other and nuzzled the wooden sides of the boat. Patrick touched Doryana's nose and whispered his grateful thanks. They too left them, jumping and somersaulting in one last display as they headed off towards the south.

The two boys were welcomed onto the boat with hugs and shouts and draped in someone else's clothes for warmth.

"Come, come," ushered Captain John, and the boys were carried to his cabin.

"Bring hot broth," he ordered. Inside the small room, Eddie, Patrick and Ellie were reunited to tears, squeals and hysterical laughter after many hours of a frightening ordeal. No one could imagine how terrible it had been. A knock on the door brought Will with the bowls of broth, and seeing his wife waking up in confusion and rather terrified, he led her by the hand to his own cabin and held her close once more. The three youngsters were alone again, and wrapped up in the bedcovers, they drank the steaming broth next to the still-sleeping mice.

"I've got to sleep," groaned Eddie

"Me too," yawned Patrick,

"And me," added Ellie, and they all crashed down on the tiny bed and fell asleep in seconds. They had been saved by the bravery of a tiny robin, two little mice and the loyalty of a seagull. Captain Avery put his head around the door and smiled. He tiptoed away quietly, a very happy man.

Chapter Thirty-seven
A sad farewell and return to the present day

At dawn the next day the clamour of battle had ceased and a thick foggy cloud of billowing white mist had settled over the river and the sea. It was peaceful and still and the whole world seemed to be resting. The woods were silent, not a bird made a single sound. All the participants of the great event had resumed their natural status; the release of power had exhausted everything. Serenity and peace had returned.

The Spirit of the Sea congratulated his loyal subjects on their most excellent execution of his orders, but insisted that the whales, Hercules and Hector, return to their place on the rocky shore and be reinstated as landmarks guarding the cove. For who could tell when their presence would be required again? They had no choice but to agree, and as they enjoyed their lives as silent guardians, lazing on the South West coast, winter and summer, they were happy. Proudly they returned, looking just like two large rocks embedded in the shingle at Sugary Cove.

Sargasso, the real hero of the day, was quietly modest and disliked the congratulations continually heaped upon him. He was anxious to return home even though his fellow brothers and sisters of the sea were enjoying an impromptu reunion. Sometimes on the farthest tip of Land's End, where the Gulf Stream surges, they met for a special audience with the Spirit of the Sea.

"You may leave," commanded the Great Spirit. "Just one word of interest to you: did you know that in the Great Scrolls of Tidings it tells us that if a soul that has drowned, his spirit may find its way back through the oceans, from time to time? … But only if he has come to us from a watery death in the deep. Keep this knowledge and remember." And the Spirit of the Sea rolled out of sight with his accompanying white horses, and disappeared. Sargasso, the seals, Solomon and Bathsheba, and the dolphins, Doryana and Diadem, all swam back through the wintry seas to Devon.

On board the *Fancy*, Captain Avery slept on and off in the Master Mate's cabin, his conscience troubling him greatly. He was relieved that the boys had returned, but knew that it was not of his doing; he had been a bystander, and had only helped at the end.

The three children had woken early, discovering Ferdinand and Isabella sleeping alongside them, nestled in their coat-bed dreamily. Ellie explained that she had picked them up when she left Sir Cedric's house and that it had not been safe at the church anymore.

"It wasn't safe anywhere," said Eddie. "Now, how are we going to get back?"

Patrick and Ellie had been wondering that too, they were all desperate to return to their own century. They heard a knock and Captain Avery stepped into the cabin.

"And a good morning it is," he greeted them. "Come, look, the mist will lift soon."

The three climbed up to the top deck and peered out. The thick white cotton wool of fog had spread like a fluffy blanket all the way from the sea to the town.

"You must leave me before the sun breaks through," Captain John told them urgently. "The Time mechanism is reversing, I feel it! Hurry! I have just time to deliver you home. We must each return to our own place, in our own time."

"What about the mice?" asked Ellie.

"They have been outside their spirit home for too long. They will return with me," Captain John told her firmly. "It is best, don't you see?"

Ellie swallowed back her tears and gulped.

"I suppose so," she reluctantly agreed.

He put his arm around her. "Nothing is forever child, nothing."

As Eddie began thinking about saying goodbye and parting forever, he remembered the medallion. He felt for the string on his neck, but it was gone. When had he lost it? Where was it now? It was a long time since he had used it. He began to worry. Didn't Captain Avery need it to get back? He seemed so sure he was going soon. And now he had all these other people: Sarah, Will, Tom, Juno, Ned, and the rest plus a large ship. What was he going to do?

"Let us go," urged the Captain and he hurried them into the green boat.

"I want you to show them the... *engine,*" he whispered to Eddie. Eddie grinned in reply and Patrick nodded in glee.

"Just watch," he told his crew who all looked over the side curiously. Eddie was overjoyed to see his little green boat again. He proudly pulled the ripcord and as the engine roared into life, the men watching from above jumped in surprise and murmured to each other in amazement, as Eddie steered round in a circle and headed towards the river, leaving a foaming wake behind them.

"It's the work of the Devil!" gasped Ned.

"It's better than rowing," laughed Will. They watched incredulously as the tiny craft buzzed along and disappeared from sight in the thick mist. Syracuse the dog, who had accompanied them, began to whine and tremble and Captain John, feeling tired and weak, wondered what was going to happen. He slumped listlessly in the stern.

"It is too late," he groaned, "the time is here, you must take me back."

Eddie and Patrick looked anxiously at each other as they entered Warfleet Creek, and Ellie could see that the house where she and Sarah had become such good friends had gone and the lime kilns had returned. Eddie swung the boat around in a tight circle and steered back out of the creek and up the river, still engulfed in thick white mist.

"Hurry!" gasped Captain John and away they went. He looked at the pink cottage one last time.

"I must make confession. I went unshriven to the spirit world, but you can hear my story now. You must!" He squeezed the words out breathlessly. "I was a pirate, selfish and greedy. I have taken too much from the world. I know now it means nothing, nothing. I beg for forgiveness. Do you understand? Although my real name is John Avery, I was known as Long Ben, and feared for my black deeds. I stole a ship and her treasure from an Indian Mogul with 200,000 pieces of gold and silver, and many diamonds. I am a liar and a cheat. Yes!" He put his hand up as the children protested.

"No, no, of course you're not! We know what you've done."

"Let me finish," he urged in a croaking voice. "I swindled my friends and sailed the seas from Madagascar and the Caribbean, to Boston in Massachusetts, and ended up here back in England.

I entrusted my treasure to a wily fellow in the London banks, and he in turn cheated me. I lost everything. I am so truly sorry now… Say I am forgiven, say it before I go," he urged them pitifully.

"We forgive you," the three youngsters said anxiously together.

"But you've helped us and been our friend, – you've saved us!" blurted out Eddie sincerely and fiercely, near to tears.

" Yes, yes you did!" agreed the other two.

"Maybe God will have mercy on me now," sighed the tired and weary seafarer, patting his dog. He had made his confession and maybe now he would rest in peace.

The *Fancy* came into view and the crew helped their captain unsteadily climb the ladder and haul up the dog behind him. He turned at the top and shouted,

"The gold medallion! Where is it Eddie?"

"I don't know." Eddie shook his head. "It may be in the sea, I can't even remember the last time I saw it. I'm sorry."

Sargasso flew from the top mast where he was perched and called loudly,

"The sun! The sun!"

"We must go," called Eddie.

"Good luck and goodbye where ever it is you go to. I wish I could come with you for a voyage of adventure."

"Look after Ferdinand and Isabella won't you?" shouted Ellie.

"Goodbye Sarah, Goodbye Captain John!"

With that Sarah appeared over the ship's side, the two mice in her hands. Isabella waved her hanky and Ferdinand shook his stick. Patrick called his goodbyes too and the sun began to pierce the mist. They turned the little boat and waving frantically, headed towards the castle, looming large now as everything became clearer.

The café was there and the car park, the battlements had shrunk, and the flag of English Heritage was flying over the castle again. The mist thinned even more and they felt the warmth of the sun. Looking back they could see nothing, just the faint mist rising out of the murky flat grey ocean, rippling rhythmically. The day began again, cool and bright, the sun trying to break through to raise the wintry temperature. It felt so very strange, sad and lonely and yet happy that the fears and stresses of the last few days were over. It was a very mixed and muddled feeling.

"We'll have to go back home now," suggested Patrick, "What are we going to tell them?"

"Heaven knows." The other two shook their heads, and made faces of dread.

"I've still got the key in my pocket," shouted Eddie suddenly, "the key to the tower, shall we go up and wave goodbye?"

"Yes, yes! Let's hurry!"

"Just tie the boat up down by the battlements," suggested Patrick. "It will save time."

So finding an old ring in the wall, he threaded the rope through. They jumped out of the boat and chased up the path, so eager to glimpse the Fancy once more. Eddie reached the door first, and fumbling, for he was in such a rush, eventually opened the door. They dashed through the kitchen, opened the tower door, and met Sargasso and Freddie at the top. The Moonmirror and the crystal signaller were both exactly where they had left them; it seemed so long ago now.

"We could signal to them one last time!" Patrick yelled.

As the mist dissolved, a line of puffy grey cloud had spread across the sky occluding the sun – but now, a slit had appeared in the greyness, and brightness shone through. A great arc of light directed rays down upon the water. The sea changed colour in

this large illuminated pool of light, glistening gold on the surface. The sun had come up out of the clouds to greet the Fancy. The hazy dark shape of the ship could be seen, sails aloft.

"There she is! There she is!" shouted Ellie jumping up and down. Eddie turned on the light of his Moonmirror and Patrick switched on the coloured lights of the crystal signaller both at the same time, and the lights shone brightly out over the water.

"Do you think they can see it?" they asked each other hopefully.

"I'm sure they can," comforted Ellie, staring out into the brightness.

On the deck of the *Fancy,* the whole ships' company, the Captain, Sarah and the two mice, blinked at the wonderful lights.

"I am content now," the Captain told Will. "Those boys, that little maid, they have made me very happy. That light is a wondrous thing they have made, but I'm best here with my own kind. Raise the anchor lads, we're off now. Ring the bell Sarah. Say goodbye."

She took hold of the ship's bellrope and clanged a loud ring several times. The ring echoed over the river, over the seas and oceans, and the Spirit of the Sea nodded wisely and with satisfaction.

"It is all over now," he whispered.

Eddie and Ellie and Patrick hugged each other,

"He saw it! He saw it! He really did!" and the *Fancy* quietly faded from sight, dimming, dimming, sinking below the waves until it could be seen no longer. They had gone to rest in a watery grave deep below in the bottomless ocean. Down, down it went to join the hundreds of seafarers who had descended before them, and who rolled eternally in the tides and oceans all around the world.

The three stood staring, not speaking, scanning the empty sea, watching the sun shining on the circle of water. They were transfixed, not wanting somehow to return to reality. The Universe Reverse Process had triggered back to normal, the earth travelled away from the moon, their paths due to cross some other time, predicted by astronomers. The children were firmly back in their own time, and a boat hooted, an aeroplane soared overhead, and a van drew up at the castle car park to prove it.

"Come on, we'd better go home to George's," said Patrick eventually. "It's too early for him to be open yet at the café."

"Let's leave the equipment here in the boxes," suggested Eddie reluctantly, somehow disinterested in his experiment now. They packed them away quickly and left the tower.

"What are we going to tell them?" Ellie's worried face gave away her anxiety.

"How many days have we been gone exactly?" Eddie wondered out loud.

"I've lost count," replied Patrick." Oh… let's just wait and see – we can't possibly begin to tell all that's happened. I can hardly believe it myself." He was tired and unsure of what to do for once.

They locked the café door and walked along the familiar path and down the short cut to the Old Bath House. Ellie tried not to look back at the church. Approaching the kitchen door, they could hear pots and pans clattering inside.

"Now we're for it." Eddie took a deep breath and opened the door a little.

"Bridget," he said seeing the dear old lady preparing breakfast in her tartan dressing gown and sheepskin slippers.

"Been out for an early morning sail in that little boat of yours, have you?" She smiled at them unperturbed, and continued, "George is still in bed, so don't wake him. He's had a terrible night with the toothache. Doctor's been here, I hope he didn't disturb you. I told him to be very quiet, those painkillers knocked him out. Just as well, he did complain so, poor man. Now, bacon and eggs alright? Tea, coffee? I expect you're starving."

Surprised by Bridget's reaction, which was one of complete normality, it dawned on the three youngsters that according to Bridget, they had been in bed and got up early for a sail. So that must mean they had only been gone for one night in their time. That made it all much easier. They were so relieved, no awkward explanations were necessary. Patrick and Eddie remembered back to the night they disappeared, and recalled George's toothache and his going back home. It seemed an eternity ago.

Feeling quite dizzy with relief, they sat in the kitchen drinking mugs of tea and tucked into a huge Bridget-style breakfast. The worry and fears they had suffered began to slip away from them and they felt safe again, and yet… none of them would ever be the same. It had been too profound an experience. They had now lost the friendship of Captain John and the amusing pair they had befriended and looked after, those infuriating but dear little mice.

Bridget took George a bowl of porridge and a cup of tea on a tray.

"What shall we do now?" asked Ellie rather gloomily, twiddling her teaspoon idly in the tea.

"Well, I'm going to have a bath, change my smelly clothes, and go back exactly where we have been, to see if it was real or not. Or did we fall asleep somewhere and dream it all?" asked Eddie, not quite sure now.

"I'll come with you," Patrick said immediately.

"And me," added Ellie, looking bright again. "I can show you where I was while you were locked up. You'll never believe it."

So determined to relive the experiences, they cleared up after breakfast and went off to the bathrooms for a good scrub.

Chapter Thirty-eight
Reunited and wise words of advice

Poor ailing George called out to them as they emerged an hour later, washed, dressed, and refreshed by a glorious soak in the bath. They popped their heads round his bedroom door.

"Hi George, how are you?" three voices asked.

"Not good I'm afraid. Bridget's driving me down to the dentist later. Now, how did it go last night? I'm so sorry I had to leave you. Were you pleased with it all?"

He struggled to sit up in his bright blue pyjamas.

"It was great." Patrick was very enthusiastic. "When the power had charged everything up, they both did give some light, and it was really good fun."

Eddie looked at Patrick and flicked his eyes at him. Nobody in their right mind could call what they had been through 'fun'.

"How about today? What's on the programme?"

"We're going for a long walk I think," Ellie told him. "That's all, just a quiet day." She smiled reassuringly.

"Very nice too," the old man agreed. "I'd better shake a leg and get myself up." He tried to smile at them, which caused his mouth to hurt even more.

Up they went to the kitchen where Bridget was putting crumbs out onto the garden bird table.

"There's a dear little robin here. He's so tame." She was delighted.

"We've got one at home like that," said Ellie, knowing very well that it was Freddie.

"Do you want us to open the tea shop for you today, if you're taking George to the dentist?"

"No dear, that's very kind of you but Ingrid from Above Town will help me out. She likes to help, she's in my knitting circle you know. How is your lovely red scarf coming on Ellie?"

"Not very well," she admitted.

"We'll sit down this evening and do some, shall we? You young ones get a good film and we'll have a cosy evening indoors. George will like that."

"So will we." The thought of it was bliss to Ellie. "That's very nice, Bridget."

Bridget went to phone the dentist and verify George's appointment. The three youngsters fetched coats and money, and Ellie noticed her jacket was missing.

"I've left it on the Fancy – I wrapped Isabella and Ferdinand in it, I remember now. Blast, I've lost that for good."

"Mum won't like that," Eddie told her, suddenly thinking of his parents far away. At the mention of the two mice, Ellie felt so very sad, and bit her lip.

"I'm never going to see them again now. The church will be so empty and boring."

Eddie and Patrick could see she was getting upset.

"There's nothing we can do Ellie. They had to go back. Come on now, where shall we start? I want to retrace my steps, and Ellie you can show us yours. It will be very interesting, before we forget."

Patrick ushered them out. Everyone was a bit touchy today: tired, bored, depressed, bewildered, all these feelings had been bottled up and shaken around. No adventure could match what they had experienced – to see the world as it used to be, to live in part of history, especially one which changed the course of events, like the end of the Civil War. Maybe as they forgot it would be easier.

"Shall we start at the church Ellie?" he asked her cautiously. "Then we can walk all the way round."

"Of course, we don't want to miss anything, let's go!"

***

It was a typically cold day in autumn, bare trees, grey clouds, and green-grey water. The early sun had vanished, making it cool and breezy. The churchyard was scattered with dead leaves, and a small car stood parked nearby as the three arrived at the church in the first step towards their reconstruction of the strange events.

"Oh, there's someone here."

Ellie noticed it was the vicar's car. Outside the door, against the stone edges of the grass, several wisps of straw were lodged, and along the gully some tiny grains of wheat were caught in the cracks.

"Look!" Eddie was triumphant. "Straw and bits of grain. How did that get here? It's got to have been blown from inside – the grain store."

The others looked carefully. He was right. When they opened the big black door and went inside, they found the vicar and the church architect prowling around, both holding a notebook and a clipboard, and making notes, scribbling furiously.

"Ah, good morning," greeted the vicar heartily. "Always pleased to see you youngsters. We're having a good look round today, we're thinking of opening a bookshop here in the church and I'm trying to find just the right spot. What do you think, eh? I think, or rather, we think, the choir vestry would be an admirable spot, it's hardly used and the old flower arranging cupboard can be pulled out. We'll find them somewhere else, don't worry. Don't want your mother up in arms do we?" He laughed nervously.

"We've come to buy some postcards," Patrick announced.

"Capital, capital. Now please excuse us." He turned to resume his discussions with an impatient and busy architect. Purchasing several cards and putting the money in the wall safe, the three youngsters left hurriedly.

Ellie was bursting. "My goodness, what an escape for Ferdinand and Isabella! They'd have been discovered and evicted."

"There. I told you so. See? Wait till I tell Mother, she'll be furious. She loves that old panelled wall, it's part of the old gallery that was removed," Eddie chuckled.

They moved on up to the castle, the tea shop, and the car park.

"All this," Patrick explained, arms outstretched, "was a huge camp. We tried to escape from the guard room – which was the café – and two great big pike men caught us. They were horrible."

He shuddered, remembering their broken teeth and bad smell.

"What happened then?" asked Ellie horrified.

"They tied us up, hands and feet, and we were roped to a horse and dragged up here … I think? But I don't remember the steps."

He frowned. They walked to the top of the steps and immediately a path opposite them, across the road caught his eye. "That's it, there wasn't a road then."

He pointed and they followed the small narrow path which wound up through woodland carpeted with leaves, bordered by ferns and mossy stumps. It came out at the top of Gallants Bower, at the foot of the Earthworks. The view was spectacular over the rocky cliffs and the huge sea beyond.

"This is where the camp was, all in here."

Patrick ran on ahead and spread his arms out again, gesturing.

"All this was full of soldiers and tents and fires and horses."

The other two followed breathlessly, climbing up on to the grassy remains. It all looked so peaceful and quiet. Eddie ran all over it, searching. In the centre was a large black circle, the remains of a huge fire; the ash and some unburnt wood remained. He put his finger into the ash. "Ouch! It's still hot!"

He looked around for a stick and poked the embers.

"Is it really?" asked Patrick, excited. Eddie nodded.

"You know I've lost the medallion don't you?" he told the other two.

"I can't even remember where I had it last. It's just completely vanished. Maybe, just the chance, I'll find it here."

Patrick disappeared over one of the earthed-up hills and called, "Up here!"

The two scrambled after him and in front of them, tucked into a grassy bank was the stone remains of a small hut.

"This is it. This is where we were kept prisoners isn't it Eddie?"

Eddie looked at the broken down stone walls, the door was missing, the roof gone.

"I suppose it must be. It's so small and it's all overgrown."

He picked up a stick and entered the remains of the sentry box. He dug with the pointed sharp end, poking around and lifting clods of grass. Patrick and Ellie sat down, looking all around them, idly eating a piece of grass each.

They stared out across the sea, watching the ripple and the roll of the waves. Talking about what had happened seemed to make them all feel better.

"Hey! Come here! Look what I've found!" shouted Eddie behind them. "You won't believe it!" As they turned around, Eddie stood with shining eyes holding up a muddy object.

"Look! It's my penknife, Patrick. Remember? That proves we were here, doesn't it?" He ran across the grass to them, eager to show his find. It was conclusive proof that they had been prisoners in that very hut, even though now it had disintegrated and fallen down.

"Oh, I thought you had found the gold medallion," sighed a disappointed Ellie.

"No, unfortunately. Still, there's time yet, we may be lucky. We found my knife."

He and Patrick felt very satisfied. It really had happened.

"How did you get away?" asked Ellie, sitting down again to nibble yet another piece of grass.

"Well, the two mice chewed and chewed to break the ropes, they really did give it everything, and when they were through and we broke free, they climbed up and pushed open the bolt. Isabella was fantastic. She fell right off the door onto the ground about three feet and winded herself. Then the soldiers came and

Soldiers camp with remains of sentry box

268

just as they were about to discover the open door, Sargasso attacked them. Then the soldiers from Plymouth drummed and shouted in the distance, just over that hill," he pointed towards Little Dartmouth, "and we took the opportunity to escape."

"Yes, and we both went in different directions," continued Patrick. "But those two pike men saw us and chased us. I was terrified; I thought he'd kill me! I ran and ran and came down to Sugary Cove, but I was trapped. I had to dive into the sea, I had no option."

"How brave," Ellie told him admiringly.

"Not really, it was that or let him catch me! Then two dolphins picked me up and I rode on one of their backs out to sea, where Captain Avery was waiting for me. It was wonderful! It seems so unreal now."

"And I hid at the top of the hill thinking I'd miss the soldiers," continued Eddie, getting excited, "and made a break for it over the five bar gate, but he saw me and fought a couple of Parliamentarians to get at me. He was drowned down by the Trip Trap bridge, in a huge tidal wave made by two whales. It was awful I suppose, to watch somebody drowning. Then I was rescued by the seals and they swam me out to Captain John as well. Patrick and I were brought to the *Fancy*, it was incredibly exciting."

Eddie lay back on the grass. "I wouldn't want to do it again. Just too much for me. I don't want to be that scared ever again."

"Nor me," laughed Patrick.

They lay in the cold grass, on a freezing morning, glad to be alive. Ellie thought to herself how the tiny mice had been the real heroes. She was now glad that they had gone back with Captain John. She hoped they would be happy wherever they were, in a new life or an old life, she wasn't sure which.

"Come on." She pulled them both up to their feet. "Now you can hear my story," and they shook the grass off their clothes and

269

she led them away down through the woods. They passed their empty house and continued down by the creek.

"Here there were farms and little cottages, and right at the bottom where the old quay is, that's where I went with Captain Avery. It was Sir Cedric Mortlock's house. Can you see the old ladder?"

They stood on the shingly shore. The tide was out.

"Come on," said Ellie, "let's go over. The house is empty. Sir Cedric's house was down at the bottom, where the garden is now. I want to go and stand there again."

"Do you think we should?" Patrick wasn't so sure.

"It will be OK, just for a minute."

Eddie wasn't the slightest bit worried; he was back on familiar territory, his beloved creek. He knew every inch of it, or so he thought. They crunched over the beach to the sandy grey-brown edge and stood at the foot of the wall.

"This was the quayside, and those lime kilns, well, they just weren't there."

Ellie pointed to all the usual landmarks in place again. They climbed up the old ladder, still firmly fastened, and stood in the garden. "This was the house," stretching out her arms and running along. "This bit was an orchard where the chickens and the cow were."

Ellie stopped suddenly and looked down. She put her hand up to her mouth and gasped.

"What? What is it? What's the matter?" The two boys ran up beside her.

"Look!" she pointed to the ground, where stretched out on four neatly tied sticks joined onto a framework was a rabbit skin.

"Will brought that home for Sarah, and we put it in the stew," Ellie told them, catching her bottom lip with her teeth and shaking her head in disbelief.

"Why are you surprised Ellie?" Patrick questioned her. "We keep seeing proof that it did happen and we were there. How much more do you need?"

"I still can't seem to believe it," she replied.

Eddie explored the garden further, his interest aroused, and he darted backwards and forewords, searching in the grass, but nothing else could be found. A voice called to them.

"I say, what are you doing in my garden?"

The three startled youngsters looked up to see where the voice was coming from, and they saw an elderly lady with white hair standing on the terrace above them looking down. She held a walking stick in her hand and she was pointing at them with the tip.

"Is that you Patrick?" she called, "I can't quite make you out."

It was Mrs Finch-Ingram, the lady he had befriended on the train from London. Patrick looked up and smiled.

"Hello Mrs Finch-Ingram, yes it's me I'm afraid. We thought the house was empty. I'm sorry. I hope you don't mind, we just wanted to sit on the quayside for a minute." He babbled on.

"Come up here, I can't see you properly, and bring your friends," she ordered him.

They had no choice but to follow the garden path through the shrubs to the old lady who had sat down, a large tabby cat entwined in her feet.

"You are trespassing you know," she chided them. At their obvious embarrassment she suddenly smiled broadly and laughed, "Didn't think you'd get caught did you? Now come and have a glass of lemonade and tell me all about yourselves," and she invited them to sit down.

"Stanley?" she called. "Stanley, where are you? I've got guests."

A small thin man appeared, dressed in a black suit.

"Yes, Mrs Finch-Ingram?" he asked anxiously wringing his

hands together. "What can I get you madam?"

"Three lemonades and a large gin and tonic," she ordered "And don't be all day about it."

"Yes madam," he replied and hurried off at once into the house.

"He was my late husband's batman," Mrs Finch-Ingram explained, smiling sweetly. "Somebody had to employ him."

The three youngsters sat politely waiting, not quite knowing what to do. Stanley brought a silver tray and handed out the drinks.

"Now," she said, "tell me what you have been doing."

Without any hesitation and without knowing why, they told her everything. She sat quietly listening, paying great attention. It took a long time, but she did not interrupt once. Her bright eyes and quick brain absorbed every detail, and she seemed to understand. At last they had finished – the whole story had rushed out like a river.

"Well, well, well!" the old lady said, smiling at them all. "You have been having an exciting time! And now it's all over I expect you're feeling a little flat. Is that right?"

They all nodded, wondering how she knew.

"In my experience life is constantly full of either thrilling adventures or humdrum everyday existence, and one is always changing into the other. You need the quiet times to recover from the exciting ones. -But, mark my words, a new adventure is always, always just around the corner, you just don't know it's there. So cheer up and carry on and it will come and find you when it's ready. You wait and see! Chin chin!" and she lifted her glass and toasted them.

"Chin chin!" they replied, laughing.

"Sir Cedric Matlock lived a long and happy life here and I've tried to preserve the quay for posterity. I am always finding

272

things in my garden that Stanley digs up. Why, only yesterday he brought me an old pewter pot – lost its handle of course, and Piper found some rabbit bones didn't you, you naughty cat." She bent down stiffly to stroke the large cat sitting quietly beneath her feet. Ellie didn't need to see the pot; she already knew it was the one Captain Avery had drunk his ale from. They seemed to have been able to tell the old lady everything without the fear of being ridiculed or challenged. She had been wonderful and they felt at ease and comfortable sitting in the weak sunshine. They sat quietly, watching the wading birds and gulls on the beach.

"And now I must go back inside." Mrs Finch-Ingram rose unsteadily to her feet, her silver-topped walking stick supporting her.

"Come along Piper," and the cat obediently got up too.

"So nice to see you again Patrick. Off you go now, you young people have plenty to do I'm sure. Just look after the creek when I'm gone – it's the most beautiful place in the whole of Devon," she said, beaming at all three of them. "Goodbye."

The two boys and the girl stood up as the old lady slowly made her way up the paved pathway. They watched her disappear, looking at her shadow and then the empty path. They all sighed, looked at each other and said, "Shall we go?"

They made their way to the quayside and the iron ladder and climbed down to the beach. They had a lot to think about. Everything Mrs Finch-Ingram had said was probably true. They felt much better and much brighter.

"We're going to have a cosy quiet night by the fire with my knitting and a film," giggled Ellie. "Is that humdrum enough for you?"

"Oh yes," laughed Patrick, "that will be perfect." Things were almost back to normal..

Later that evening the phone gave a loud ring making everyone jump.

"I'll go," insisted Eddie and jumped to his feet from the great squashy sofa beside the fire.

"Hello Dad!" he said brightly and a long conversation ensued. Ellie got up and waited by Eddie for her turn. Eventually she got her chance, and chatted away, finally saying her goodbyes. Both the children were very pleased to have spoken to their parents; they had almost forgotten about them.

"Well?" said Bridget.

"Oh, they're having a wonderful time. Mum won some money at the Casino in Estoril. The NATO exercise has finished and they're all going on leave. Mum and Dad are flying back together and the ship is staying in Lisbon. They will be back in four days."

"Good, good, that all sounds just fine," said George, beaming from his armchair. He was slowly recovering from his painful ordeal at the dentist.

Patrick sat quietly enjoying all the excitement. His parents hadn't phoned once, and he tried not to mind.

"When are you going home Patrick?" asked a sharp-eyed Ellie noticing his silence.

"Probably at the weekend. I've got to go on the train again to London. School begins next week, so I have to be back for a new term."

"Bed now I think." Bridget folded her knitting away. "You've done well Ellie, that scarf of yours is nearly finished."

"Oh I've a lot more to do yet," laughed Ellie.

In a mood of optimism they said goodnight and disappeared each to their own comfy bedroom, to reflect on the day's happenings. It had been a day of readjustment, coming to terms with what had been, what was now, and what was to come. The wise words of the old lady came back to them as they thought it all over. Would they ever truly forget?

Chapter Thirty-nine
A memorable Autumn Council Meeting

Outside in the darkness the birds had gathered on every available branch. Dark shapes filled the trees where the owls hooted in unison. The autumn council meeting was to take place the following morning, because the unusual events of the past few days had made it necessary to postpone it. Now, no one wanted to miss it. The news had travelled far and wide, and even in retirement birds flew back just to be there. It was going to be a momentous occasion.

Freddie the robin, who had taken up temporary residence in Bridget's porch, was dreading it. He kept remembering how rude he had been to the buzzards. Could he possibly have said those things to the lord and master of the woodland? Where had he found the courage? What was his punishment to be?

He needed to talk to someone. The last few days had weakened him and made him feel old. His red breast had a few flecks of grey and his beady black eyes were not quite so bright. He was very keen to resign from all his responsibilities and take life a little easier. He was bound to be banished from the woodland. Perhaps he would be escorted to the Freedom gate and pushed over into the outside world, left to the fate of the wind and weather? It was a worry. At last, in desperation, he flew to the bell tower of the church to talk to kind Belvedere and Boadicea.

In the second ash tree on the right, Oliphant heard a loud knocking at his door. Not more squirrels looking for accommodation! Feeling exasperated, he wrenched open the sturdy door and shouted "Yes?" very loudly. He almost fell over his own doorstep when the dark shadow of huge wings filled the doorway. It was His Grace the buzzard. Trembling and blinking furiously, he bowed.

"My lord, welcome."

The buzzard who was too huge to fit inside, greeted him and perched outside on a nearby branch.

"Ah Oliphant, take me to that cousin of yours, Tolivera, would you?"

"With pleasure your grace," bowed the owl again.

Freedom gate

"I'd be much obliged. What is the time by your Dark Dwellers clock? Owls keep such strange hours I remember."

"Why it's MOONRISE your grace, a good time for owls."

"Let's go then. Lead the way."

The owl hastily picked up his compass and his map, which he fastened inside his wing. He closed the door behind him and stepped out into the dark night. The buzzard followed him closely. Up the hill they flew, to the top of Gallants Bower, to the huge ash tree which overlooked the estuary. It was a perfect spot for spying, or observing, as Tolivera would have it.

The two birds stopped sharply outside the oval door in the ash tree's grey-green bark and one knocked loudly. The door creaked open by itself, and the buzzard glimpsed the welcoming interior with gleaming polished wood and soft lighting. Warm scented air floated out into the cold.

The buzzard entered, the doorway being larger than that of Oliphant's more humble home.

"Good evening," purred the low deep voice of the most senior and powerful bird, one rank below the buzzard. He was seated in his favourite plush chair which was carved out of conker wood and polished to lustre with mouse grease. It was upholstered in grey fur. Wreaths of smoke plumed from his long pipe and smelt of lawn clippings. He was an imposing figure, and a rather sinister one.

"Good evening," the buzzard replied, sensing no fear in Tolivera's demeanour– he was not subservient in the slightest. It was a new experience for the Lord of the Woodland.

"Recovered from your little tussle with the humans?" asked the owl with a twinkle in his eye.

"All is now peaceful, all are safe," replied the buzzard coolly, sensing just a smatter of criticism in the tone of his underling.

"Humans never change in my opinion, your grace. Conflict, killing, death, that's how they solve everything, always have. You'll never change them my great master." And he smiled a slow and deliberate rather cheeky sort of smile.

"Come and sit down, I'm forgetting my manners. Come, let's drink a small cup of the Mists of Time. It's a good and peaceful year – 1970 I think."

The buzzard first and then the small, nervous owl seated themselves in the luxurious chairs and relaxed visibly in the comfort and seduction of wealth and obvious good living.

How does he manage it? thought the buzzard. *Why, this is more comfortable than the Citadel. Mine is fine, but this, this is… well opulent,* and he cast a quick eye around the shining furniture and skin rugs. Crystal cobwebs gleamed with glinting droplets, a pile of luscious fruits lured him, feather cushions plumped themselves against him, and a strange collection of little animal sculls, creamy-white and polished, were grouped on a shelf, neatly labelled. Quill pens and elderberry ink stood on a heavy desk alongside sheets of bark paper held down by an amber pine-resin paper weight; a small dragonfly was trapped in the translucent solid crescent for eternity. It was all in astoundingly good taste.

Tolivera handed the precious liquid to his guests in iced glasses. It steamed slightly with an unrecognisable odour. They sipped it in silence, appreciating its warm glow.

"Now you are here for a reason my lord, what could it be?" wheedled the voice of Tolivera at its most persuasive.

"I'd like to look at the Happenings of January 18th please, all of them," the buzzard insisted firmly.

"And so you shall," agreed the owl, "I'll get them ready for you at once," and tipping the rest of his drink into his beak all at once, he got up to go to his root cellars and manufacture that

278

day's history.

"Go with him," hissed the buzzard to the startled Oliphant. "I don't want him destroying any of it, or spilling it. Go on!"

The small owl arose nervously. "Cousin, wait for me," he called. "I'd like to watch this, It must be fascinating," and tripping over a fur rug on his way, he followed.

Down in the earthy depths below ground Tolivera set to work turning taps and gauges and watching the dates flick by. At the right date he pulled a stop lever and held a flat, wide silver dish beneath a brass tap. He turned on the tap and out poured a multicoloured striped liquid which spread out into a picture. He immediately stopped the tap.

"Tell his lordship, His Grace the buzzard, to get himself down here at once, there's a good fellow Oliphant," he ordered sharply. "Hurry up."

The little owl scurried off to fetch him. The large buzzard squeezed himself into the root-crossed cellar and sneezed in the musty air.

"Take a seat, my lord," invited Tolivera. "Ready?"

Slowly he turned the tap on. The pictures appeared in the silver dish and when it was full it overflowed neatly over the lip into a narrow pipe and was sent back into the system. The whole scene of the Universe Reverse Process was visible, just like watching television in the flat silver dish, with no sound of course. The two boys, the soldiers, the camp, the little mice arriving, the sea gull; the whole thing repeated. They watched very carefully, saying nothing, nothing at all, even though it was most exciting. The chase, the whales and the dolphins, the good ship Fancy and Captain Avery were all there.

"It would appear my lord, if you'll pardon me, that the boys were not saved by us, but by two mice, who were not Woodlanders.

Your Grace?" Tolivera was in for the kill and he wasn't going to let him get away with it.

"Well of course I knew it was happening but we don't like to interfere. The robin suggested I could do something with my power. Of course one has to be careful," nodded the buzzard benevolently.

"The robin accused you of not doing anything, of cowardice and indecision, if I'm right, eh my lord?" continued Tolivera.

"Oh no, no, no, he was a little excited, but I'd made up my mind already to release the Power."

"I see." Tolivera was furious. "And what rewards are the seagull and the robin to receive tomorrow?"

"Rewards? Umm, well, I shall have to see."

"Make sure you do my lord. There's not much time left now. The council meeting will begin at sunrise, if I'm correct?"

"Yes, yes, sunrise," agreed the buzzard. Silence fell between them. Tolivera puffed away on his obnoxious pipe furiously. The buzzard longed to be at home preparing his speech for the meeting. Oliphant felt small and confused; he was a solitary little person, who did not like hob-nobbing with the hierarchy of power. A very faint dawn chorus began twittering.

"Is that the time already?" pretended the buzzard, "Must be going, must be going," he flustered.

"I shall see you later no doubt, my lord," drawled Tolivera, and with that the buzzard took his leave, led by the nervous little Oliphant, who touched wingtips with his cousin and tripped up again as he left the doorway.

"Steady, cousin," chuckled the portly owl from the warmth of his room, and closed the door.

At the Citadel the squirrels had been preparing refreshments at a frantic pace during the night. The bluetits had laid the autumn carpet, magnificent in its glorious colours, glowing brightly. They were expecting crowds. It had been many Woodlander kingdoms since the Power had been released. These buzzards and their three sons would be marked in history. This united effort of the Spirit of the Sea, the Power of the Woodland, and the lesser might of the Skywingers had produced an enormous surge of energy and strength.

As the sky began its subtle changes from black and inky night to watery blue tinged with pink, the silent migration started to the high Citadel for the great Autumn Convention. Creatures of every ilk surged forwards from their shelters and congregated at the foot of the tall pine trees, jostling for the best view.

The buzzards, eyeing their audience arriving from a hidden vantage point, were stunned by the huge crowd and a shiver of anxiety ran over the Lord of the Woodland. Tolivera had unsettled him and he tried not to think about him. His wife, his most loyal supporter, calmed him and his arrogant young princes clawed each other in playful mock combat, their tawny feathers smooth and shiny with youth, their beaks razor sharp, their eyes bright and piercing.

"Oh to be young again," sighed the buzzard, "and free of this weight of decision-making." Suddenly he was weary of power. His authority had been questioned, his actions disapproved of, his absolute belief in himself shaken, and over what? An inferior, inconsequential bird who had overstepped the mark and actually insulted him. No! It could not be allowed. Once someone doubted him they all would. His father had given him some advice as he relinquished power: "Never apologise, even if you are wrong, a crack turns into a chasm, indiscipline turns into chaos, anarchy rises out of weakness. Keep them on a tight rein my boy, and never let them get the bit between their teeth."

They had been wise words. One other thing worried him: who would the Spirit of the Sea send to represent him? A huge white albatross? A wise black cormorant? Surely not the deadly black-backed gull? He gave up. The time was approaching. All was prepared and rank on rank of all dwellers sat murmuring and musing, renewing acquaintances in expectation and excitement.

The buzzard appeared on the topmost branch and cleared his throat, to rousing applause and cheers. He bowed and spread his huge wings to make himself larger, obscuring the sun momentarily. He was an imposing figure; the tiny creatures looked up in awe. The buzzard waited for complete silence and surveyed the crowds. He was scanning for the robin and the seagull but did not see them. He was surprised. Attendance was compulsory for the robin as a council member and the black rooks had not told him of any absences.

He looked down momentarily through the green pine needles to the knotty boughs beneath, where the senior members sat proudly. The spot where the robin should have been was still empty. How dare he defy him! Anger swelled inside him, making him look even fiercer. At the recess for food he would send his sons to fetch him, dead or alive, he didn't care which, so great was his rage.

His wife, discomfited by his mood, prompted him. "We must wait dear, for the other two representatives. They will be here soon, I'm quite sure. Just a few more moments my lord," she shyly nodded.

He had temporarily forgotten his manners in his anger. "Quite so dear, quite so. I'll just do a short general welcome, shall I?" Without hesitation he began:

"Greetings, dwellers of all places in Sky, Sea and Woodland. Your representatives will be here soon, and we shall begin our

282

autumn council meeting. Thank you all for coming in such great numbers. We are all honoured indeed. But we have much to celebrate as you will hear later."

Lots of the animals and creatures whispered to each other excitedly, hoping to hear more of the extraordinary happenings of recent days.

A violent flapping suddenly startled everybody and the pine tree branches shook furiously as a golden eagle from the craggy peaks of Dartmoor shot into view and extended his large feathered legs and huge talons onto the topmost branch. The little creature dwellers shivered in fright and clutched each other, but then calmed down, knowing that he couldn't and wouldn't hurt them on this very special occasion, when the hunter and all who he hunted met on equal terms.

"Welcome to you, Most High and Supreme of all the Skywingers," greeted the buzzard and the proud and haughty bird accepted graciously the warm invitation to join them.

"I have heard amazing tales from my people lord. All true I expect?" he queried gently.

"All true, Eagle," proudly replied the buzzard. "You will hear in due course," holding back the moment when he would disclose the Happenings.

He looked around a little anxiously; what manner would the Spirit of the Sea take? He wished whoever it was would hurry up before everyone got restless and bored waiting. He noticed creatures looking upwards to the clear blue sky, its welcome sunshine filling the expanse with light. A billowing mist was crossing the sky like a huge carpet. It was held on its corners by four beautiful white kittiwakes, and sitting aloft, taking a human form with flowing white curls, was the Spirit of the Sea. He had come in person to the Gathering. It had never been known or spoken of

before. He was magnificent. Furls and fronds of mists of green flowed over and around him. He ordered the birds to stop and his cloud hovered above the pine tree. The creatures all ceased their hubbub and looked up in wonder. The buzzard and the eagle dared not speak first, as they knew his power far surpassed theirs.

"I am come to your Gathering, Lords of the Sky and Woodland. I have much to say," echoed the deep and resonating voice which seemed to fill the whole sky. The sun was covered by the huge engulfing mist and the air was cooled, causing the little creatures to shiver. The Spirit of the Sea seemed to fade and reappear in different places, as the mists swirled around everything and everyone. They could hardly see as its blanket of dewy softness covered them.

"I shall be brief in my explanation," boomed the melodious voice again, echoing around the gathering. "At the eclipse of the moon, the time mechanism became held fast, and then to try to free itself went into a reverse procedure. This caused us all to spin backwards into times past we could not remember. Three of our human friends – yes, they were friends, Lord of the Woodland, I point this out to you most particularly," (at this obvious reference to himself the buzzard felt sick and dizzy) "…these friends were in great danger, and heroic and brave action was taken by five members over our combined territories."

A great murmur went up from the cold but intensely interested audience, and whisperings and wonderings spread through the crowd.

"Our human friends were freed and escaped to the sea with the help of a fleet of my subjects, who shall be honoured in the Seafarer way. Freedom to travel the mighty oceans of the world for as long as they wish, whenever they wish, is granted. I insist that the other gallant heroes receive the same honour. The State of Freedom is the greatest one we can offer. Buzzard, Eagle, you surely must agree?"

Asking that question to themselves, from under his endlessly moving green and dazzling garments, peeped Ferdinand and Isabella. He had resurrected them from the deep, their spirits his alone to control, but only for this meeting. When their freedom was granted, who knew where their spirits might wander in the oceans?

The eagle, who was the first to compose himself, looked up to the sky to try to see the Spirit of the Sea through the dense mists, and asked, "Who are these other subjects, great one from the sea? So we may know who we are honouring."

"A good question and I shall answer it," rumbled the voice, and from the cloud a vast hand appeared. Cupped comfortably in it were a seagull with one leg, a small robin, and a bat.

When the buzzard saw the robin he gasped. So that's where he was! And he was to be honoured now and revered and given his freedom for ever. He didn't like it at all. But the crowds below didn't agree. When they saw the assortment of animals and birds crossing all sections of creatures of sea and sky, they nodded their approval and clapped and cheered. It was a popular decision.

At this signal of approval, the green and grey mist seemed to roll back to the pine tree and hover like a carpet again. The Spirit of the Sea could now clearly be seen, the figure of a great man with wafts of white locks blending into a frothing beard, wearing a billowing sea-green gown which fell in tumultuous folds and joined the mist in an inseparable way. It was constantly moving, undulating and wreathing, but the palm of his hand could be seen outlined with the little creatures and the grey and white seagull held in it. They looked over the edge curiously.

The buzzard knew he was beaten. He could resist no longer against the power of a majority such as this. He gathered his good sense together and drove out his feelings of resentment and anger to a small dark place in the deepest recesses of his mind. He tried to be himself again.

"Great Lord of the Sea, you do us an immeasurable honour to come in person to our Autumn Gathering. You and I worked together during the Release of Power in the unusual circumstances of the Universe Reverse we all experienced. As you know it was in my woodland territory that the Happenings took place. I directed and instructed from the Citadel. Here, the immediate response was activated to resolve the plight of the girl, boy, and the boy stranger, who are all personally known to us here. Spirits were awakened who have been long lying in our earth. At your request, the honours due shall be bestowed on those in my kingdom. Only say the word, and it shall be done, Great Ruler of the Oceans."

The buzzard dipped his wings in reverence to the Spirit of the Sea. The eagle followed the buzzard's example and spread his wonderful shiny feathers in a mighty span, dipping them towards the cloud. The crowd clapped and cheered but the Spirit of the Sea hushed them.

"As the sun strengthens, so my mists weaken, and the Scroll of Honour must be read before I leave you all. If we are agreed and harmony has been reached between us, I shall proceed. Do we all agree?"

"Yes lord," nodded the buzzard sweetly.

"Yes lord," blinked the eagle adoringly.

"Very well. From this day, freedom of passage in earth, sea, and sky, unhindered and unchallenged is offered in gratitude for unselfish heroism to Sargasso the seagull, Freddie the robin and Belvedere the bat. Ferdinand and Isabella, the two white mice in the good ship Fancy, will roll in the deep evermore.

"Special mention and privileges also to Solomon and

Bathsheba the two seals, Doryana and Diadem the dolphins, my two petrified whales Hector and Hercules, and a flotilla of flying fish drawn to our waters to help, like so many."

Cheers and applause followed, rippling through the crowd. What a morning it had been!

"We have a great role to play in our world, every one of us, and co-operation is essential to keep our lives happy and peaceful. Buzzard, Eagle, this has been a memorable day and I thank you."

And with that the sun pierced through the mist, blinding the gathering with its brilliance, creating a huge golden pool of light. Everyone shielded their eyes, and when they looked again the Spirit of the Sea was gone; only the white kittiwakes could be seen, flying away in the azure sky. The audience followed the flight of the birds in silence until they had disappeared. The buzzard and the eagle stared after them, unable to comprehend what had just taken place. They were shaken and stunned by the appearance of the powerful spirit. The buzzard had never dreamed of him actually taking the form of a human. He tried to take control again.

"We have been highly favoured, everyone. You have witnessed a great sight. Let us celebrate now with a sumptuous feast. Please make your way to the buffet breakfast, and eat and drink your fill."

All the gathering cheered and a mad clamour ensued, the hard work of the squirrels was demolished in a very short time. What a spectacle had evolved in front of their very eyes! How lucky they had been to witness it all. Everyone had a wonderful time in the winter sun, eating and talking and gossiping about the morning's events. The buzzard and the eagle went into conference for some serious talking, and the young princes joined them.

Tolivera had enjoyed every minute of it, knowing from his vast wisdom that something was bound to happen, and the buzzard had got what he deserved, in his opinion. Gradually all those who had gathered so eagerly in the early sunrise, full of the morning's events, the excitement, and the delicious food, began to take their leave and to disappear as quietly as they had appeared in the dusky dawn. The black rooks waited for a signal from the buzzard to dismiss the council, but none came. Eventually they took it upon themselves to permit them to leave; hesitantly said goodbye to each other, and tiptoed away.

Tolivera joined the buzzard and the eagle who were the only two left. He didn't care if he was intruding; it was not in his nature to be sensitive. The eagle seemed happy that two Skywingers had been celebrated and forgot about other mundane matters due for discussion until the Spring Gathering. Many of those present had been waiting to hibernate and now they could.

The buzzard, who had been unsettled by the whole affair, seemed a little petulant. The eagle and the owl persuaded him to forget the Robin incident, it wasn't important; there was great strength in mercy, the eagle pointed out. The buzzard, with his sons watching, gave in with dignity. They all heaved a great sigh of relief. The two black rooks, eavesdropping as best they could, touched wingtips and smiled gratefully at each other. The moment had passed. The world moved on. The buzzard had clung on to his position, but only just.

Chapter Forty
A shock for Eddie, and Patrick returns to Scotland

Gradually, just like holidays do, the journey back into the past began to fade for the three youngsters. Every now and then they would remember things and talk about them, sharing the memories, but the present day kept forcing itself in, and soon they began to forget to think about it altogether. Time moved itself relentlessly on, minute by minute, hour by hour, until several days joined themselves together seamlessly and they didn't talk about it at all.

The three fell back into their old patterns for the next few precious days: sailing, fishing, walking on the cliffs, picnicking, going downtown, eating and drinking in the cafes and sitting on the front looking at the boats. They felt relaxed and agreeably content to wander. In the evenings, warm and well fed they all sat together, playing cards, knitting, watching TV, films, or talking. Life was pleasant and unexciting – just how they wanted it to be for a while.

On Patrick's last day it rained heavily, a cold and miserable day, and the boys decided to walk the short distance to the castle, pay the entrance fee, and have a really good look around. Ellie went to town with Bridget, shopping for groceries to put into Watermill Cottage before her parents came back. She tried not to think about the two mice, now gone from her life forever. She mustn't dwell on it, it made her too sad. Ellie concentrated on her parents' return, planning to make it welcoming for them.

Eddie and Patrick were about to buy their tickets from the

small English Heritage shop when the Keeper of the Castle recognised them.

"Hello boys." he said in a friendly way, "come to see our new
treasures?"

"What treasures?" asked Eddie curiously.

"We've just opened a new exhibition down in the Battery –
relics and remains from the Civil War with explanations and diagrams and some artefacts. It's in co-operation with the Education
Department, trying to bring history to more people. I'm rather
proud of it. I'm supposed to charge but I know you both, you're
locals and if you tell lots of other people for me, we'll call it an
advertising expense. Off you go, I'll look the other way!" and he
grinned at their surprised faces.

Calling "Thanks Terry!" they raced off down into the castle
through the side door.

"That was lucky wasn't it?" laughed Eddie. "He's a really
good bloke, and it is raining!"

They made their way through the empty rooms. The exhibits
were in glass cases and had overhanging lights to illuminate the
complete history of the Civil War, condensed well and made
very interesting. Several life-sized model people stood dressed
in appropriate costumes. One of the Governor of Dartmouth was
rather fine and in beautiful colours. There were several soldiers,
including one dressed as a footman and one as a cavalier, with
their clothes faithfully reconstructed but the helmets real. These
had been discovered elsewhere on a dig and donated to English
Heritage. For Eddie and Patrick it was horribly real and the
memories of being frightened out of their wits returned. They
moved on to a mock up of a camp fire, cooking utensils, food,
and two hideous female camp followers. The boys had seen it
before in reality and they quietly laughed together,

The last exhibit was a small case of precious items – a piece of jewellery, a small leather purse with moth-eaten strings, several uninspiring silver coins, some shot from a pistol, a belt buckle, a short sword and a gold medallion; all rather run-of-the-mill museum stuff. Eddie and Patrick peered at the case, more out of a sense of duty than of interest. They stared for a long time through the glass, reading the inscription on the medallion: *'To Captain John Avery. In gratitude for your devotion to duty. Governor of Jamaica. Port Royal. 1630.'*

"But it can't be!" Eddie spoke aloud softly, staring and staring again at the gold medallion in its velvet case.

"It must be," Patrick replied, shading his eyes to try to get a closer look. "There can't be another one, can there?"

"I don't know. I suppose not. Where do you think they got it from? I'm going to ask Terry Come on, he'll know." Excitement and disbelief spread through him. He had lost the medallion somewhere, that was a certainty, but where he couldn't tell. He just couldn't remember.

Terry was coming down the stone steps to see how they were enjoying his new exhibition, and what comments or criticisms they had. He was eager to hear.

"Finished already?" he smiled at them.

"No, no, we were coming to find you to ask you some questions."

"Good, I'll answer them of course if I can, now, what was it you wanted to know?" He beamed encouragingly at the two in front of him,

"Come on," and he led them back down into the gloomy and slightly musty room. Eddie took him over to the cabinet and pointed to the medallion.

"Ah!" said Terry, "Now that's an interesting one. I'm glad

you've chosen that one. It's not exactly from the Civil War, you see it's a bit earlier."

"Yes?" Eddie couldn't help himself interrupting. Patrick put his hand gently on his arm to restrain him.

"However it does have connections because it was washed out on the beach here, below this cove, with some other relics from the Civil War, when we did some excavating for our new path down to Castle Cove. Several bodies were found, well, what was left of them, and one had this attached to it in the leather purse. We reckon a soldier who drowned or was thrown over the cliff, stole it."

"Really?" remarked Patrick, remembering the manic chase down to the waters' edge both he and Eddie had endured.

"Oh yes, and the most interesting information is...." he proudly continued, while Eddie writhed in anxious anticipation, "I've done some research and the Captain this medallion was inscribed for was a real pirate who lived in the West Indies. Made himself very rich indeed, plundering and capturing wealthy ships, and came back to Devon in some sort of disgrace and died here a pauper. So somehow the medallion ended up here by chance and we managed to salvage it. It's a real find. Would you like to see it closer?"

"No! NO! No, thank you!" shouted the two boys at once, quite shocking poor Terry.

"Well, of course not if you don't want to. I only thought…"

"It's very kind of you," Patrick interrupted this time hastily, "but we didn't realise the time. We must be back for lunch at my godfather's or we'll be in real trouble. We're often late you see. We promised today we would be on time."

"Yes we did, didn't we?" agreed an ashen-faced Eddie.

"Well I understand of course," smiled the gentle Terry. "Off you go then. I hope you enjoyed it." And he led the two boys up the stone steps and out into the cold, wet daylight.

"Thank you for coming," he said politely.

"Thanks Terry, we really enjoyed it," and off they went. Patrick turned back,

"We'll remember to tell lots of people, don't worry." He raised his hand in thanks. Terry smiled and nodded.

Eddie made for the nearest seat and sat down heavily. "My God, I can't believe it." He thumped both his hands down on the slatted seat which was below the shelter overlooking the sea. "Nathan or Edwin must have found the medallion and had it with them when they chased us. They both fell into the sea didn't they? It must have been one of them. How stupid of me, I'll never, never get it back now; I'll never see him again. Never." He was so distressed and upset that he clenched his fists to try to stop tears filling his eyes. "I'd always hoped we'd find it again you know, and we could go on making him come back. It was stupid of me wasn't it? Silly and childish and stupid." He buried his face in both his hands.

Patrick looked out to sea. He didn't know how to comfort him. There wasn't any way of making it easier to face the loss of the medallion. It was gone for good, trapped in its glass case for all to see, a reminder of a very special time for all of them. A time that they had glimpsed. He had to let go. Perhaps it was just as well, Patrick reflected. How could it have ended better in a way? He knew Eddie could not have resisted holding the medallion tightly for just one last time. Now he couldn't. Ever. But there were always other adventures waiting around the corner, wasn't that what Mrs Finch-Ingram had told them cheerfully that sunny morning? A flapping and a squawking broke his thoughts, and Eddie sat up abruptly to find Sargasso sitting by his feet, putting his head against his leg. Eddie stroked the smooth, soft feathers

294

without saying a word. They weren't necessary. Eddie fingered the back of the seagull's neck lovingly. Patrick and Eddie sat in silence. Eddie found Sargasso's presence very comforting. It reminded him of the years that had gone by, and how long he had been friends with him.

"It's over now," he told himself. "Got to get on now, find new things to do. Dad will be back soon, we'll get a bigger and faster boat."

"Fancy a boat of your own Patrick?" he suddenly said to his friend, grinning, just like the old Eddie.

"Aye I do," replied Patrick, "and what'll be the cost of that?"

Eddie laughed. "You Scots are all the same. It'll be a fair price, don't worry. I'm thinking we might sell *Sargasso* maybe. You could keep it at the Old Bath House in the shed for the winter. Dad and I are hoping to get a bigger boat for racing. What do you think?"

Patrick thought carefully. "I'll talk it over with George first," he said.

"That's fine by me."

"OK let's go shall we? Go and see if we can find some more fun somewhere else?"

"You're on."

Eddie turned to the sea and took one lingering glance at the wide ocean, and said his final farewell. It was well and truly over.

***

Bridget left Ellie outside the cottage with her shopping bags.

"I can manage Bridget now, I'll be fine, Thanks so much for bringing me home. I'll see you at suppertime," and she kissed her goodbye.

Ellie wanted desperately to be alone. She was glad Bridget had gone. She opened the front door and was pleased to see her comfortable home again. Carrying the bags she went into the kitchen. She laid the table up for two, put candles into two holders, folded napkins, put glasses out and wrote a welcome home card from her, Eddie and Patrick. She put the contents of the carrier bag, the supper she had planned, into the freezer, and placed the flowers in a tall glass vase with a little packet of flower food to keep them fresh. She fetched a duster and spray polish to freshen up the furniture and make the whole place smell nice. Then she opened the windows for a blow through of fresh cool air, as the house had been shut up for a few weeks.

"There!" she said with great satisfaction when she had finished. "I hope Mum and Dad like it." She went to the cupboard and found the biscuit tin. Taking out two biscuits and crumbling them up in her hand she opened the window, and immediately the robin woke up.

"At least you're still here Freddie," she whispered. The two mice had been charming, naughty, irresponsible, delightful, and a huge worry to her. They had gone back where they belonged, with someone who cared for them. It had been a happy ending after all, no matter how much she would miss them. It was for the best. She thought of Patrick, soon leaving them to return to his sad life in Scotland, and was suddenly filled with a longing to see him again. She liked Patrick.

I shall miss him, she thought. *He's so reliable and sensible – not like Eddie and me,* and she smiled to herself. *Come on you've finished here, back to the Old Bath House for a cup of tea and a natter with Bridget, it's the least you can do.*

She made up her mind to finish the red scarf she was knitting and give it to Patrick as a present, a sort of farewell gift. Ellie said goodbye to the robin, took one last look at her handiwork, and satisfied, she closed the windows and finally the front door. Mum and Dad would be back tomorrow. She was looking forward to it.

She had missed her mother, especially during the bad time when she had lost Eddie, but all that was over now, thank goodness.

***

Patrick prepared to leave, watched by Eddie. Ellie shyly gave him the completed red scarf. He held it appreciatively in his hands, remembering her difficulties in getting the stitches right.

"Thank you Ellie. Are you sure?"

"Oh yes!" she laughed. "Take it away. It may be the last thing I ever knit in my entire life."

"You won't forget about the boat will you?" Eddie pressurised him again.

"Indeed I won't. I can't think of anything I'd like better. There are a lot of memories in that boat." They all agreed whole-heartedly.

"I don't want to go, you know!" Patrick suddenly burst out, "I'd rather stay here. I really don't want to go back to that school ever again."

The others looked at him in surprise.

"You've never said anything about it before."

"Well, I've never had a choice, have I?"

There was no answer to that. They all knew it. They had to be resigned to the inevitable. George was taking Patrick that afternoon to catch the 4.55 train from Totnes to London. Patrick was meeting his father at Paddington station and they were flying back to Edinburgh together. It was all settled. Eddie and Ellie decided not to go to the station. They knew it would be an emotional wrench for all of them. They had been through such a lot together in a very short space of time. They felt bonded for life, inseparable from one another, in a very special kind of way.

Bridget packed him up a snack for the journey and fussed and petted him. He succumbed to her attentions good-heartedly. He felt as if Eddie and Ellie were actually his own family, his own brother and sister, and could hardly bear to think of their parting. The clock rolled on, ticking away and the time to go arrived. George took his bags out to the car and they all trooped after him. Bridget kissed and hugged him making him promise to ring as soon as he got home.

Patrick kissed Ellie, shook hands with Eddie and said in a strangled voice, "I've got to go now. I'll never forget this holiday as long as I live. See you very soon, I hope. Bye for now."

He got into the car and looked straight ahead. He didn't turn round and he didn't wave, and George just felt it best to drive away quickly. Eddie and Ellie stood watching the car disappear, feeling sad, lonely and left behind. It was heartbreaking. Nobody could think of anything to say that would make it feel better, so nobody did. Bridget slipped away inside, leaving the two youngsters together.

They'll get over it, she told herself. *They've got so fond of each other, it's a shame. That boy's been so lonely. It's not right.*

She busied herself in Patrick's room taking the sheets off the bed and collecting the towels for the laundry. Eddie and Ellie were going home. There would be just the two of them again. She didn't mind, school terms were short and holidays long; it would all come round again for certain, summer sun and sailing. She felt a little better.

Eddie and Ellie gloomily trudged down to the bedrooms to begin their own packing-up.

"Do you think he'll write?"

"Course he will, every week I should think."

"It was an amazing adventure wasn't it?"

"It was incredible, I can hardly believe it myself now."

"Some of it was fun wasn't it?"

"Well, until the Civil War it was."

They laughed together, remembering things that Isabella and Ferdinand had done, things that Captain Avery had done, and somehow everything had been a kind of bittersweet experience.

"I haven't looked at my Moonmirror or the crystal signaller since that night you know."

"But you've still got them haven't you?"

"Of course, and I'm very proud of them, wait till I show them to Dad."

Suddenly they were excited at the prospect of going home, seeing their parents again, and being looked after by them. Bridget and George were wonderful but it wasn't the same as your own Mum and Dad.

George came back and they all ate supper together.

"He wasn't happy at all to be going back," said George, shaking his head,

"Not happy at all. I reckon you've spoilt that lad Bridget, waiting on him hand and foot."

He winked at Eddie and Ellie across the table.

The phone rang, making them all jump. It was Patrick's father: he wanted to know where Patrick was, and why he wasn't at the café on the station at the usual place by the window. He was very angry.

"But I put him on the 4.55 to Paddington myself," George assured him. "He waved me goodbye out of the window. I saw it leave, and it was exactly on time. I don't understand."

A conversation followed in which it was obvious that George was getting the very rough end of Mr McNab's tongue.

"Well let me know when he turns up at once, won't you? I'm very sorry indeed." And with that George put the phone down and sat, bewildered, on the sofa.

"Where do you think he is?" asked Bridget gently.

"I've no idea. Really." George put his hand up to his head and sighed deeply. Eddie and Ellie gave each other a knowing look across the table, smiled, and continued eating. The phone rang again, and…

But that of course is another story.

Totnes station